"THE WILDWOODS WEEKLY READER"

Have fun *(signature)*

By

Don Oakland

Oak Press
904 Broadway Avenue
Wausau, Wisconsin

SECOND EDITION

Copyright© 1985 by Don Oakland

ISBN 0-9615242-0-0

First Printing 1985
Second Printing 1987
Third Printing 1988

Published by
Oak Press
904 Broadway Avenue
Wausau, WI 54401

Distributed by: Adventure Publications, Inc.,
P.O. Box 269
Cambridge, MN 55008

PRINTED IN THE UNITED STATES OF AMERICA

This book is dedicated to my wife, Kathy, whose marvelous sense of humor has tolerated my somewhat exaggerated view of family life. Without her encouragement and patience, this book would have never been attempted. To my mother, Helen Oakland, Madison, WI, who has always supported my attempts at creative writing. To the editors of the *Wausau Daily Herald* copy desk who wrote the column headlines and kept me editorially tethered so my writing couldn't follow my imagination into the realm of bad taste and questionable grammar. And special thanks to Cynthia Schley, whose outrageous sense of humor constantly tries to corrupt her artistic talent, and to John Froelich, a very talented photo-journalist and close friend.

CONTENTS

CHAPTER ONE

THE WOES OF THE WOOLLY BEAR

Dear reader, please bear with me this week. I feel compelled to write the following. Good judgment has played no part in what I'm to present here.

The other day I was riding my bike down a rural road in Lincoln County when suddenly I came upon a woolly bear caterpillar. I nearly hit and squished the little critter.

That made me feel bad.

How I can get worked up over a lousy caterpillar constantly astounds my wife.

Anyway, I got off my bike and walked over to the caterpillar. I picked him up to see if he had suffered any shock from the near miss.

It was then I got to thinking: Just how perilous it is for a caterpillar to cross a road.

I couldn't get this thought from my mind. I decided then and there to conduct a scientific study. Since this study would not involve any money, I figured I needn't worry about Senator William Proxmire's golden fleece award.

I measured the caterpillar. He was just over an inch in length.

Then I tried to measure how fast he moved.

That was darn hard. Ever try to make a caterpillar run a straight line down a ruler? Took the better part of 15 minutes before I was able to get an accurate reading.

This sprint caterpillar did seven inches in four seconds.

When I got home I sat down at my desk calculator and began figuring.

Well into the night I was still figuring.

It was about midnight when my wife came storming out of the bedroom and threw a thick paperback book at me. The book bounced off my head and nearly knocked me off my chair.

"Normal people don't do this, Donald!

"Normal people go to bed at night.

"AND, normal people don't give a darn about CATERPILLARS."

She slammed the door.

I regained my concentration and resumed my calculations. An Oakland, like a Newton, is not easily derailed from scientific pursuit.

I began thinking out loud:

"If a caterpillar crept seven inches in four seconds, how long would it take him to cover 20 feet?

"Well, 20 feet is 240 inches," I muttered.

"If he can cover seven inches in four seconds, first I've got to know how many seven-second periods in 240 seconds." I tapped out the numbers on the calculator.

34.285714

Times four seconds.

137.14285

Divided by 60, equals...

2.2857141 minutes.

"Now given that a car has four tires and each is about seven inches wide, what are the odds of a caterpillar surviving a trip across a road?"

I had reached my limit.

I cried out. That same cry I used in fifth grade when I was unable to figure out a story problem. It used to bring sympathy from the teacher.

Not so with my wife.

She returned to the bedroom doorway and glared at me. She didn't say one word. Just glared.

It was then I decided it would take a computer to figure out those odds. I decided that I'd try to let this question rest.

But, I have one regret.

There are millions of woolly bears out there who will never know the odds they face crossing the road.

$$* * * * *$$

WOOLLY BEARS AND THE "FUZZ"

Woolly bears are driving me bonkers.

The little creatures are becoming an obsession with me. Things are simply getting out of hand.

It all started a few weeks back when I wrote a column about my attempts at calculating the odds of a woolly bear caterpillar making it across a road without getting hit by a car.

Thus far I've not found a satisfactory answer to my problem. But, that's not my problem.

My problem is that ever since writing that darn column I have encountered hundreds of woolly bears as I drive home from work each day.

You have no idea of the number of woolly bears that try to cross the road in the fall. It's as if something in their DNA makeup is telling them: Woolly bear, cross that road!

Maybe that's how woolly bears determine who's macho among them.

Anyway, since publicly expressing my concern for the woolly bears' lifestyle, I have had this overwhelming compulsion to avoid hitting them on the highway.

Have you ever tried to avoid hitting a caterpillar as you drive down the road at 55 mph?

You think trying to avoid hitting a deer is rough! That's nothing compared with trying to save the life of a jaywalking caterpillar no bigger than a forefinger.

I see them now. I never used to. Like all of you nice people, I went merrily along annihilating woolly bear after woolly bear with innocent abandon.

Now I see them inching their way across the highway. I can spot them about ten yards away. That gives me about a second and a half to react.

I crank the wheel to the left, sending my car into a violent swerve. Tires squeal, rubber burns and a long black mark is left on the highway.

My car jumps across the centerline. I throw the wheel right. The car hops back into its right lane.

The woolly bear continues inching its way across the road.

It wouldn't be bad if I had to do this only once or twice. But, after doing this Le Mans driving six or seven times, I'm almost car sick.

This explains why I have no appetite for supper. Despite my wife's concern for my good health, I have yet to reveal the reason for my nightly malaise.

Thank goodness I've never encountered a cop on my travels home. He would surely think me intoxicated and pull me over.

"No officer, I'm not drunk," I tell him in a calm voice. He shakes his head.

"I was trying to avoid hitting this woolly bear caterpillar as it crossed the road," I tell him. He winces.

"You were what?"

"I was trying to safely maneuver my car to save the life of a woolly bear caterpillar," I say in a stern voice.

"Hey, fella, normal people don't do that," he replies.

His face turns pale. He realizes this is no drunk he is addressing but a full-fledged wacko.

"You do this often?" he asks timidly.

"Only in fall when the woolly bears migrate," I reply.

How the officer or I would fare after such a conversation, I'll leave to you to decide. But, I'm willing to bet I'd be on some psychiatrist's couch within a day.

If you think this is the last of my writing about woolly bears, you're wrong. I have become an expert on the creatures. They aren't just caterpillars.

4

Someday I'll tell you about how the great woolly bear spirit helped me find a lost pen. I'll reveal the location of the Center for Woollyworm Studies. And, I'll scoop the National Enquirer with a true story on how woolly bears and Dolly Parton are alike.

* * * * *

THE GREAT SPIRIT (GENUS WOOLLY BEAR)

I was recently up in Canada canoeing with a bunch of guys through the back country.

At times I thought: You know if you get sick or break a leg, you might not get out of here alive. The guys might figure it's not worth the effort of carrying you out along with a few hundred pounds of gear.

I mean, it would be a whole lot easier saying: "Well, Mrs. Oakland, uh, a bear ate him."

It wouldn't be totally untruthful. You leave someone for dead in the wilderness, something is bound to eat him.

I worried about this for a while. But, those concerns went away the minute I saw a woolly bear caterpillar on a leaf.

I knew I was safe.

The spirit of the woolly bear would watch over me.

You ask: What's this spirit of the woolly bear business?

Look, I don't think it's a coincidence that at every portage and at every campsite I found at least one woolly bear.

They were my good luck charms.

You laugh.

Let me tell you how I came to believe in the woolly bear spirit.

About a year ago I wrote about my concern that woolly bear caterpillars had an awfully difficult time crossing roads. I tried to figure the odds of a woolly bear getting hit by a car.

I've never found an answer.

In writing about the woolly bears, I developed an awareness about this otherwise innocuous insect. I felt compelled to learn more about this furry creature.

I learned the woolly bear is a keen weather forecaster: The width of the bands on his body foretell the severity of winter.

I developed a fond respect for this little creature.

Since last fall, I have always avoided hitting a woolly worm with my car or bike (something which has caused me to perform some rather acrobatic driving maneuvers).

Well, the woolly bear has shown its appreciation.

One day last fall I lost a rather expensive pen. I had absolutely no idea where I had put it or dropped it. I gave it up for lost.

A couple of days later I was at the Marathon County Public Library reading a magazine article about woolly bear caterpillars. Suddenly, from out of nowhere, came a thought.

I remembered two days before I was in the library reading a newspaper in the very chair in which I was seated. It was one of those big easy chairs. Perhaps while I was sitting there, the pen slipped out of my pocket?

I swear the following is true and not exaggerated.

I put my hand between the chair and its cushion, pushed down and my fingers found my long-lost pen.

Another example.

The article I wrote on the woolly bear was one of three which earned me an award in a state newspaper contest. I have to think it was the woolly bear article that attracted the judges.

Another example: Everyone on that canoe trip got banged up— everything from a cut finger to bruised shins.

I was the only one who spent six days in the wilderness and returned unscathed.

Further proof:

My photographs of the trip came out better than I expected. And, unlike a previous trip into the outdoors, I didn't lose any of my film.

I'm convinced that, had I gotten lost, the woolly bears would have rescued me.

The little creatures would have joined together, placed their bodies on a big leaf and formed an arrow pointing the way out.

6

Now you might think this is all so much foolishness.

You might go on squishing little baby woolly bears as they cross the road.

You might even stomp them underfoot or sic a dog on them.

But, think of this. Woolly bears don't bite. They don't smell. They don't fly around your ears. They offend no one. They just want to live out their lives among the fall colors.

So the next time you see a woolly bear, tip your hat, smile and pass by. Maybe pet him gently. Your luck might change.

* * * * *

OF WORMS AND MEN

Never let it be said this column is afraid to tackle questions that others fear to ask.

This is the story of one such question.

It was raining hard that night. I put on my "Mad City" T-shirt, my Hawaiian flower print swim trunks and grubby sneakers and ventured out the front door.

I made my way across the front lawn, past the sidewalk and onto the boulevard. I knelt and began watching the grass.

"Donald! Get in here this minute," my wife screamed from the front door.

"Can't, dear. They're coming..."

"Who's coming?

"Worms," I yelled back, my voice a bit impatient with the interruption.

"WORMS," she hollered back. My wife quickly glanced at the homes of our neighbors to see if anyone was looking. "Why do you always have to embarrass me like this!"

"Shhhhhh!" I replied.

She slammed the door. Next thing I knew she was staring at me from the picture window. I could see her shaking her head and biting her knuckles.

What she didn't understand was that I was in pursuit of a most serious question: Why do earthworms come out when it rains?

Why do these creatures leave the safety of the ground and risk almost certain death when the rain stops?

After about an hour of worm watching in the rain, I arrived at a hypothesis, which I'm prepared to deliver in this column.

I suspect, but cannot prove at the moment, this will have some lesson for mankind, or as they say in the pornographic trade, some socially redeeming value.

Imagine yourself as an earthworm. You spend all your time day and night crawling around in dirt. You rarely encounter a fellow worm. Once in a while you run into a grub or two. But, you hate grubs because they're so ugly looking.

All you see, smell and taste is dirt. You begin to despise dirt.

And, you suffer constant anxiety from knowing that any moment someone might dig you up, throw you in a smelly cottage cheese container with two or three dozen other worms and throw the container in a refrigerator for days.

But, that's not the worst of it. Imagine knowing that at any time you might be ripped from your home, impaled on a fishing hook, drowned in a lake or eaten by some fish.

As you worry about your fate, you hear a thumping above you. You squirm to the surface and immediately get whacked with a rain drop. It washes the dirt from your body.

For the first time in your life, you feel clean!

You crawl out farther. Suddenly you notice other worms doing the same thing. You're overcome with an urge to party.

Hundreds of worms begin mingling. You feel wet and wild in the company of your peers.

Well, you know how it is when you get a bunch of strangers together. Some hustlers pick up dates and retire to more secluded settings. Earthworms are no different, but the consequences are more dire.

As the evening progresses, these wormy couples slither off only to find themselves rolling headlong over the curb and into the flow of the water rushing down the curb.

When daybreak comes, the waters dry up. The worms wiggle around trying to find their newfound friends instead of trying to find a way out of their predicament.

Soon the sun burns their delicate bodies and—well, the rest you know.

I got a bit misty eyed as I hunched over the curb. I thought how cruel nature is.

It gives us all, from man down to the lowly earthworm, a need for companionship. Yet, nature sometimes doesn't give its creatures the capacity to share their lives with others.

And, in the earthworm's case, it punishes them with death when they try.

* * * * *

A WORM NEEDS A FRIEND IN WINTER

Earthworms have been on my mind lately.

We think we have it pretty rough during our Wisconsin winters. But, what of the plight of the lowly nightcrawler when things turn cold?

What the heck does a worm do in January?

He can't go south like the birds do.

He can't crawl inside someone's warm house like the mice do.

He can't hibernate in some cave like the bears do.

I suppose he just buries himself deeper, digging fast enough to stay one step ahead of the frost.

I just hope worms aren't claustrophobic.

Think about it. In summer earthworms wiggle themselves out of the ground every so often. But in winter they can't do that because the frost forms an impenetrable lid.

9

Nature has not treated earthworms kindly.

She forces them to live in dirt.

If they try to escape, nature created birds to swoop down and gobble them up.

And, they're hunted down by humans who use them as bait for fish.

I hope earthworms are dumb or else they must live terribly anxious lives.

I think that mother nature ought to have given the earthworm some means to better live in the northwoods.

Something like a fur coat.

A worm must get terribly cold in winter. I mean, we'd be mighty uncomfortable running around naked this time of year.

I think fur-covered worms would be kind of neat.

You could watch them slither across the snow or slide down snowbanks.

After a new snow, you could look outside and marvel at the intricate patterns of worm tracks crisscrossing your backyard.

With fewer birds around, worms could lead more peaceful lives.

And, being fur-covered, I don't think they'd make good fish bait.

But, alas, nature has not seen fit to correct this obvious flaw.

So, it is up to us to make the earthworm's life during winter more comfortable.

"Well, if you think I'm going to knit a wool coat for a nightcrawler, you're nuts," says you.

I'm not suggesting that.

Why not do for the worms what we do for the birds?

Let's build wormhouses.

Why not be the first person on your block to have a wormhouse in your basement.

That shouldn't be difficult to make. Just take a couple of 2 x 12s, make a box and fill it with black dirt. Every so often throw some coffee grounds in there to feed the frolicking dirt crawlers.

Come spring you can take the dirt and worms out to your garden to use as highly fertile compost.

You could try building something on the order of an ant farm and mount it like a picture on one of your living room walls.

I think it would be relaxing to sit and watch earthworms undulate through the soil like tropical fish through water.

And, like fish, earthworms don't make noise.

And, since they thrive in dirt, you'd never have to clean the tank.

And, I doubt if earthworms eat that much. Earthworms are economical.

If you colored the soil, the tunneling done by the worms could create an awesome display of abstract art in motion.

Your children could really impress their classmates and teacher by bringing an earthworm farm to show and tell.

You know earthworms are rather unique creatures. For one thing they are both male and female. That's a trick even new wave punk rockers can't match, though they try so hard.

Come on people, let's pay back the earthworm for all those big fish they have sacrificed their lives to give us.

* * * * *

OF ANTS AND ANXIETY

Ants suffer from high levels of anxiety.

A ceramist from Milwaukee and I were discussing this the other day. Not often can one find someone who will indulge in the highly intellectual level of conversation this subject requires.

Ants do suffer a lot of anxiety.

Ever watch an ant? Ever seen a more nervous creature? He's moving all the time, can't stop until he burns out and—well, we won't get into that here.

When you see an ant, what's he doing? He's working.

Have you ever seen an ant not working?

I can't imagine anyone saying: "Hey look at that lazy ol' ant over there laying up against that blade of grass smoking and drinking dew."

When ants aren't working, what are they doing?

They are holed up with a couple of million other ants in a cold, drafty hill. They're shoulder to shoulder with creatures that look exactly like themselves.

Ants suffer identity crises to almost a psychotic degree.

Imagine yourself in your bedroom with your wife. She looks exactly like you do. Now imagine a hundred other people in the room, each looking exactly like you and each looking at you and your wife.

Well, now you have some appreciation for what an ant goes through day in and day out.

Some just can't take it and fling themselves on a sidewalk to be crushed by a human's shoe or a dog's paw.

The peer pressure in an ant colony is tremendous

If you don't work, they throw you out of the hill and you're left to wander until you're eaten by a beetle.

In an ant colony, there's no going down to the neighborhood tavern to lift a few with the boys. There's no YMCA where you can run off the day's frustrations.

Ants never get a break: from work, from their friends, from themselves.

Life begins to really wear on them.

Some brave ones get fed up and flee from the hill. In the cold, alone and without shelter, they search for a new home. Maybe your home.

Yes, the ants you find scurrying across your kitchen floor are refugees from a society of terrible abuse. They are free spirits who yearn for a better way, a slower pace, a more meaningful existence.

And, what do you do?

You put gooey stuff on pieces of cardboard. These bold adventurers, seekers of a higher consciousness, die in the night, poison strangling their veins.

Ah, they're just running away from a little hard work, you say.

But, ants never get vacations like you do.

They don't have major medical or a pension plan.

This adds worry to the young ant trying to bring up a family. I mean, if he should fall off the hill someday, there wouldn't be anyone to care for his family.

This stress causes some ants to crack up.

So how can we help the ant?

I've got an idea.

We get some scientists, those guys who breed sterile Medflies in California, to develop a laid-back species of ant. These ants would be dispersed throughout the ant kingdom.

Eventually, the behavior of these ants would rub off on others. In a couple of years, ants would be living at a more leisurely pace—like people living in Southern California.

I can see ants building mounds instead of building hills.

I can envision this conversation between an ant foreman and a couple of his workers sometime in the not-so-distant future.

"Hey, you guys, let's get this hill built. We've got to get this done by sundown."

"Hey, man, I'm in a very mellow state at the moment. I'm not into building this afternoon," the ant says as he drinks a droplet of dew. .

"I want you to pick up that particle of dirt and put it up there," the foreman yells at another ant and points to the top of the hill.

"Yeah, I'll get to it—I'm busy at the moment, on break, yah know—Hey, you got a smoke, good buddy?"

* * * * *

WEAVING A WEB OF DREAD

Company was coming so it could no longer be avoided.

But, I really didn't want to do it.

I knew HE was down there.

I don't mind going down in our basement to grab something out of the freezer or to do a load of wash. But, cleaning the basement, well, that's different.

The basement is getting warmer as spring approaches. And, as the temperature rises, I know, he will be aroused from his winter's slumber.

He's a spider.

13

I know every basement has its spiders. You can find cobwebs even in the best-kept homes.

But, he's no ordinary spider. He's a multilegged, man-eating monster.

I know, I've seen his tracks through the sawdust on my workbench.

My wife thinks I exaggerate because of my general dislike of spiders.

I don't know why I possess bad feelings toward spiders.

Maybe it's the way they do their grocery shopping.

It's gruesome to think of some poor creature suddenly becoming trapped in a web, helplessly struggling before the malevolent eyes of the hungry octopod.

And, I dislike a spider's lack of concern about where he puts his web. I hate it when I inadvertently walk through a spider web. And, doubly unnerving is finding an irate spider dangling from the tip of your nose, glaring at you as if it was entirely your fault his web was broken.

Anyway, I'm convinced that lurking in my basement is the granddaddy of all daddy longlegs.

Even the cat won't take it on.

My wife's cat doesn't mess with mice, but is death on insects. Trouble is, most spiders reside in places she can't get at. So while our millipede population is scarce, spiders are spreading.

The more I thought about cleaning the basement, the more I thought about that spider. I began imagining what it would be like facing him...

"Do you see any sign of him?" I ask in a trembling voice.

"Quiet! With you talking I'll never hear him coming. I feel like bait for an alligator," she says angrily.

I climb up on top of the washer and sit down crosslegged. I lift my 12 gauge semi-automatic shotgun and pull back the bolt.

"All you've got to do, honey, is yell and duck; I'll do the rest," I instruct as I watch the shell go into the chamber.

Suddenly a shadow shoots along the west wall.

"DONALD!" my wife screams, diving for the floor.

BLAM—BLAM!!

My wife gets up on her knees and peers through the gunsmoke.

"Donald, you just killed the furnace!" The furnace looks like a soup can that kids peppered with .22's.

"There he is!" My wife points toward a closet door.

14

"Die, spider," I yell.

BLAM—BLAM!

Pieces of cloth float down like snowflakes.

"Donald, those were my good sweaters and winter coats!" She begins crying.

"Hold still, you lousy legged web slinger!"

BLAM!

A box of laundry detergent explodes, filling the entire basement with fine white dust.

Through the white cloud I watch as the gray, basketball-size creature crawls up the wall and out an open window. I take chase, my wife close behind.

We look out the window just in time to see it break through a screen and crawl into our bedroom. We turn to each other in horror...

Suddenly my mind shifts back to the present. I hear my wife coming up beside me.

"Come on, Donald, I want that basement cleaned."

"Uh, maybe tomorrow, dear." A look of dread crosses my face. I feel like a fly bound for a web of doom.

* * * * *

WHO YOU GONNA CALL?
SPIDERBUSTER!

Ever since my wife put the cat's food dish down in the basement, the spiders down there seem to be thriving.

I often thought mice were the worst creatures to have in one's home. I was wrong. You don't know terror until you've come face to face with an overfed spider.

It's an awesome experience.

We put the cat's food in the basement because our baby amused herself by playing in it, and on more than one occasion, dining on it.

Eating cat food didn't seem to bother the baby, but it gave the cat conniptions.

Despite having to walk a bit farther for supper, I think the cat appreciated the basement because it offered coolness and a lack of competition from the baby.

Everything was fine until one night I awoke to a sound like someone was walking up the basement steps. Flashlight in hand, I investigated. With a great deal of anxiety I opened the door to the basement and turned the flashlight on the steps.

I don't know if it was my scream or the crashing sound when I fell head over heels onto the kitchen table. Anyway, my wife came rushing in just as I picked a salt shaker from my mouth.

"What is it?" she said in a half worried, half groggy voice.

"Spiders," I replied, as I fought the urge to scream again.

"I tell you, there are spiders big as hen's eggs rappelling from the ceiling to the basement steps. Listen to them."

For a moment we both stood silently and listened to the thud—thud—thud coming from behind the door.

I peeked through the doorway once more.

There were a dozen spiders hopping down the stairs toward the cat's food dish. Some were already in the food, devouring it with great abandon.

Some looked like overhead cranes as they dangled on strands of webs and grabbed bits of kitty chow with their eight legs.

I locked the door and my wife and I returned to bed for a very uneasy sleep. I kept waking up thinking I felt something crawling up my leg.

The next morning, after rather strenuous urgings by my wife, I returned to the basement to do battle with the eight-legged devils.

With a softball bat in one hand and a bottle of Stroh's in the other, I cautiously edged past the cat's dish. Suddenly one of those big black bugs appeared on the ceiling. Held by a single strand of web, he plopped down inches from my face and growled at me.

I quickly stepped back and sprayed him with beer. That didn't faze him, so I dropped the bottle and swung my bat with all my might.

Ever hit a tomato with a baseball bat? That's what it was like batting that bug. I had spider guts from head to toe. It was absolutely gross picking spider legs from my beard.

16

Meanwhile the cat had come down the stairs to watch the battle. I grumbled that I shouldn't have to do the cat's work cleaning up those marauders.

Suddenly, one of the ugly critters charged at me from behind a box.

I whipped around, grabbed the cat and threw it at the approaching monster.

For the first minute I thought the spider might win, but the cat seemed to catch a second wind and outwrestled the bug to a rather gory and fatal conclusion.

I marveled that this was the first time the cat had shown any enthusiasm for something other than being fed. Of course, fighting for one's life tends to bring out the best.

Buoyed by her first success, the cat took after a few more spiders. Boxes and papers flew. At times the cat leaped high above the debris, wailed fiercely and dove back in.

I tell you, olympic wrestling wasn't half as exciting as watching that cat roll around in the dust with a huge miltilegged attacker.

Any spider that tried to retreat up the walls, I nailed with the bat.

The carnage lasted about 45 minutes. The cat finally appeared—victorious—licking off the spider legs dangling from her whiskers.

I think we got them all.

But every night when I get into bed, I have this uneasy feeling that somewhere on the ceiling, hiding perhaps in a dark corner, is a lone surviving spider.

A creature bent on revenge for the massacre of its family. A big ugly thing itching to get its hairy little legs around my neck.

* * * * *

TUB WARS: A CLOSE ENCOUNTER OF THE WORST KIND

Ever been attacked by a shower spider?

It's horrible.

The other morning I was about to take my shower when I discovered I wasn't alone in the tub.

There by the drain was this huge, furry, eight-legged creature staring up at me.

He had apparently crawled up through the drain. Normally the drain has a screen over it, but I haven't been able to find one that fits. But, that's another story.

I pushed my body against the corner of the tub opposite the spider. I hoped it was a male spider because I wasn't wearing anything. I didn't even have a washcloth to cover my nakedness.

I felt both a sense of violation and vulnerability.

The spider began moving away from the drain. Suddenly he paused, turned and started walking toward me.

I quickly grabbed a bar of soap and whipped it at him. The soap flew past him, glanced off two sides of the tub and ricocheted back, striking me in the shin.

Still he kept coming.

I frantically looked around for another weapon to dispatch this arrogant arthropod. For a moment I considered dousing him with shampoo, but I only had a bit left in the bottle.

Opening the water faucet on him wouldn't kill the big bug, it would just wash him down the drain. He'd only return a couple days later twice as mean, I told myself.

18

I thought about leaving the shower, running into the bedroom, grabbing my wife's cat and throwing it into the shower with the crawler. However, I dismissed the idea figuring the cat would make such a racket it would awaken my wife. I thought I'd rather deal with a spider than a prematurely awakened woman.

I concluded I had no choice but to go one on one with the creature, hand to leg combat so to speak.

You know it is one thing to go after a spider when you are fully clothed and wearing Playtex gloves. It's quite another thing fighting the crawler when you are totally exposed.

Somewhat apprehensively I got down on my hands and knees. The spider seemed to have quickened its pace toward me.

For a moment we both held perfectly still, each of us staring into the eyes of the other. This was no daddy longlegs. This was a killer spider, bred and reared in the harsh insect jungle that is my basement.

I lashed out at it with my right arm. Unfortunately the sudden motion caused me to lose my balance and my entire body rolled over on the slippery tub surface.

Flat on my back I looked around for the creature. I figured I had probably crushed him underneath my quivering body.

Then my eyes caught a hint of movement down by my navel. What appeared to be a tiny clump of hair began moving. But, it wasn't my hair—it was the spider crawling out of my navel.

He seemed to shake himself off, then proceeded to crawl toward my chest. Thank goodness I have hair on my stomach to impede his progress, I thought to myself as I watched the little bugger struggle past each hair.

I had him now. All I had to do was let him get close enough and then whack him dead with my hand.

It tickled terribly as he moved. But, I resisted the urge to brush him off. I had to let him get close enough so there would be no chance of missing him with my flattened palm.

It nearly grossed me out when I discovered he was spinning a web from hair to hair as he traveled. When he comes over the top of my pectorals, I'll get him, I told myself.

Leg by leg his ugly body appeared.

WHAM!

There was no evidence of the spider, but I knew where his remains were. I kept my right hand curled as I turned on the shower faucet.

That morning I washed myself twice. I did not want to go to work wearing spider guts.

I was drying myself when I felt an itch on my big toe. I leaned over to scratch it and saw to my horror another spider perched on the toenail.

I swear there was vengeance in his eye.

* * * * *

THE MUCH-MALIGNED MILLIPEDE

The other day I was watching a bunch of young boys attack a hornets' nest.

They'd run up to it, dump something on it, and take off running as the hornets came swarming out.

Heck, I used to do the same thing when I was a kid.

Things never change.

You'd think after being stung often enough, my generation would pass the word on to younger generations that you don't mess with bees.

Anyway, I got to thinking how intimidated man can be of a bug no bigger than his pinky.

I mean, here are these kids running full tilt from something only 100th their size.

If we're so smart and talented and superior in all ways, how come we let an insignificant insect push us around?

On the other hand, we really do a number on insects who can't protect themselves.

Lately, I've been getting pretty incensed about the way millipedes are treated at the Daily Herald offices.

20

A millipede is a multilegged creature that resembles a skinny caterpillar. The minute a millipede is spotted in the newsroom, chaos ensues. Men scream; women shriek. Or, is it the other way around?

The meek leap to their desks; the brave take after the swift-legged creature.

The bravest usually overtakes the poor thing and SQUISH—the millipede becomes but a smear on the floor.

What have millipedes ever done to deserve such treatment?

They don't buzz.

They don't bite.

You don't see screaming headlines in newspapers: "Child attacked by millipede; dies in mother's arms."

They don't infest.

You don't even see a millipede on Raid commercials.

Why, then, do we squish them at first sight?

Maybe we're jealous.

I mean, many of us have a hard enough time running on two legs. A millipede effortlessly runs dozens more. A lot more coordinated than most of us, I'd say.

OK, millipedes aren't pretty.

Admit it. We are prejudiced against unsightly insects.

Hey, how many of you have put the boot to a butterfly? That's right, you never see butterflies smeared on the floor.

You don't see people run for the hills when a butterfly flits past.

But, put an ugly spider within a quarter-mile of some people and they'll have a coronary.

Maybe we have a bias against legs?

I mean, a spider has eight of them and we all hate spiders.

Centipedes have ten and I've never heard anyone with a kind word about them.

But, think: If you took all the legs off a millipede, what would you have? One mad millipede. You'd also have a big worm or a little snake, neither of which would appeal to most of us.

I guess they just can't win.

Maybe if we grew to understand this multilegged creature better, this malevolent millipede mayhem would end.

OK, millipedes aren't the most sociable of creatures.

But, I'm confident if we get to know the millipede—you know, spend a day with one—we'd gain a better respect for this much-maligned creature.

21

The next time you see a millipede racing across the floor, don't send the dog after him.

Pick him up. Give him a name. Give him lunch. (Hey, I don't know what millipedes eat—give me a break).

Relate to him. I don't know how you would relate to a millipede. How do you relate to a dog? You pet him, so...

Maybe race him across the room—you need the exercise more than he does.

Let's pledge to get to know our multilegged friend and to build a better bridge between ourselves and the poor little millipede.

* * * * *

A TALE OF TICK TERROR

The following column is R-rated. Anyone under 17 cannot read this unless accompanied by an adult.

The producers of recently released horror or thriller movies are really missing the boat.

They have produced a wide variety of movies about psychopaths, monsters, devils and other macabre creatures of the night. And, these movies seem to be doing quite well at the box office.

But, they have neglected the most terrifying creature of all. Why, the mere mention of its name makes people nervous. Some Wisconsin people I know get downright paranoid.

It's the tiny tick.

Scared already, aren't ya?

I once wrote a column about encountering a woods filled with ticks and how I kept finding them on me for days after my woodland visit.

After publication of that piece, people came up to me on the street and began telling me horror stories about their own encounters with ticks.

I suspect there hasn't been a movie about ticks simply because there aren't any ticks in Hollywood.

I suppose I could send them a few just so they could get some idea of what it's like to find a tick burrowed into your flesh, snacking on your blood.

Instead, I'll send them the following script and wait for them to come banging on my door.

DBO productions presents: "Tick Terror" Rated R.

The movie begins with a scene of a shaded woodland glen where three young and beautiful girls are seated around a campfire. They're Girl Scouts out for an afternoon adventure. They're laughing and singing.

Suddenly the camera pans away from them and focuses on a nearby bush. The leaves are mysteriously shaking.

The camera quickly shifts to a stand of tall grass quivering.

Ominous music builds to a crescendo.

Soon all the foliage around the girls is vibrating, but so quietly the girls don't notice.

(Out of respect for my editor, I will not include in this column a description of the ensuing scene. If you feel disappointed, you've seen too many R-rated thrillers and should be ashamed of yourself.)

In the next scene, the lone survivor is home alone in bed. She is trying to sleep, but can't. Nightmares of the day before keep reappearing.

Ominous music begins.

The girl tosses and turns. On her sheet a small dot begins to move. In the moonlight it casts a tiny shadow across the white sheet. Soon another dot appears and begins to move toward the girl's head.

For some reason the girl opens her eyes and glances down the bedsheet and sees...

The scream can be heard throughout the house. Her parents run to her room. But, it's too late.

The following day the father is driving home from the cemetery. The camera shifts to his rearview mirror. There on the top is a smiling, hungry tick.

THE END.

23

Of course, I'll be adding other scenes, each progressively more vile and grisly. Using the standard R-rated thriller format, I suspect I'll kill about a dozen people.

And, of course, I'll write it in such a way as to make a sequel.

Move over "Friday the 13th" and "Texas Chainsaw Massacre"—"Tick Terror" and "Return of the Tick" are coming soon to your local neighborhood theater. Watch for them.

* * * * *

THE NIGHT OF THE INTRUDER

This being close to Halloween, I thought I might recount this story, which is true with one exception that will be noted later on.

Evidence indicates that what attacked the young woman that night wasn't human. It was a creature having no emotion or remorse—just an inhuman desire for her blood.

The attack occurred shortly after midnight on July 22, 1977. She was alone in her one-bedroom apartment located on a quiet street in a small Wisconsin city.

No one heard her scream that fateful night.

No trace of the assailant was ever found.

At approximately 11 p.m., the 27-year-old woman was sitting in bed reading a paperback novel. The night air was humid and hot; so hot one would think the noonday sun was still shining. She couldn't sleep.

Then she remembered that she had forgotten to open the bedroom window. She got up, opened it and returned to bed.

She didn't know that evil was watching her from outside, waiting for an opportunity to gain entry to her room.

A gentle breeze blew lace curtains apart. Like cool stream water, it meandered across the room to where she lay. The breeze parted her long blonde hair and pushed her curls across the silken pillow.

24

At approximately 11:45 p.m. she set down her book and turned the light off.

A short time later the breeze disappeared. The curtains became still. But, she didn't notice for she was fast asleep.

A nearly full moon slipped from behind a cloud, its light striking oak leaves outside her window. The combination created eerie shadows.

Suddenly, a bat flashed into the moonlight. Startled by its exposure, the creature dived back into the darkness and disappeared behind a tree.

A neighbor's dog began barking wildly as if disturbed by an intruder.

"Shaddup, you mutt," someone screamed. The dog ceased barking. A window slammed shut.

The moonlight filtered through the lace curtains, which hung in long curves on either side of the window. The soft light crossed the room and fell upon the sleeping woman.

The curtains moved as if hit by a single gust of wind, then became still again. A shadow appeared on the window sill, so faint as to be hardly seen.

The shadow crossed the sill. As it did, it grew larger, as one's shadow grows at sunset.

Except for the woman's gentle breathing, the room was quiet. The intruder made no sound.

The intruder jumped off the sill, but instead of falling to the floor, it floated as if held by the moonlight. Silently it moved next to her, its head very close to her pretty face.

For a moment it stared at the sleeping woman. It studied the soft features of her face. It glanced at the shape of her body beneath the light sheet.

It watched her lips tighten in a smile. Her dreams were perhaps pleasant this summer's night. There was no hint of foreboding, only a somnolent peace.

The creature, satisfied his presence was undetected, drew even closer to her. Its body once again entered the stream of moonlight.

It had an ugly, unshaven face. Its small eyes bulged slightly. From its mouth appeared something long and narrow, something resembling a dagger.

It placed this needle-sharp protuberance directly above the soft flesh of her neck and without hesitation plunged it into her.

"AAAAAAAAIEEEEE!" she screamed as she jumped up, the sheet tumbling to the floor.

WHACK!

"Darn mosquito!"

Epilogue: As I said at the outset, this story is true with one exception. The victim wasn't a young girl, but myself. But, heck, it's more fun writing about young women.

* * * * *

ZAPPING THE ZAPPERS

Remember the television show, "The Twilight Zone"?

It was a a half-hour program back in the early 60's in which Rod Serling brought us stories of common folk placed in bizzare and frightening situations.

With horror stories in vogue nowadays, I offer his tale loosely based on a conversation I had with a co-worker.

Mr. and Mrs. Jones were a Wausau couple living comfortably in a suburban, ranch-style home. During the summer they'd spend a lot of time sitting in lawn chairs in their backyard and enjoying barbecue meals.

Mr. Smith was their neighbor to the north. A quiet man who enjoyed the quiet of the suburbs. He loved to sit in his backyard in the summer, sipping on a beer and listening to the sounds of nature.

One hot July day, Mr. Jones brought home a large, blue-lighted electric bug killer. He thought he would make his life in the backyard more comfortable. But, he was soon to discover, he had just bought a ticket to the "Twilight Zone."

The following day, Mr. Jones installed the bug killer on a post in the middle of his backyard. Almost immediately it began electrocuting flying insects.

Mr. Jones smiled and sat down in a chaise lounge near the killing machine.

Day in and day out, the device killed. It was never turned off. Piles of burnt bugs began appearing at the base of the pole.

Next door, Mr. Smith sat in his lawn chair with his hands over his ears, his face tight and red.

The sounds of nature he once enjoyed had been replaced by ZZZZZZZZZZZZZaaaap, zzzzzap, sizzzzzle, zap. Hour after hour, night after night, the sounds of carnage continued.

He had asked Mr. Jones to shut it off during the night, but Mr. Jones refused. He had paid too much for it to sit idle.

It was early August. Mr. Smith had become increasingly nervous and distracted. He had had enough.

One night he sneaked into Mr. Jones' yard and threw a mug of coffee into the bug killer.

ZAAAP sssssssssssssssssssssssss.

Next morning, Mr. Jones found his bug killer covered with sticky goo. "Wow, must've been one big bug that hit that baby," he said, shaking his head.

He cleaned the unit and plugged it in again.

Mr. Smith stood by the fence staring at the blue light and the tiny puffs of smoke around the coils.

He wished a bolt of lightning would hit it. The ultimate ZAP!

Then he smiled. He had a plan.

It was about 3 a.m. Mr. and Mrs. Jones were awakened by a buzzing sound. It grew louder and louder. It seemed as if the entire house were filled with bugs.

Mr. Jones rushed to the window. It was covered with June bugs. The buzzing grew louder. A housefly alighted on Mrs. Jones' nose. She screamed and ran in terror toward the basement.

CRASH, tinkle, tinkle.

A June bug shot through the window, hitting Mr. Jones in the eye. He reeled backwards, tripped and fell, his head hitting a nightstand. The buzzing ceased for Mr. Jones.

In the darkness outside, Mr. Smith put down the shotgun into which he had loaded a blank shell and several June bugs. He shut off the recorder on which he had a highly amplified tape of a beehive.

As he listened to Mrs. Jones' screams, he walked over to the bug zapper, took it off the pole and carried it off to his garage.

Mr. Jones had sought refuge from nature, but found retribution and a first class suite for eternity in the Twilight Zone.

27

* * * * *

LEGION OF LEECHES MAKE BATH MEMORABLE

I have developed a profound dislike for the leech.

On my list of least-liked creatures, I put the leech right up there with the wood tick. In fact, the leech is worse.

Mosquitoes and flies are nuisances. Sure they bite and cause itching wounds, but you can always brush them off or swat them.

You can't swat or brush off a tick. When he has a hankering for your blood, it almost takes a Vice-grips to pluck the little rascal off.

However, ticks usually don't attack en masse. They're more the solitary guerrilla fighter waiting to make some heroic leap for your leg.

But the leech attacks you with an army and each soldier has tenacity equal to the tick.

This fall a legion of leeches attacked me as I bathed in a Canadian stream.

I decided that after five days of paddling a canoe, I was about due for a bath. When the fabric of your shirt starts disintegrating, you know accumulated sweat has gone beyond foul to corrosive.

I knew there were leeches about when I jumped in, but I figured a soap-covered human would be of little epicurean interest to the Canadian leech.

I should have known better. I had already discovered how sneaky they are.

The morning before, I found one rolled up dead in my sock. Apparently he had latched onto me while I was wading the canoe through shallow water and decided I would not only make a good

28

supper but breakfast as well. I guess during the night my foot odor suffocated him, poor creature.

Despite the chilly water, I had a rather nice leisurely bath in that Ontario river. It felt good to finally see flesh again.

As I dried myself, I happened to look down. To my shock I saw. at least—and this is a conservative estimate—three dozen baby leeches lunching on my left foot. Their momma was halfway up my calf, about to dine herself.

Apparently the babies use momma as a personnel carrier and fan out like a SWAT team when she finds a warm-blooded host.

Within moments they were chomping on my skin. Some found a shortcut by sipping on cuts I had incurred during the trip.

I flicked the mother off with one stroke, but the hungry babies already had their hooks into me. They didn't budge.

And, when a few did break loose, they immediately dug into my fingertips. I had to fight them on two fronts.

When I picked them off with my other hand, they'd cling to those fingers.

Fiddling with my fingers made me forget about the grand banquet being held on my left foot.

I thought about jumping into the water to drown them but realized: Cripes, that's where they live. I'd probably end up with twice as many on me.

I also thought about running back to the campsite and sticking my foot in the fire. The thought of seeing those leeches fry seemed worth the first-degree burns. But I discarded the idea, figuring my compatriots wouldn't understand such self-abuse.

After about ten minutes of picking, I managed to rip them off me—or at least those I could see.

Staring down at my bloody left foot—they had opened every cut and made some of their own—I decided there was no way I was going to put my socks on. So I walked barefoot through the woods back to our campsite.

I suspect that's how I acquired the poison ivy on both feet.

So for better than a week I sat itching my feet—thanks to those lousy leeches.

Next year I'm buying a bunch of leeches and using them as fish bait. I won't even care if I catch fish. I'll enjoy such satisfaction with each cast. Die leech!

* * * * *

CHAPTER TWO

TALKING TO THE ANIMALS

Recently I read that scientists are close to being able to communicate with dolphins.

Who the heck wants to talk with a dolphin?

Geez, couldn't you pick some more interesting animal to establish conversation with?

I can just picture the first conversation with a dolphin...

"Hi."

"Hello."

"Uh, nice day, isn't it?"

"Wouldn't know."

"Uh, yes, I forgot you spend most of your time underwater. So, how's the water?"

"Wet."

"Been busy?"

"Been swimming."

"See much?"

"A lot of water and a lot of fish."

"Oh, really. What kind of fish?"

"Big ones and small ones."

"Must be neat being a dolphin?"

"Yeah, it's a real gas. Hey, can I have something to eat now?"

I'm hard pressed to come up with anything valuable a dolphin can offer me.

And, the bad part of all this is, once we establish communication we are bound to corrupt whatever we're talking to.

I envision the following conversation with our same dolphin.

"Hey, dolly, you want a bucket of minnows?"

"Sure," the hungry dolphin says eagerly.

"OK, here's all you got to do," the human says as he looks around to see if anybody is watching. Then he looks in the water to see if there are any fish around.

"All you have to do, my friend, is tell me where those schools of tuna are."

"Why you want to know?"

"Oh, I don't know—maybe it's just I like to look at them."

"I don't know..."

"Trust me... Anyway, if you tell me I'll give you two buckets of minnows."

"Two buckets!"

"Yeah, two big buckets of delicious fish for your tummy."

"Well, you can find those tuna..."

And then the human sends out the tuna fleet and, well, the rest you can figure.

If it were up to me, I'd work to establish communication links with squirrels. Now, that would be worthwhile.

I envision this conversation with a local grey squirrel.

"Hi, Fred."

"How ya doing, Donny boy?"

"Not bad. Here, have a nut."

"Thanks. Here, take this dollar bill I found while looking for acorns. It's of no use to me."

"Well, Fred, what's new?"

The squirrel looks around to see if the two of them are alone.

"I've got lots for you, Donny boy, lots."

"Give it all and don't skimp on the gory details."

The squirrel smiles.

"Tuesday I was sitting on the limb of a maple tree outside the bedroom window of George and Mary down the street.

"Boy were they going at it. George was madder than a bluejay because Mary blew $500 on a new dress and coat.

"Mary blasted him for spending too much time at the golf course and getting drunk.

"Well, he denied getting drunk and then she said, 'I talked with Emily down the street and her husband told her that you were so drunk that you stole a hardboiled egg from the buffet and tried to drive it off number one tee.'"

"That sort of stopped him dead and things got pretty quiet so I left to drop over to Stan's. I made like I was looking for acorns while Stan played poker with his cronies.

"Who joined me in the trees but a bunch of detectives!

"The police have been staking out Stan's home for quite some time. Seems ol' Stanley has run one too many basement poker parties. Stakes have been getting a bit too high. Heck, there were more poker chips on Stan's table than I got nuts in my tree.

"From what I can gather, Stan's wife turned him in. One day I heard her lambast him because he sold her china to meet a gambling debt.

"Hey, I've got another hot story for you. You know that blonde down the street, well..."

A conversation with a squirrel would surely be more enlightening and entertaining than talking to some slimy fish.

Trouble is, you can't trust a squirrel not to talk about you.

* * * * *

EASEL COME, EASEL GO

Visiting the bird art exhibit at the Leigh Yawkey Woodson Art Museum made me recall the time I tried being a wildlife artist.

I figured it might be an easier way to make a living than working for a newspaper.

I borrowed an easel, bought some paint and ventured out into the woods to creatively capture nature's colorful creatures.

It wasn't long before I found a squirrel snoozing in an oak tree of beautiful bronze leaves.

Perfect.

I quickly set up my easel, put paint on the palette and began painting the somnolent squirrel. I figured since the squirrel could up and leave at any moment, I'd best do him first. The trees and flowers I could finish off later that afternoon.

I was working on his tail when a large acorn glanced off my head.

I rubbed the sore spot for a moment and just as I was about to resume my artistic endeavor another acorn hit me in the eye.

I looked up in the tree and saw the squirrel standing on its hind legs. It had one of its paws cocked back ready to throw another acorn.

"What do you think you're doing?" the squirrel yelled.

"Huh?" I was stunned. Since they're rather introspective creatures, it's not often a squirrel will yell at you.

The squirrel shipped another acorn at me, just missing my left ear by inches.

"Hey, buddy, I'm talking to you."

"Uh, I'm painting your picture."

"Did you ask if you could paint my picture?" the squirrel asked indignantly.

"Well, no."

"Don't you think you should respect my privacy?"

I smiled.

"Animals don't have privacy."

The squirrel let out with a loud chirp, picked up another acorn and threw it at me. It bounced off my cheek.

"Whadaya mean, animals don't have privacy? Who says?"

"Well, I don't see any signs..."

"And, I suppose I'd find signs in front of your house," he snapped.

"Well, no."

"How would you like it if you got up from a nap in the living room only to find a dozen members of the J. P. Boggs Memorial Nature and Man Watching Club gawking at you?"

"Well..."

"How would you like it if you stepped out of the shower as members of the Everett Edward Peabody Art Club drew charcoal sketches of your dripping body?"

"But, you're a squirrel," I countered.

"Does that mean I don't have feelings? Have you ever seen pictures of squirrels? They're disgusting."

"Ah, come on."

"Hey, when you see a picture of a squirrel, what is he doing? He's eating. You guys portray us as a bunch of lazy, fat acorn eaters."

"Well..."

"Or, you see photographs of squirrels in birdfeeders. People think we're all thieves.

"Look, I wouldn't have minded the attention if I was immortalized by professionals. But, no, squirrels get all the amateurs," he groaned.

He hopped off the limb and a moment later was on my shoulder.

"What's that gray spot that looks like someone sneezed?"

"That's you."

"You are the worst excuse for an artist I've ever seen. I don't think you could even paint a house. I want no part of such incompetence." He disappeared into the woods.

Well, that hurt. I put down my brush and returned to writing because, as everybody knows, squirrels can't read.

* * * * *

HUMANS CAST SHADOW ON GROUNDHOGS' TALENTS

"OK, groundhog, it's show time!" I yelled into a large hole in a town of Texas woods.

"Come on, you lazy critter, time to make your annual prediction. Tell us if spring will be early or late this year."

"Ah shaddup!" came a growling voice from within the hole. "Go away, you jerk."

"Listen groundhog. It's February 2 and it's your duty..."

35

"Duty my foot!" the furry creature yelled as he popped his head into the cold February air. "Darn it all, a groundhog can't get any sleep with jokers like you running around."

"Tex, all you have to do is look for your shadow. No big deal, just give a quick look around and head back to bed."

The groundhog shook his head.

"Look, yoyo brain, I'm through taking the rap for spring being too early or too late.

"You know, it's you humans who are making the predictions, not us. You never ask us."

"If I recall, I asked you back in November what winter would be like and you told me it would be warmer and wetter. You were wrong, buddy boy."

The large groundhog smiled.

"I think if you look at the past 100 winters, you'll find our winter on the whole has been milder. And we did have a white Christmas this year," he replied.

"And, I made my prediction without the benefit of my shadow," he snapped. "You know, there isn't a groundhog who believes that shadow nonsense."

"Then why do you do it every year?" I asked.

"Because turkeys like you come banging around waking us up!

"I admit some of us like the publicity. I mean, except for Groundhog's Day you don't hear much about us. It's like we're useless for 364 days of the year.

"Oh, occasionally you hear that disgusting little ditty— How much wood could a woodchuck chuck if a woodchuck could chuck wood?

"There are some of us who get a real charge out of seeing you humans freeze your tails off in the cold morning air waiting for our grand appearance."

The groundhog laughed heartily.

"But, really, this shadow business is needlessly hurting our reputation as weather forecasters," the groundhog said in a serious tone.

"You see, we do a lot of consulting work. Like we tell geese the best time to fly south. Deer contact us every fall to find out how severe the winter will be. We also help bears determine how long to hibernate."

"How do you do it?" I asked.

"Experience. For thousands of years the animal kingdom of North America has relied on the weather forecasting abilities of the groundhog. This business with the shadow is an unfortunate fad," he said.

"Years ago we groundhogs used birds to exchange weather data. Now we use radio teletype," he said, pointing to a large beam antenna hidden in the trees.

"Each day weather information from around North America appears on the screen of my Wang computer. Let me tell you, our data is a lot better than what humans have.

"You think you're such hot stuff with your weather satellites. Hey, all they do is take pictures of the tops of clouds. What do pictures tell you? Nothing!

"We get our information from migratory birds who actually fly through the clouds. They not only see them, they smell, taste and feel them. We don't just watch the weather, we have an intimate relationship with it," he said proudly.

"OK. What does your intimate relationship say about spring?"

"It's going to be early this year. And, right now indications are it will be a wet one."

* * * * *

GRUMPY GROUNDHOG GIVES IT A GO

He was right once,could he be right again? I thought to myself as I weaved my way through a woods in the town of Texas.

It wasn't long before I came upon his home, a foot-wide hole in the ground in front of a large fallen oak.

I gave the hollow log several raps with my walking stick.

"$%**%%&*!!!" growled a voice deep within the hole.

"Tex, is that you?" I cried out.

Like a cork from a champagne bottle, the head of a groundhog popped out of the hole.

"Cripes! A groundhog can't get any sleep around here. Who's doing all that pounding up here?" He glanced my way."Ohno, not you again."

"So you remember me."

"How could I forget? It took me two days to get back to sleep after you awakened me that February morning and wanted me to make some off-the-wall prediction about winter."

"And, you were right," I replied with a smile.

"Right?"

"Yup, we had a short winter just as you predicted. Take a look around—don't see much snow, do you? And, the air, notice how warm it is?"

"Too early for spring, I'm going back to bed,"he said with a tone of disgust.

"Well,before you go back to snooze, could you please tell me what spring will be like?"

The groundhog shook his head.

"You woke me up from a sound hibernation to ask me what spring will be like! Look fella, I've got to get my sleep or I'll be ornery as a hungry cat."

I smiled.

"Well, I just thought since you did such a bang-up job predicting a short winter, you might be able to tell me when I should put in my vegetable garden."

"Look, creep, I'm a groundhog, not a county farm agent."

"But..."

"Geez, I haven't gnawed through logs as hard as your head," he said, glaring at me.

"All I'm asking for is an indication of what lies ahead weatherwise."

"Look, clown, I'll give it to you straight. I'm a groundhog, not a weather bureau cloud watcher!"

"But everybody knows creatures of the woods are closer to nature, that they have a feel for nature that we humans don't possess. Nature reveals herself to you lower animal types."

The groundhog flashed its two large teeth.

"Whadaya mean lower animal types! You're the one coming to me for answers."

"Come on, you know what's going to happen," I replied. "Just give me a little of your insight."

The furry animal glared at me again.

"Yeah, sure. It's going to be wet. Plant your early vegetables about April 15. Then dig a big hole next to them and jump in."

"Jump in?"

"Yeah, that's what you do when you plant yourself. I mean, a nut like you ought to produce a really nice fruit tree."

I tried to ignore his remark and his snickering.

"Will spring be warmer than normal?"

"Hey, man, groundhogs only do winters, they don't do springs!"

"Aw, come on."

"Other animals have the franchise for spring predictions. I don't know who, maybe geese or rabbits..."

"You're avoiding the issue. Either you give me a prediction or I'll keep you up till May 1..."

"OK! You let me get back to what's left of my hibernation and I'll give you a groundhog's view of spring. But, don't spread it around that I gave you this. I can just see some irate goose hassling me about treading on his turf."

I got out my notebook.

"Spring will be warmer than normal and goodbye!" he said and disappeared.

* * * * *

Take a Gander at That Goose

You've got to admire bird watchers.

They'll go out into the most god forsaken areas in the worst of conditions just for the opportunity to view birds.

And, unlike some who enter the woods,bird watchers leave things as they find them.

I don't know what it is about us humans that we have this penchant for invading the privacy of other creatures. I'm not casting any moral judgments here. I'm as guilty or innocent as most.

Why, I remember once climbing a 40-foot tree in the middle of a swamp just so I could get a better view of a couple of herons in a rookery.

Can you imagine if I climbed a tree of similar size to get a better look at my neighbor?

In no time someone's husband would probably shoot me out of the tree or I'd find myself shackled in some locked room with a couple of psychiatrists huddled over me shaking their heads.

I have no trouble with bird watching until I begin thinking from the bird's perspective.

Notice, I didn't say thinking like a bird.I don't need to give people more reason than they already have to call me bird-brained.

Birds don't care that they are being watched, you say.

How do you know that?

Humans assume that just because the members of the animal kingdom don't speak the king's English, they don't communicate. They might just be more subtle in how they converse than we humans.

So, for a moment, let's see bird watchers from a bird's point of view, which, of course, is bird's-eye.

"Harry, they are looking at us again," says Henrietta, the blue jay.

"Try to ignore them," Harry replies as he pecks away at a worm.

"I can't.They disgust me so. Look at them gawking at us. There's that lady again wearing that repulsive pith helmet.Look at her pointing at us. She always points," Henrietta laments.

"Look, those humans don't have anything better to do, poor creatures. They'll become bored with us and move on. Tolerance my dear, tolerance," Harry says.

"Tolerance, my beak!I have a good mind to fly over them and..."

"HENRIETTA," the jay interrupts. "Doing something as vulgar as that would lower yourself to the level of humans. Such actions reflect poorly on our species.

"I want privacy, Harry.I want to be able to eat alone, raise my young alone... Why, everytime I take a bath, there are a hundred human eyes staring, "Henrietta says, her feathers ruffling.

Harry downs another worm and glances at the huddle of people whose binoculars are all pointing at him.

"Give'em a show,I always say, " Harry jokes. "Anyway, you should be flattered they look at you. You never see them admiring a crow."

"I have no intention of being another Bo Derek, "snaps Henrietta.

"Who?"

"That's the lady on the outdoor movie screen where a few of us girls perch every Monday night.Humans seem to spend a lot of time gawking at her as well."

Harry shakes his head.

"Now calm down, I don't want you to throw out a wing muscle again. Look, they're leaving. See, they're going over to bother that cardinal again..."

"Yeah, and that cardinal loves it,vain old bird that he is," Henrietta says with a sarcastic tone.

"And, Harry, go wash your beakout—you've got worm breath.""*

* * * * *

THE BIRDS DO IT BETTER

Do you realize we are the only animal who flies who requires someone else to tell us how to get back down?

And we think we're so smart.

Look, I've seen a billion bees land in front of a hive and I have yet to see one mid-air collision. I haven't even seen an aborted approach.

Ma Nature never intended man to fly, but we went ahead and did it anyway. So we must pay a price.

Other winged creatures were given their own system of navigation, sort of internal air traffic controllers.

I've seen dozens of blind bats fly tight patterns and never collide.

Man, on the other hand, was denied all faculty for flight. Therefore he had to create his own external means of flight and navigation.

Such a system has been in the news recently.

Right now, I'd be a bit wary of flying with a human, but I'd fly anywhere with a duck. With a duck, I'm assured of getting there in one piece.

I mean, we talk about the space age and point with a lot of self-pride that we can get from New York to London in a few hours. But, really,when you look at it,we have to take a back seat to the birds.

They get where they're going without fossil fuels.

They take off and land without the need of an O'Hare Field, tickets or baggage handlers.

They might get there slower, but they don't need to slam down a half dozen martinis just to obtain enough false courage to endure a high altitude flight.

Let's look at it another way. What would happen if birds adopted our system, say at Horicon Marsh?

"This is V-victor one ought ought four niner two—we're a 14-goose V coming in from northern Illinois—request permission to land. Over."

"Victor one ought ought four niner two, this is Horicon control. We have you on our screen, vector eight at 220 degrees, altitude 1,800 feet. Turn left two and a half degrees and begin approach to pond one zulu four. Over."

"Roger, Charlie Mother Goose."

Meanwhile, in Horicon tower a big goose waddles up to a group of geese sitting at a panel of radar screens.

"Hey, who's watching V-victory one ought ought four niner two?" he yells.

"I am, sir," a goose replies.

"Well, take a gander at your screen, boy. You've just steered them into two oncoming V's and a half dozen solo geese in final approach," he yells as he brings his huge wing down upon the head of the controller.

Suddenly a red collision light begins flashing. The young goose sits up and grabs his microphone.

"Victor one ought ought four niner two, assume emergency descent—you have two V's at three o'clock and are in a collision trajectory—drop to 500 and resume approach at ought four degrees north."

"Roger, Charlie Horicon tower—but, isn't that going to put us into range of those hunters down there?"

"Oh my gosh! Get out of there!"

"Too late,Horicon tower. We're getting fire, two are down—make that three—request clearance to ascend two triple ought..."

"Victor one ought ought four niner two,denied—you've got a V right above you—permission granted to dissolve your V at 500 and disperse."

"Roger, Charlie."

The big goose in the tower just shakes his head. The lowly goose controller is honking profusely, tears running from his eyes.

"Hey, boy, no time for regrets. You've got four other V's coming in and two in final approach."

"But, sir, all those birds..."

"Fact of life, son," the big bird says. "We've got 20,000 birds to bring in daily—most make it. Don't blame yourself, it's the system. Shake it off,boy, you've got three V's coming head on."

The young goose snaps to attention and begins speaking rapidly into his microphone.

"Baker Charlie forty-four descend immediately to fiver fiver four and land in pond 226—Zulu 50 turn 10 degrees left, descend to..."

* * * * *

RETWEET TO WISCONSIN

If robins are anything like humans, I can't believe they'd be that anxious to head back to Wisconsin.

Take Henry and Regina Robin, current address, a cypress tree in Boca Raton, Fla.

"It's that time, Henry," Regina says.

"Shhhhhhh!" Henry replies, his attention focused on a big earthworm lying on the moist lawn of a seaside resort.

"Don't shush me, Henry Robin!"

The earthworm slithers into the sod and disappears.

"Regina, ya dun it again. How ya expect me to eat with you yapping all the time?"

"You could afford to lose a little weight," she replies sharply.

"Remember last summer. Who was sitting in the nest when the bottom fell out? Who was it who fell on the hood of the shiny new Cadillac leaving a dent the size of a saucer."

"Well, if you had built the nest better," Henry replies.

Regina's face turns as red as his breast feathers.

"How come I have to build the nest each spring?"

"Well, someone has to engineer it and someone has to build it. Nature endowed the male with the ability to properly design nests."

"Nature endowed males with the ability to be lazy."

"And, nature endowed females with a big yap which is supposed to be used for carrying nesting material, not creating noise."

"Well, hear this, fella, we head north tomorrow."

Henry shakes his head.

"Hey, it's still cold up there. Remember last year? We spent three weeks huddled up next to some smelly chimney trying to keep warm."

"Look, if we don't get up to Wisconsin early, all the good nesting spots will be gone. And, I've got this feeling about having a family."

"Let's not have a family this year. I mean, year in, year out the same squawking bunch of ugly birdies who do nothing but make a mess of the nest."

"Now, Henry, you know we have a duty to perpetuate the species..."

"Well, let someone else perpetuate this year. I want to have some fun this year."

"Nature won't allow it."

"Hey, I don't want to and nature can't force me," Henry says defiantly.

"Look, pretty soon Old Lady Nature will put a bug in your ear and..."

"Well, you go up to Wisconsin by yourself and I'll stay here. That'll fool Mother Nature.

Suddenly Regina's expression turns suspicious.

"Why are you so insistent on staying behind?"

"Why not?"

"OK, what's her name?"

"What???"

"I've seen you eyeing those young southern birds. What they see in a fat slob like you, I don't know."

"Hey, I..."

WHACK! Regina's right wing flies into Henry's face, knocking him from the limb to the ground. Henry lies dazed.

Regina glares at him.

"It amazes me that Wisconsin would pick such a loathsome creature as its state bird."

Regina flies down, digs her claws into the back of Henry and lifts him up.

"We're going to Wisconsin and that's that."

Henry groans.

"I have a feeling perpetuating the species this year is going to be a real treat," he says under his breath.

* * * * *

A Snake Has "Hissssay"

The story and pictures the *Herald* ran about the snakes in the home in Kronenwetter brought a call from the American Snake Association. Not fluent in snake, our switchboard operator had a difficult time with the caller.

Naturally, she referred the caller to me. Now I speak some snake. A little garter, some pine—I have trouble understanding rattler because they tend to lisp their words.

"Hissssay, this is the American hissSnake Association, Idalou, Texas, calling and we're kinda miffed at the press hisssome of our hisssnakes have been gettin up your way," the snake spokesman said.

"We'd liked to print the other hissside of the hissstory," the snake said.

"Look," I said, "A couple of pine snakes were found in this house while this lady was taking a bath, no big deal."

"Front page news," the snake hissed. "We hissssaw the picture of that poor hisssnake being hissstrangled so his tongue would hissstick out!

"How'd you like it if hisssssomeone grabbed you by the neck and as you turned blue and your tongue became like a necktie he cried out, 'Hissssmile for the photographer?'" the snake said indignantly.

"OK, I'll hear you out. But go slowly, I have trouble with southern snake," I said.

"Hisssay you lived in a lonely hissswamp, but lots of people lived next door. Can you honestly tell me that on occasion you wouldn't wander over for a peek?" the snake asked.

"Well, that's all that hissssnake did. He was just curious. So what if he ended up in the bathroom while this woman was taking a bath. Why, you guys in the media made him out to be Jack the Ripper.

"Hissssnakes have had a bum rap from the beginning. Ever hissssince the devil used a hissssnake to deliver Eve's apple, everybody's been down on us.

"We are terribly persecuted. People hissscream when they hissssee us. How do you think that makes us feel?" the snake said in a sorrowful tone.

"Well, snakes do bite," I replied.

"Hissss-so do dogs. But, you don't hissssee people going around with shotguns blowing dogs off the face of this Earth.

"You reporters write really heart-wrenching hisssstories about little children getting bit by hissssnakes. But, you completely ignore the millions of hissssnakes humans kill each year.

"I bet you didn't know that last year over two million hissssnakes died on our nation's highways. More than 350,000 were murdered by humans.

"You married? Well, imagine your teenage daughter out on the back lawn hissssunbathing. Hissuddenly, over the fence hops a man with a gun and without warning he blows away your little darling.

"Well, almost every day hissssnakes hissssunning themselves on railroad tracks and woodland trails are killed that way by trigger-happy humans," the snake said venomously.

"And what do you teach your children? You tell them hissssnakes are hissslimy, vicious things that will only hurt them.

"If you had no arms or legs and a big giant picked you up and hissstarted hissstrangling you or twisting your body, what would you do? You'd bite him. It would be your only way of telling him: Lay off, jerk!

"What you humans forget is hissssnakes help you everyday. Why, if it weren't for hissssnakes, you'd be knee deep in mice and rats."

"Well, how can we help?" I asked, trying to calm the caller.

"Just leave us alone. We don't hissseek you out. We're like other wild animals; we have absolutely no desire to associate with your hissspecies.

"If we get in your way, just pick us up and put us aside. We love to be cuddled."

"Pick up a rattler? You've got to be kidding!" I exclaimed.

"Well, rattlesnakes, they're a mite bit particular about who picks them up. Rattlers seem to have no hissssense of the value of good public relations.

"But most of us aren't hisssuch a pain in the grass."

* * * * *

WOLF PACK TOUGH TO SIGN

With the actors' strike in Hollywood, television producers are seeking animal replacements for actors in commercials.

This is a well-kept secret.

Also, they're looking for animals to star in series. You've probably noted the increase this season of television programs revolving around animals.

Let's face it, animals don't have a demanding union.

I have it on good authority that right at this very moment Hollywood producers are in the Wisconsin northwoods looking for animal talent.

The producers have brought along animal stars to further entice wildwoods creatures to sign.

Like this bald eagle who does automobile commercials and poses for political campaign posters. He was brought to Lincoln County just the other day to persuade that bald eagle who resides near Lake Alexander to star in an upcoming car promotion.

The eagle told the Lake Alexander eagle how he came from the Mississippi Bluffs to Hollywood. He was dined on imported fish and given a carpeted nest on a hill above Bel Air.

Lots of animals are making it, the eagle said.

Take that cougar who does spots for Mercury, the eagle tells the Wisconsin bird.

He was a scruffy old cat eating cactus in the Mexican foothills before a group of producers discovered him.

His big break came when another cougar who starred in Walt Disney shows was kicked off the set of a Mercury commercial. It seems he decided to get sick while sitting in a new car. He ruined a $12,000 automobile and sent a beautiful young model into hysterics. The old Mexican cat was brought in and he handled the part with ease. In fact, he now is the pet of a Hollywood starlet.

Not all negotiations with animals go so smoothly, sources report.

We have learned that a group of CBS producers are negotiating with the wolf pack up in western Lincoln County.

The wolves are playing real hard ball.

The producers have a TV series in mind that would center on the wolves' struggle in a hostile land. Isolated from their Minnesota cousins, they suffer alone all the trials of Wisconsin pioneer life.

Sort of a furry "Little House on the Prairie."

"You've got a natural story out here, wolves. I see both a U.S. and a foreign market," the producers told an agent for the wolves.

"We're not impressed," the agent replied. "What's your offer?"

"We'll put $5,000 in trust for the wolves each season."

"You're nuts," the agent screamed.

A huge male wolf showed his teeth and growled viciously.

"Our pack wants nothing less than $25,000 a year in trust, a 100-acre wildlife sanctuary in Canada and a provision that during filming you guys keep the DNR boys off our back. Cripes! Our wolves can't move without some snooping wildlife manager making a federal case of it."

"Well, the $25,000 is no problem, but a wildlife sanctuary?" the producers asked.

"Once this show is out you can't expect the wolves to live in Lincoln County. Why the area would be overrun with little kids seeking autographs. A horde like that would terribly upset the deer herd."

"I don't know," the producer said, shaking his head.

"Look, in addition to the cash, our wolves want ten percent of any cable and five percent of any international film rights..."

"Hey, we've got a wolf up in Ely that will sign for half that," the producer interrupted.

"We ain't impressed..." the agent countered.

Negotiations are continuing.

* * * * *

49

GRIZZLY DOESN'T DESERVE
BAD NAME

It seems grizzly bears have an advocate in Washington these days.

His name is Russell Dickenson, director of the National Parks Service.

In a recent speech before Wisconsin park officials meeting in Wausau, he said it is time to think about closing portions of the Glacier National Park to backpacking and camping because of the bear problem out there.

"The bears in Glacier National Park are fighting back," he said.

After making a few remarks that people are intruding upon the bear's turf and not the other way around, he concluded with this statement:

"I'd like to let the back country (of Glacier) belong to the grizzly bears for awhile."

About time.

So often we hear about the grizzlies chewing up campers. A couple of years ago there was a movie about a grizzly who did rather nasty things to pretty young actresses.

Anyway, all of this is giving the grizzly a bad name. Really, he doesn't deserve it.

For a minute, pretend you are a grizzly bear.

Picture yourself walking through mountain forests or open meadows bathed in summer sunshine. The winds carry the scents of wildflowers and voice of John Denver singing "Rocky Mountain High."

Life's great. You've got plenty to eat and you're big enough that nobody bothers you.

So one day you stroll along a pristine trail and lo and behold, you come upon a couple of campers. Not having seen campers before you move in a bit closer.

"Oh my God, John! A bear, a BEAR!" this woman screams as she jumps up and down wildly.

You think that looks kind of funny and decide to watch.

Well, good ol' John jumps into the tent and comes rushing out with something in his right hand. Turns out it's a .44 magnum handgun.

And good ol' John begins shooting at you for no apparent reason, at least from your perspective.

You dash off as bullets whiz by your head and hit your backside.

After a couple of encounters like this, wouldn't you be a bit ornery?

Let's go one step further. Let's say, grizzlies could talk.

You're a grizzly, used to being lord of the mountain valley. You come upon a group of campers. What would you say?

"Hey, man, what you think you're doing?"

The campers look up. One camper gives you an obscene gesture and throws a beer can at you.

"Get outta my valley. You guys do nothing more than scare the other animals and throw beer cans around."

"We have a perfect right to be here," cries out one of the campers.

"You have no rights out here. This ain't Chicago, ya know," you reply.

"Bug off, bear," pipes one skinny camper, peering out of his Gor-Tex parka.

Getting a bit impatient, you'd probably growl a bit. Grizzlies like to growl.

"Look, what would you humans do if I wandered into downtown Skokie and set up residence in your backyard? You'd throw me out. You'd say I was trespassing," you say.

"Well, I say you're trespassing, you and all your foul smelling, cigarette smoking brothers. And, by the laws of nature, I'm throwing you out."

Well, when a grizzly tries to throw a human out, it's like a bulldozer trying to pick up an egg.

Consequently, the humans end up not only thrown out of their campsite, but out of the world of the living.

51

I think if you and I were grizzlies we'd agree that until humans learn they tread the back country at the pleasure of its inhabitants, they ought not to be welcomed.

* * * * *

GROUSE GROUSE ABOUT HUNTERS

When I'm in the woods I often listen to the sounds of its inhabitants.

Typically, we humans think any sound an animal makes has something to do with mating. Of course, we never apply the same principle to ourselves. Heaven forbid.

Well, I think the animals are talking about us. Take grouse. When they "coo" or drum, it isn't that they're cruising the woods for chicks. They're telling hunter jokes.

Frank, Fred and Felix grouse are sitting around having a brew—a can of Grain Belt left by a sloppy hunter. They begin trading hunter jokes.

"You know what a bear hunter is?" asks Felix.

The other two shake their heads.

"A nudist with a Winchester."

The group coo and cackle loudly.

"Ah, but do you know the difference between a goose hunter and a duck hunter?" asks Fred.

"A duck hunter will blow away two boxes of shells shooting behind a flying duck while a goose hunter will blow away four boxes of magnum shells shooting at geese a mile and a half high."

Frank pipes up.

"Yeah, that's like that drunk goose hunter from Chicago who blasted away at a high flying goose until his equally drunk partner pointed out he was shooting at a Republic Airlines jet."

Felix pours another round. He shakes his head.

"I can't figure it, guys. A grouse hunter will spend most of his weekend tramping through brambles, through swamps and risk getting lost about three times daily just to get a shot at a tough little bird he'll probably miss anyway," Felix mutters.

"Heck, he could get just as much fun swinging on clay pigeons all day and go to the supermarket and buy himself a chicken," Fred adds.

"Well, everybody knows how stupid grouse hunters are," says Frank. "I've heard it said a grouse hunter is a guy too afraid to hunt deer, too uncoordinated to handle a bow and arrow, too afraid of water to hunt either ducks or geese and too afraid of his wife to stay home," he says.

"Hear about the guy from Chicago who practiced his bird shooting by blowing away Frisbees thrown by his two boys at his home in downtown Evanston?" Frank says. "His practice ended when he suddenly pulverized his neighbor's picture window."

"Or that guy from Chicago's lakefront who took pot shots at golf balls at a driving range. He was getting pretty good until he nailed the club's pro teeing off," Fred adds.

Grouse love to tell Chicago hunter stories. These three birds are no exception.

Frank stands up, swallows the last of his beer, pauses for a moment and then recites his favorite Chicago hunter jokes.

"You can always tell a Chicago hunter—he'll wear a camouflage shirt and hunting boots with a three-piece Brooks Brothers suit."

The other two are kicking the ground and flapping their wings trying to handle their laughter.

Frank, seeing he's rolling, continues.

"There was this guy from Cicero who went after grouse with an M-1 rifle. No one in Chicago told him what a grouse was. He thought it was a rat with wings."

Felix and Fred are breaking up.

Felix raises his wing.

"Hear about the yahoo from Wilmette who went bear hunting and got so drunk one morning he shot a black Volkswagen as it went down the highway..."

"And, it wasn't until he tagged the front axle he realized his mistake," interrupts Frank.

The three birds cackle hysterically.

"Boy, hunters are funny," Felix says as he finishes off the last drop of beer.

* * * * *

RHINO RAISES RUMPUS

I was reading one of those hunting magazines the other day when I came to an article about rhinoceros hunting. It was one of those "I-have-three-tons-of-death-coming-at-me-and-no-cartridge-in-the-rifle-chamber" stories.

After reading through half the story, I found myself rooting for the rhino. I mean, what chance does an unarmed rhino have against a hunter holding what amounts to a baby howitzer?

I put the magazine aside and finished a bottle of Rhinelander beer that I had been nursing. For a moment my thoughts took a slight detour from their normal rational course.

I wish Wisconsin had rhinos, I thought to myself.

Wiscoinsin needs rhinos. Wisconsin likes feisty animals, else it wouldn't have allowed the University of Wisconsin to pick the badger as its mascot.

What this state's animal community needs is a little African muscle.

Remember those cowboy flicks in which a town is continually harassed by baddies until some dude with a fast gun arrives to show the townsfolk how to fight their oppressors?

The rhino could teach our woodland denizens a thing or three.

Take for instance highway accidents involving wildlife.

Nine out of ten times, the animal ends up on the short end in such accidents. While some motorist is crying because his fender is bent, some deer is breathing its last.

Nobody cares except the insurance company that is out a few bucks and some warden who is dragged out in the night to tag the carcass.

Now if there were a few rhinos about, people would begin to care. Maybe even drive a bit more carefully.

I got myself another beer and sat down to consider the possibilities. In my mind, a car appeared...

It's Happy Harry toolin' down the back road trying to show his date, Sally, that his little ol' Datsun is a Formula I racer.

Suddenly his front headlights catch the glimmer of two eyes off to the side of the road.

"Dumb deer," Harry tells his date.

In an instant the eyes are directly in front of the car. Harry hits the brakes. The car slams into the flank of a three ton rhino.

The Datsun folds like an accordion. The rhino doesn't move. He's got the car outweighed two to one. However, the noise and the smell of gasoline disturb him.

Happy Harry isn't happy anymore as he scrambles out from the wreckage. Sally follows closely behind.

The rhino turns and ambles down the highway about 20 yards, then turns again to face the car.

He snorts once. Suddenly his huge flanks shiver and his massive chest surges. All at once his body is set in forward motion.

He bows his head so that his mighty horn becomes a jouster's lance.

Kaaaaah BOOM!

Like a football off the foot of David Beverly, the Datsun goes sailing in a lofty arc, disappearing into the darkness.

About five seconds later comes a terrible crash as metal and glass weave themselves into a grotesque heap.

Wide-eyed Harry looks at the roadway. The only remnant of his car is a slightly cracked rearview mirror shining in the moonlight.

The rhino looks at Harry. Then he glances at Sally. He gives what appears to be a wink, then snorts. As the rhino leaves, Harry swears the beast is laughing.

Yup, with rhinos around, police would sure have some interesting accident reports to write, I say to myself as I finish another bottle of Rhinelander.

WANNA LLAMA FOR A PET?

The rage in Southern California is to buy a llama for a house pet. A llama is a creature that looks like you took a sheep, stretched its neck ten times its length and jacked up its legs.

A llama is to a camel what a Volkswagen is to a Cadillac.

Truthfully, I can't fathom why anyone would want one of these Peruvian creatures as a house pet. I'd rather have a Dalai Lama who does housework.

Llamas are big and ugly and I suspect not housebroken.

What are you going to do with one?

I mean, they don't bark. There's no such thing as a watch llama.

I suppose you could ride them. But, it would be like owning a horse. Can you imagine the Marlboro man riding up on his llama?

I suppose being the first on your block to own a llama brings a certain status.

But, I suspect that newfound status might be offset by some newfound problems.

"Get your *&&**&%&* llama outta my garden, Oakland!"

"Gosh, I'm sorry. He must have jumped the fence again," I say apologetically. I grab my lasso.

"Look at my prize petunias—petunia blossoms all over my garden like confetti!" he sobs.

Twirling the lasso over my head, I jump the fence and charge the llama, who stands contentedly nibbling on rose petals.

"AAAAAAAAAGH!" Mr. Smith screams as he spies the errant creature among his roses. His scream scares the llama back over the fence into my yard.

56

"That beast has eaten its last bud, by golly—I'm going to blast that **&&% thing to kingdom come," he says, running into his house.

"SURRRRRIIEEEEKK!"

I whip around only to see my llama eyeball to eyeball with old lady Jones, my neighbor to the east.

"Be calm, Jrs. Jones," I yell. "Llamas don't bite."

The same thing can't be said of Mrs. Jones' dog, which is half wolf/half canine mayhem. Always afraid of burglars, Mrs. Jones bought this trained-to-kill-on-command dog, whom she affectionately calls Poochie.

At the moment the dog is cowering under a picnic table, scared out of its mind by the odd-looking llama.

"I'd fetch my llama, Mrs. Jones, but your dog would have me for lunch," I cry out.

Mrs. Jones doesn't say a word, her eyes still locked on the llama's expressionless face.

Suddenly Mr. Smith bursts from his back door. In his hands is a double-barreled shotgun. He runs across his yard, leaps the fence as if it were a hurdle on a high school track and makes a bee-line for the llama.

"Bye bye, llamee," Smith says, putting his shotgun to his shoulder.

BLAM!

Mr. Smith, although a heckuva gardener, is no shot. His buckshot flies past the llama and Mrs. Jones and squarely hits Mrs. Jones' handcrafted porcelain birdfeeder. Instantly the feeder is but a cloud of gray dust settling over the green grass.

That brings Mrs. Jones out of her trance.

"You hoodlum!—Poochie, sic em."

With a growl the big dog shoots out from under the picnic table and heads full tilt toward Mr. Smith, who has thrown aside his shotgun and has begun a 440-yard dash for his back door.

Mrs. Jones' command also elicits a response from the docile llama. He licks her face. Mrs. Jones faints.

With the dog occupied, I sneak into Mrs. Jones yard, lasso my llama and drag him home. I lock him in the garage, go inside, pop a can of beer and wait for the sirens, followed by neighbors screaming, followed by a lot of llama lawsuits.

* * * * *

WILDWOODS THE LOCALE FOR "JAWS IV"

News Item: Something rose from the depths of Island Lake south of Hurley and bit a 13-year-old girl swimming—It probably was a muskie.

Wildwood Productions presents "Jaws IV."

Da dah—da dah—dadadadadadada...

A group of Girl Scouts frolic in the waters of Island Lake, unaware of the danger lurking below.

A camp counselor on shore spots something breaking the surface of the water. Her eyes widen.

MUSKIE! MUSKIE!

Pandemonium ensues in the swimming area as the girls fall over one another in a frantic race for shore. Within minutes they're all lying on shore coughing lake water from their lungs.

One of the girls looks out over the now calm water. A large painted turtle pokes his head up.

"Some muskie, Mrs. Jones," the girl says sarcastically.

Da dah—da dah.

The counselor suddenly realizes she forgot about the girl sunbathing on a small rectangular wooden raft about 100 feet off shore.

A large fin silently slices through the water next to the raft. The girl innocently lies on her stomach, soaking up the sun and listening to the radio which is drowning out the cries from her fellow scouts on shore.

A loud splash awakens her and she lifts her head just in time to stare into the gaping jaws of a monstrous muskie. She screams and dives off the raft just as the muskie's mouth chomps down on it as if it were a chocolate bar. But the raft becomes wedged in the muskie's

58

mouth like a stick between an alligator's jaws. The big fish thrashes about as the young girl swims safely to shore.

Da dah—da dah—dadadadadadada.

It's early morning. Clyde and Ernie have just lowered their bass boat into the waters of Island Lake.

"I tell you, Clyde, that muskie is ours," Ernie says confidently.

"I don't know about this, Ernie. That's supposedly one big fish."

"Yeah, I'm ready for it. I've got my special bait tied to 3/8-inch-thick steel cable attached to a winch on the bow. I tell ya, Clyde, I could pull in a whale with this rig."

"But, Ernie, this ain't no perch we're after. It's a man-eating muskie!"

"That's why my lure is going to work," Ernie says as he attaches a Barbie doll to the end of the leader. He tosses the line out. "Let's troll!"

A few minutes later the line rips out from the boat. In a moment, the winch is empty and the boat is being pulled out into the lake.

Clyde quickly throws a chain to Ernie on the pier and he fastens it to one of the posts. The boat starts making cracking sounds as the pier pulls away.

"Ernie, get that tire chain out of the four by four, tie it to the pier and the front bumper, then start pulling," Clyde yells frantically as cracks appear across the hull.

Ernie fastens the chain, hops into the truck and puts it in low gear. The tires dig deep into the ground, but the truck starts sliding backwards as the pier disappears underwater.

"Oh, lordy, lordy, lordy," Clyde cries out. "I don't want to be some fish's breakfast!"

Faced with certain death, an idea flashes into Clyde's mind. He runs to the back of the boat and starts up the 75-horsepower motor. He turns it full throttle as he loosens the support bolts.

With strength that comes only with stark terror, Clyde lifts the whining motor over his head and heaves it like a huge shotput toward the fish. Mistaking the motor for something to eat, the big muskie turns and takes it like some big lure. In an instant, the muskie is mushkie.

Da dah da dah dadadadada.

* * * * *

DOUBLE ON THE MOO-ZARELLA, PLEASE

The other day I read a very disturbing article by our farm editor, Jane Hanousek.

She wrote about some University of Wisconsin Extension prof who says cows are perfectly capable of enjoying pizza.

Hey, if this weren't America I wouldn't worry about such strange ideas. But, in the land of opportunity, I fear such thinking may lead to...

The scene is outside a Wausau pizza parlor. A large truck pulls into the parking lot. A man gets out, walks to the back of the truck and lowers a ramp. He opens the back door and 40 Holsteins amble out.

Without prodding, the cows line up at the front door of the establishment. The man squeezes between them and enters the restaurant. A couple of cows follow him in.

"I'd like 20 extra-large cheese pizzas, ten medium pizzas with pepperoni and five with pepperoni and black olives..."

"MOOOOOO!" one of the cows bellers.

"Uh, hold the olives."

The clerk furiously jots down the order.

"Will that be here or to go?"

"Here."

"OK, that will be about 30 minutes. You and your cows can find seating over by that pen in the corner."

Meanwhile, a guy and his date walk through the door. The guy, obviously upset and with a disgusted look on his face, turns to his girl.

"Cows!"

"So?" the girl replies blandly.

60

"Hey, I'm not going to eat pizza in the same room with a bunch of cows."

"Why not? It's no big deal," she says, uttering a long sigh.

"They smell..."

"Half the guys I date smell," she snaps back.

The guy shoves the rear end of one cow and pushes another aside to get to the front desk.

"I hate cows, especially Holsteins. They're such obnoxious eaters. They just can't keep quiet at the table," he snarls.

Suddenly he stops dead.

"What's wrong, Sam?"

He grimaces. Slowly his eyes lower and for a moment he stares at his shoes.

"Look what that lousy animal did to my shoes," he screams.

"Calm down, honey," the girl says, tugging at his elbow.

"I will not! My good shoes, ruined!" His face turns red and his nostrils flare.

Without warning, he swings around and slams his fist into the side of a masticating bovine. The cow continues chewing.

"Sam, what are you doing?"

"Shaddap!"

Suddenly the cow swings its flank into the man. He goes flying across the room, bounces off a group of Holsteins and crashes into a table.

The rest of the cows begin mooing and moving about.

The clerk, sensing a melee, calls the police. He and the girl grab the young man and carry him outside.

He returns to his desk and turns to the farmer.

"Hey, I've got nothing against cows. They're good customers. Always tip well. But, I can't take this intolerance."

The farmer nods in agreement.

"Why can't people and cows get along? I know they come from different backgrounds. I know they speak different languages. But, cripes, you'd think they could sit down and eat a pizza without going at each other's throats."

Several burly policemen rush through the door, in their hands electric cattle prods.

"OK, where's the trouble?"

"We sent the troublemaker packing," the clerk replies.

One officer sighs. "Thank goodness. I've busted up three cow-man fights this month. Hey, I'm a professional, but sometimes I feel like a rodeo clown. Ya know, I don't even like milk anymore."

* * * * *

CHAPTER THREE

THE GOOD OL' BEARS STRIKE BACK

Once upon a time there were these two good ol' bears, Billy Joe Bear and Bartholomew Bear, Bart for short. Unlike other Wisconsin black bears, these two were restless winter sleepers. Hibernating was hard for them, simply unbearable.

One January day a procession of snowmobiles awakened the two bears from a light sleep.

"I can't get a wink of sleep around here," Bart said as he stretched out his mighty front paws and arched his back like some huge black cat.

"I tell ya, them things give me one heck of a headache," B.J. replied.

Believing they'd not be able to return to sleep, the two went for a walk in the woods. Soon they came upon two deep ruts in the snow, ruts which followed an old deer trail.

"Cross-country skiers, I'm afraid," Bart said, shaking his large head. "No privacy, I say, no privacy at all these days."

Then Bart smiled and clapped his front paws together. "You know, B.J., I feel like having a little revenge on those intruders," he said.

"Let's play a game of tag with the first group of skiers to come down this trail. We'll hide behind that big ol' oak and when they come by we'll give chase," Bart explained.

About two minutes later a group of six skiers came sliding down the trail. As they swished by that big oak, the two 400-pound bears let out with fierce growls.

The skiers stopped cold. The skier who brought up the rear turned slowly, he didn't want to see what he thought he had just heard.

"Bears! he screamed.

With Bart and B.J. barreling full tilt down the trail, that skier nearly jumped out of his bindings. He dug his poles into the snow and gave a mighty kick. He never bothered turning forward so he didn't see the skier ahead who was frozen with fear.

The two skiers collided and fell into a tangled heap. The two bears leaped over the screaming skiers. They were in hot pursuit of the remaining four skiers.

The poles and skis of the skiers moved like high speed pistons. They cared only for speed and ignored the finer points of trail navigation.

Skier No. 4 hit a dip and careened off the trail like a stock car off a high-banked curve. A broad white pine abruptly ended his flight.

Skier No. 3 spotted a low limbed pine and figured he'd try to climb to safety. Didn't seem to bother him that he still had on his skis. Halfway up he slipped and came to hang upside down, his skis firmly held by several limbs.

Skier No. 2 made the mistake of looking back and seeing Bart only a few yards behind. The sight caused him to cross his skis. He went end over end for about 20 yards before landing like a brightly colored cheeseball with toothpicks stuck in it.

Skier No. 1, the best of the bunch, gained more speed by the minute. Thinking about nothing but gaining more speed is fine as long as the trail remains straight.

It didn't. It made a sharp turn to the right to skirt a 30-foot drop.

Like a man off a ski jump, he went flying—sailing over treetops like some huge bird of prey and screaming like a teenager at a horror movie. But his screams grew faint as he disappeared into the branches.

As sounds of breaking branches filled the stillness of the woods, Bart and B.J. rolled in the snow. Vengeance was theirs.

* * * * *

B.J. AND BART ON A BUMMER IN WESTON

Back in February I devoted a column to reporting on the exploits of two good ol' bears, Billy Joe and Bartholomew, who had a penchant for harassing cross-country skiers.

When I heard about two bears harassing the good citizens of Weston, I figured it must be the same two. Through connections I have with the animal underworld, I was able to locate Billy Joe up in Langlade County.

I found him sitting upright against an oak tree, his front paws clenched to his massive head. His tongue was half hanging out.

"Oh, do I have a headache. Wow! I'm still seeing stars," B.J. moaned.

"This is worse than the time I raided ol' man Schneider's honey yard and got attacked by a million bees and the buckshot from ol' man Schneider's shotgun," B.J. said.

"Hey, were you in Weston the other day?" I asked.

"Sure was. Let me tell you, those people are anything but hospitable. Heck, you'd think Bart and I were the plague," he said in an angry tone.

I asked him what happened.

"Well, ol' Bart and I were getting a bit restless. Food was scarce. All the other animals were on edge because things were so dry. Everyone expected the woods to burn down at any moment.

"It was a real bummer with everyone so down on life. We decided we'd just leave for a couple of days and see if we could find ourselves a couple of female bears and a good time.

"Boy, what a mistake that turned out to be," he said, shaking his head.

"We were still two lonely bachelor bears when we encountered the town of Weston. Normally, we'd pass by during the night and no one would be the wiser, but we were impatient. We decided to try to sneak through.

"We were spotted right off. Then all hell broke loose. People flocked around us, yelling at us, calling us nasty names and trying to push us around.

"You know, messing with humans is like foolin' around with whiskey—the longer you indulge, the worse your reward," B.J. said with a smile.

"Bart wanted no part of this nonsense and hightailed it for the woods. I sort of liked the attention and played the part of a dumb animal for awhile.

"Well, all this was mighty exhausting. Later that night I found myself a nice tree and took a snooze. The next morning I wake up and find all sorts of people below me and one of them is pointing a gun at me.

"Well, I about died."

B.J. got up on all fours.

"Suddenly the jerk with the gun fires and I'm hit. Things go crazy! Oh, wow! Everything begins spinning, then the world goes black. I lose my balance and tumble out of the tree."

B.J. rolls to the ground demonstrating how he fell.

"Next thing I remember, I'm sitting by this tree nursing a throbbing headache.

"I tell you, never again am I coming into town. You people are crazy.

"You walk into my woods, my friends and I don't surround you and call you names and point guns at you. No sir, we animals have some semblance of class.

"Heck, it's not as if I came to town to rob your banks, rape your women and eat your kids. Maybe I might bounce a garbage can or two, but really, that's no excuse for coming after me with guns," he growled.

I figured I'd better leave ol' B.J. as his demeanor was taking a turn for the worse. I got the distinct feeling he'd love to take out on me the abuse he experienced from my species.

* * * * *

B.J. Shoots for a Full House

Normally this time of year bears are settled in for a long winter's sleep.

Not so with two good ol' bears, Bart and B.J.

"I'll take two, Bart," B.J. says, staring at his poker hand.

"Going for that full house, aren't cha?" Bart asks, smiling.

"I wish."

Bart pushes two cards B.J.'s way, then leans back and looks at his own cards.

"Dealer takes, ummm, three."

"That bad, huh?"

"It's been one of those nights," Bart says, staring at the pile of blueberries in front of B.J.

He looks up at B.J., concentrating on his eyes. B.J. doesn't flinch. He pushes four berries into the center of the long, flat log where a pile of berries has already been built.

Bart continues staring at B.J. He glances down at the cards in his hand and takes one more look at B.J. "Call."

"Two pair."

Bart throws down his cards and growls.

"Sorry, ol' buddy," B.J. says as he scrapes the berries to his side of the table.

Bart shakes his head. "I just can't get tired. We've been at this stupid game—let's see..."

"Four weeks, Bart, four long weeks..."

"You don't say."

"Trust me."

Bart smiles. B.J. starts dealing.

"Ya know, it's getting harder and harder to get to sleep. My nerves, they're shot," Bart says.

"I know whatcha mean."

"It begins in the fall, B.J. First it's the nature hikers, craziest group of yahoos I ever did see. The woods are filled with these nuts gawking at everything. If humans didn't taste so bad, I'd eat a few of 'em."

"Know whatcha mean. You want to open?"

"Then come these guys with guns. First they shoot at anything that flies, then they take after anything on four legs. I'll put in two."

"Did I tell you I had dogs after me this year? Went up a tree and lost them. Dogs are so dumb." B.J. smiles. "I'll see your two and raise you two."

"You're out for blood this time, B.J. ol' pal."

"Hey, I'm just testing your will," B.J. replies.

"I'll see your two."

B.J. leans back.

"Ya know, I've been thinking. It's time I settled down."

"What's her name this time," Bart says with a smirk.

"She lives up in the hill country about 15 miles north. Oh, she's a black beauty—broad shouldered with fur that has a shine like mink when the sunlight hits it."

"I see, love at first sight."

"Hey, this is deeper than just, well, you know, a momentary attraction."

"You've had more momentary attractions than I've got teeth. You want to play cards or daydream?"

B.J. glances down at his cards. "Dealer takes one."

"One???"

"Yeah."

"Gimme two," Bart replies.

"I tell you, I've got to get away from here. I just think it's time to settle down, find myself a good female and start a family."

"Now what would you do with a family, B.J.? You can hardly take care of yourself," Bart says.

"Hey, I could do it. Well, she could do it—I'd sort of help in between card games. How much you going to put in?"

"Three."

"Well, I'll see your three and raise you three," B.J. says confidently.

"Call!"

70

"Two pair," B.J. says slamming down his cards.

Bart smiles. "Well, family man, have a full house."

"Hmmmm."

"Well, B.J., it's apparent you won't be supportin' your new family playing cards," Bart laughs.

"Shaddup and deal," B.J. snarls.

* * * * *

BART AND B.J. GO BEAR BAITING

"I tell ya, B.J., nature payed a cruel trick on us bears," Bart says as he eases his black hulk into a woodland stream.

"How so, Bart?" the good ol' bear from Langlade County replies as he floats by on his back.

"Well, she gives us this big black fur coat that's perfect for keeping us warm in winter, and then makes us hibernate through the season.

"In summer when we're real active and it's hotter than asphalt in the afternoon, we have to carry this hairy hide around with us. I tell you, it's downright..."

"Don't say it, Bart!"

"Unbearable."

"The only thing unbearable is your lousy puns," B.J. growls. "Actually, it ain't too bad as long as we're sitting in this cool stream."

"You got a point there, B.J.. Trouble is you can't play cards in the water. Eventually you've got to head for shore and misery."

"Well, not today, ol' buddy, too $$%$&&*&*!! hot," B.J. says as he dives underwater.

Suddenly Bart's ears perk up.

71

"B.J., somebody's coming."

B.J. swims up behind a large bush and looks upstream. "Darn it anyway, another trout fisherman."

"That's the second one this week," Bart says disgustedly. "I tell you, they're peskier than flies on garbage. This one's a persistent little critter, though. Why, he must have walked a half mile through bramble and scrub pine to get here."

"I'd say they're more dumb than persistent. Doesn't make sense to go to all that trouble for one or two lousy trout," B.J. says as he fires his right paw into the water and pulls out a 13 pound brown trout.

"I can't for the life of me figure out how humans expect to catch fish flicking some string around on a thin stick. I'd have to be one dumb fish to go chase after a string," B.J. continues.

"Speaking of dumb, that loco human is walking right toward—and goodbye, Charlie!" Bart laughs as he watches the fishermen disappear into a deep hole.

"I suspect filling his waders would be mighty refreshing," B.J. laughs.

The man works his way back to shore and empties his boots. A few minutes later he's got them back on and is walking downstream.

"I tell you, the more misery a man can put himself through, the more macho he feels," Bart says, shaking his head.

"Macho, smaacho! Remember what we did to that trout fisherman last year?" B.J. asks.

"Darn, that was funny. As I recall, you were crouched down hiding behind this bush as the guy made his way downstream. Just before the fisherman would have seen you, you dove into the water and disappeared to the bottom of a deep hole."

"Yeah, I was sitting there holding my breath waiting for the dude to flick his fly over my way. Didn't take long before I saw it plop down right above me. Well, I grabbed that little fly between two claws and pulled her down to the bottom."

Bart starts laughing hard. "I swear, that fisherman thought he had a whale on. He got all nervous and started stumbling toward the hole. He was just about to reach for his net when you surfaced, front legs outstretched, teeth and claws bared and roaring like momma missing her cub.

"I tell you, B.J., I have never seen a human jump so straight and so high out of the water in my life. Why, his legs lifted outta those waders like they were blasted from a double-barreled shotgun.

"And, when he hit water he started swimming so fast he looked like a water bug with hemorrhoids,'" Bart says, holding his stomach.

"Well, Bart, let's see how far this ol' boy can jump," B.J. smirks as he disappears underwater.

* * * * *

RESPECT IS A TEN-FOOT, ONE-TON GRIZZLY NAMED GUS

Not all bears hibernate for the winter.

We know two good ol' bears from Langlade County who use winter as an excuse for a marathon poker tournament.

"Raise you 50 acorns," Bart says confidently. "Your luck has got to change."

B.J. smiles from behind a huge pile of acorns. "You could be right, Bart ol' buddy. Why, 24 straight days of winning is darned embarrassing.

"Call," B.J. says boldly.

Bart folds down a full house, queens high.

"Masterful, really masterful," B.J. says with a hint of jealousy. He slams down his two-pair, eights high.

Bart smiles. "Heck, maybe by March I'll be even."

"Ah, but remember how fleeting the finger of fate is in poker," B.J. cautions.

"We'll see. Deal, you bum," Bart snaps back.

"You know, Bart, bears have an image problem nowadays. We don't get any respect," the big ol' bear says as he deals out the cards.

"How so?"

73

"I think it started with Smokey the Bear, you know that wimp whose face is plastered all over the place."

"You mean the dude in the funny hat?" Bart says as he studies his poker hand.

"Yeah, that's the one," B.J. says with disgust. "Darn it all, Bart, people think all bears are like Smokey: Always smiling, always friendly. Heck, people think we're all a bunch of teddy bears who love to eat out of the hands of humans."

Bart shakes his head. "Somebody tries that I'll take his arm off right up to the neck!"

"I tell you, people are making us out to be wimps. Like the other day I see this commercial on TV for some fabric softener. And, on it is this little pink teddy bear talking like a sissy. Madison Avenue thinks we're a bunch of pansies!"

"Yeah, and we're really such meanies," Bart laughs.

"Time was men would think twice about going bear hunting, especially with a bow and arrow. Nowadays you got women out there hunting. They must think we're as threatening as deer."

"I'll take two, B.J."

The bear throws down two cards.

"I bet they'd change their tune if my cousin Gus was around."

"You mean that ugly old grizzly from Montana?" Bart asks, looking up from his cards.

"He may be ugly, but he stands ten-foot tall and weighs in at close to a ton. And, mean—you look cross-eyed at him and he'll make you look like you've been through a Cuisinart!

"I can just see some Wisconsin bowhunter coming upon Gus in somebody's back 40. Just as he would draw back his bowstring, ol' Gus would turn around, stand up on his hind legs and give that hunter a look that said, "Go ahead and make my day."

"Why that hunter wouldn't stop running until he reached the next county. Heck, against ol' Gus an arrow would be about as deadly as a toothpick."

Bart laughs. "Yeah, it would take a howitzer to bring cousin Gus down."

"Can you imagine tourists trying to feed Gus? They'd putter up to him in their little foreign cars and Gus would give them that 'I eat Toyotas for lunch' look."

"Knowing Gus, he'd probably eat it, too," Bart says. "Grizzlies aren't subtle."

"With Gus around, we bears would get some respect around here," B.J. says proudly.

"Speaking of respect, when you gonna respect my poker playing abilities?" Bart asks, laying down a trio of kings.

B.J. raises his eyebrows and smiles. Then very slowly, card by card, he lays down a full house. "When you start winning boy, when you start winning."

* * * * *

CHAPTER FOUR

RACCOONS MAKE CHICKEN OF CAMPER

The thing I like about camping is you're never alone— especially after the sun goes down.

"AAAAAAAAAAIEEEEE"

My half-awake body bolts from the sleeping bag as my wife's scream echoes through the tent.

"Something just walked over my head!" she yells frantically.

"Nonsense," I respond, groping for my glasses and a flashlight.

"On the other hand, it could be a mouse."

"DONALD!"

I find my flashlight, but am unable to locate my glasses.

"Hurry, hurry!"

"I can't find my eyes, dear."

"I think I can hear it," she says in a whisper.

"Gotcha!"

"AAAAAAAIIIEEEE"

"Whatcha screaming for?"

"What kind of animal is it?"

"Animal?" I hold up my glasses in front of the flashlight. "Now where's this intruder?"

My wife points to the far corner of the tent. I shine the light over there. Nothing. I shine the light over to the front flap of the tent. It's closed tight.

"Dear, there's no way..."

"What's that?"

"What?"

"Outside, what's that rustling?"

"Probably a raccoon."

"Noooo, I bet it's a bear."

"Nah, it's just a raccoon looking for food."

"How do you know? You can't see him."

"There aren't any bears around here," I say in a calm, reassuring voice.

"My father says polar bears actually stalk and kill men and a grizzly will kill for no other reason than that you happened into his territory."

"Dear, there isn't a polar bear within 5,000 miles that isn't behind bars.

She listens intently. "There's another one."

"Probably several."

"Bears?"

"RACCOONS," I say with more than slight irritation.

"Well, go out there and scare them away. Why are they bothering us? Why don't they just leave?"

"Hey, they were here first."

"I don't care, they're scaring me."

"Look, they aren't going to come in here. They're only interested in food, not you..."

"Sure, remember up north? I was floating on that rubber raft 25 yards off shore when I felt something on my back and it turned out to be a huge garter snake?"

"Dear, it thought you were a warm log."

"I resent that!"

"Look, all he wanted to do was sun himself. Everything would have been all right had you not panicked and sent both of you into the drink."

"I never swam so fast in my life."

"Ha! The snake beat you to shore."

The rustling outside the tent continues.

"There must be an army of them out there," she says in a worried voice. "What if they attack?"

"Sure, I can see the headlines now: 'Wausau Couple Killed by Angry Horde of Raccoons—raccoons believed to be part of a radical animal terrorist group bent on driving campers from campsites...'"

78

"Stop your joking."

"Could be worse, dear."

"How so?"

"Remember the opening sequence in the movie 'E.T.?' That's what's out there—snooping extraterrestrials."

"Donald!"

"A small army of funny looking, gooey space creatures poking around in the weeds."

"DONALD!"

"They're coming to take you away, hey, hey. They're coming to take you away..."

"You're disgusting," she snarls as she flicks off the flashlight and buries herself in her sleeping bag.

* * * * *

OF MEN, BOYS AND BACKPACKING

Backpacking quickly separates the men from the boys.

But, some people's definition of what is manly will kill you.

On every backpacking trip a leader emerges. If no leader emerged, no one would get out of their sleeping bags in the morning.

A leader determines the style of the outing.

Some leaders' style resembles that of a Marine sergeant.

Why is it, when you backpack with someone who was in World War II, they keep talking about forced marches and 20-mile hikes with 50-pound packs?

What happens is the more these veterans talk like this, the more the backpacking outing resembles a forced march.

I'm not complaining.

Forced marches have their advantages.

79

You usually get to the next campground faster than any other backpacker on the trail.

The main disadvantage is you have to get up at some ungodly hour of the morning.

Never go backpacking with anyone over the age of 50.

People over that age require less sleep than, say, a person of my tender age.

Consequently, you and the old man go to bed at the same time, but he wakes up at 3:30 a.m. raring to go and you cry out for permission to sleep until 8.

However, with everything there is a bright side.

The older backpackers are usually the first to get the campfire going. There is nothing finer than a fire before sunrise.

You would think an older backpacker would have trouble keeping up with the younger members of the party.

Just the opposite is true.

My legs grew wobbly about the same time my older friends started getting their stride.

They were sorry when the day's hike was over. They wanted to plunge on another 14 miles because they were just getting warmed up.

On the other hand, all I wanted to do was get that (blank) pack off my back and plunge my swollen toes into a cool brook.

One nice thing about backpacking with the more mature hiker is he requires less food. He can go a whole morning on a cup of coffee and a cup of instant oatmeal.

On a breakfast like that, I can go about two and a half feet before feeling an empty stomach and a weak constitution.

The advantage of this is you don't have to carry as much food. The less weight in the pack, the less pain in the knees.

The disadvantage is you tend to starve.

When you're all prepared to devour a grand breakfast, the others in your party are packed and ready to hit the trail. It's either travel on an empty stomach or travel alone.

You never want to travel alone backpacking. You need someone to listen to your complaints.

It's always best to hike the trails with experience.

An experienced backpacker might get up early, break camp early and hit the trail with all the zeal of a teenager, but he'll take the time to appreciate things around him.

He'll pace himself. He'll pause to notice the leaves turning, the mushrooms sprouting up from fallen logs, the tracks of deer and the beauty of wildflowers.

He'll take the time to build a campfire from fallen wood (never live wood) because he knows a campfire is a lot warmer to the spirit than some modern backpacking stove which has a habit of blowing up or burning out.

He's fun to be with in the woods because he respects nature. It's not a respect gained from reading some book or subscribing to some pop land ethic.

It's a respect gained from years hiking and sincere appreciation of what enjoyment nature has given him.

* * * * *

THE HANDY, DANDY WALKING STICK

For his birthday, my father-in-law received the ultimate gift for the outdoorsman: A custom-made walking stick.

This walking stick, perhaps one of a kind, was fashioned by Helmut Schwab of Appleton who, when not busy being a chemist, does wild things with exotic woods.

Helmut took a sturdy limb down to his basement workshop and attached to it a wooden box with a hinged top. Into this box he placed items essential to a backpacker's survival.

Like toilet paper.

Most backpackers carry a couple of sheets of toilet paper in their packs. That supply usually runs out after the second day, leaving the poor backpacker to forage the woods for whatever substitutes the trees may yield.

But, the ever resourceful Helmut was able to build his box so that it could accommodate an entire roll of toilet paper. An added touch is that the tissue is dispensed from a hole in the bottom of the box.

Helmut had the uncanny foresight to include in his walker's box hemorrhoid medication.

Why, any seasoned backpacker will tell you, if you get hemorrhoids while out in the back country, you're done for. A week of rain and a legion of mosquitos would inflict less suffering.

I'll bet half the hikers lost in the Rockies are lost because they leave the trail in search of a drug store that carries Preparation H.

Also included in the box is a notebook and pencil. I suppose that's in case the hiker meets a bear. If you meet a bear on the trail, you'd best have something on which to write your last will and testament.

Another item: Lipstick remover.

Today's backpacking is a liberated affair and it's common to find women on the trails. It's very uncommon to find your wife among them.

And—well, I'd like to say more about this, but my wife will read it and never let me out into the woods again.

Knowing my father-in-law is an avid hunter, Helmut attached a slingshot to the stick. It's a nice touch, but I wonder if ol' dad can bring down a grouse with one shot.

Included in the box are a whistle, compass, Band-Aids and a map of the world. Funny thing about becoming lost: You never know it until you are.

I always say when the birds look like they're wearing tuxedoes or the persons you encounter are wearing Mao jackets, you're lost.

I hold the belief that every backpacker should carry provisions to cope with doom.

Hence, I always pack a pint of Jack Daniels.

Helmut was a bit more cosmopolitan. He packed kirsch, a Swiss drink of some sort that probably tastes as bad as it sounds.

He also included a small bottle of tequila. Not good. Tequila is useless in cases of doom that occur north of the Texas panhandle.

There's a deck of cards in the box. Good choice. Why, many times I've sat down in the pitch blackness of a woods at night and played solitaire. It becomes intriguing recreation after you discover you can't read the cards' markings.

I have saved the best for last.

Although small, this item is immensely important to the outdoorsman. Among all those other things, Helmut snuck in a roll of Rolaids. What a stroke of genius!

Let me tell you, quite often—especially after a steady diet of freeze-dried food—the campfire isn't the only thing burning.

* * * * *

WINTER IS ULTIMATE CHALLENGE—FOR SOME

My wife is complaining about winter already.

Heck, it hasn't even gotten cold yet. I can always tell when it's cold. My beard frosts up.

I can sympathize with her. She's from Ohio where the air pollution keeps things lukewarm most of the year. She doesn't have Wisconsin blood to keep her warm in the state's freezin' season.

Let winter come, I say. I'll laugh in its face no matter what Ma Nature hurls at us.

Summer is fun. Fall is beautiful. Winter, well, winter is an adventure, a primordial challenge.

And, man thrives on challenge. He needs it. A bit of adversity is like a shot of brandy before bed—it's good for the system.

I really feel sorry for people out in Southern California who can't experience winter. They have perpetual summer and chronic sunburn.

That's why 96 percent of them—almost everybody except my relatives out there—are loony.

California weather simply bakes their minds. The farther you go north or up mountains in California, the greater the chance of winter weather and the greater the chance of finding folk who are somewhat sane.

83

The exceptions to this are San Francisco and Marin County, bastions of the bizarre.

The only purpose Southern California serves is providing a standard for societal zaniness. Or, put more symbolically, California is the Fruit Loops of America.

We who are of Wisconsin blood are fairly levelheaded sorts because we experience winter every year.

Winter whips us back to reality: Life's not all Jacuzzis and surf boards.

Reality is trying to push a two-ton car out of a three-inch bank of snow situated on a slight incline. And, having that two-ton car roll over your left foot in the process.

Man, does it wake you up!

It's like that television commercial or an aftershave which shows a man's face being slapped and the man saying, "Thanks, I needed that."

Some think winter numbs the mind.

On the contrary, winter's cold causes the blood to surge, bringing new and refreshing energy to the brain. It forces you to think harder:

"How the heck am I going to stay warm around here."

They say winter brings on various illnesses like colds and flu.

Bah!

As I keep telling my Ohio-born wife, I could stand stark naked on a snow drift for two hours and not catch a cold. I might die of exposure, but that's not the point.

It's only when we come indoors to its warmth and the company of disease-ridden friends that we catch colds.

You see, cold germs can't survive outside during a Wisconsin winter. They don't own down-filled jackets, you know.

So the next time you see a picture of sunny California—a shot of a man on a verdant green putting—pity those poor people who are slowly sinking into dementia.

And then think how fortunate you are as you stand in a puddle of icy water, its chill sinking into your toes, and look at your car stilled by a dead battery.

Remember, without winter, spring would not be as refreshing, nor would it carry a spirit of rebirth and optimism.

* * * * *

84

Chapter Five

The Cat That Swallowed
the Turkey

A while back someone asked Ann Landers if animals could get drunk.

With her usual eloquence she explained how bears have been stopped by wine, snails killed by beer and goldfish revived with scotch.

"So—in answer to your question—yes, animals can indeed tie one on," wrote Ann.

As I put down Ann Landers column, a broad smile crossed my face. I uttered a sinister laugh and thought about my wife's cat.

"Hee hee, that cat's going to get it now," I whispered to myself.

On my way home from work I stopped at the liquor store and picked up a bottle of Wild Turkey. Knowing that my wife was going to be at a meeting that night, I figured the cat and I might party a bit.

Nothing would please me more than drinking that lousy cat under the table, I thought to myself.

That critter deserved nothing less than a grand slam hangover.

And, I knew I could do it. Everybody knows journalists are legend among the premier boozers of the world.

I said nothing to my wife, but gave the cat a sly grin. It arched its back, hissed and disappeared into the bedroom.

"We'll see you about ten," my wife said as she walked out the back door. As I watched her pull away, I grabbed the whiskey bottle and opened it.

"Here, kitty kitty," I said softly as I poured a shot of whiskey into her water dish.

The cat came up to the dish, took a sniff and turned away.

I picked up the dish, put it on the kitchen table. The cat jumped up beside it.

"Now look, you stupid cat, all you do is take a sip," I said as I took a swig of the whiskey.

The cat took several licks of the spiked water, stopped and looked up at me.

I took another swig.

The cat took a few more licks.

Well, this went on for the better part of two hours. The cat had gone through two bowls of water spiked with three shots of the "Wild Bird."

I finished off my sixth glass and gave the cat a mean stare.

"Derrrrr ink up, you loll-see kitty," I said.

The cat glared at me.

"Come on, don't be a partee poooo purrrr." I smiled and grabbed the half empty bottle.

The cat bent over, took several licks of water and began purring loudly.

"Yeah, I feel like singing too. Hum a few bars, I'll remember the words..."

The cat responded by taking a few more sips of water and again looked up as if to challenge me to take another sip.

"No lousy catz gonna derr ink ME under the table, noooooh way," I yelled.

The cat let out with a loud and long meow.

"Yourrrr h'on."

I dumped another shot into the cat's dish and filled my glass to the brim.

"Cheerz!"

Suddenly the back door opened and my wife walked in.

"DONALD!"

"SuussssssssH, the cat and I are involved in some seer-ee-ous derr-innking."

I turned to the cat. "I think we iz in trouble royal. Let me do the talking."

"DONALD, YOU'RE DRUNK."

"Ssssh, not in front of the cat."

"WHAT HAVE YOU BEEN DOING WITH MY CAT?" she shouted as she picked the cat off the table. The cat was purring loudly.

"We've been getting to know one another, haven't we, cat?"

The cat hissed.

I lifted myself off the chair and got to my feet, but suddenly my knees gave out and I went crashing to the floor between the table and the chair.

The last thing I remember was looking up and through the fog seeing that cat in my wife's arms. I could have sworn that cat was smiling.

* * * * *

Kitty Diet Cat-astrophic

I swear, Cosmopolitan causes more problems with its flaky advice to women.

Last month an article told women how to diet with their cats. It had lo-cal cat reducing tips ("no table scraps") along with your normal rabbit food menus for humans.

After reading this pop-health propaganda, my wife turned and smiled at her cat. "Mittens, you and me are going on a diet." The unsuspecting cat just purred.

"Great. I always figured that cat ate more than it was worth," I piped up. "You know, that cat wouldn't have to diet if it did something other than shed fur."

The cat glared and hissed at me.

"Ah, but she is such a pretty kitty," my wife said. "And, we're going to be even prettier." The cat purred.

87

Well, day one of the diet went reasonably well for the dynamic duo. However, I noticed the cat had a particularly desperate expression as she watched me eat supper.

Day two, things started getting unpleasant.

Meeeeeoooooow!

"Shaddup, you stupid cat!" I screamed as I lifted my head off my pillow. I looked at the clock.

"Cripes, its 3 a.m. Go feed the lousy thing so it will hush up," I told my wife as I shook her shoulder.

"Can't. The diet expressly prohibits snacks before breakfast."

"Does it expressly prohibit sleep?"

The cat began moaning in the basement like she used to do before we got her fixed.

"Please find a mouse!" I muttered as I buried my head in the pillow.

It was no use. The pillow couldn't muffle the soprano cat cries or the baritone growling of my wife's stomach.

At breakfast I spent the whole time pushing the cat off the table as she made bold charges toward my cereal. I wanted to complain to my wife but I could tell she was in a foul mood as she chewed on half a grapefruit.

Things really turned strange at supper.

I sat down to a plate of warmed-up chicken leftovers, semi-mashed potatoes and lukewarm canned peas, a feast which I had to prepare myself. My wife figured since she couldn't eat supper she wasn't obligated to cook it either.

She sat chewing a carrot and giving me pained expressions so I would feel guilty eating in front of her.

I was just about to chomp into a drumstick when I looked up and saw the cat on top of the refrigerator. She was hunched over like a mountain lion about to pounce on some innocent prey. Her yellow eyes were glued to the drumstick.

"Darn cat's after my drumstick," I whispered to my wife.

"Stop picking on the kitty."

"Maybe she's after me."

"Quiet!" my wife scowled as she grabbed another carrot.

"Dear, at any moment that creature is going to leap down on me, kill me with a swift bite to the jugular vein and drag me off behind the couch to feed upon my carcass!"

"Don't be gross..."

"If you don't call off your cat, I'm going to get my deer rifle!"

"Don't be ridiculous."

Suddenly the cat leaped onto the table, grabbed the drumstick in its mouth and disappeared down the basement steps.

"See, see! She's coming after me next."

My wife sighed.

"Look, if this diet is going to drive you paranoid, I'll just have to quit." Suddenly she grabbed my plate and slid it in front of her. She started forking down food frantically.

"I'll feed the cat in a minute," she said between mouthfuls.

"Thank goodness, you're too young to be a skinny widow."

* * * * *

THE BRAWL THAT WASN'T

It was like walking into a bar and suddenly realizing the whole place was about to explode into one big brawl.

That's how it felt walking into the veterinarian's office with my wife's cat, a female cat with a bad case of the hots.

Her heat was keeping us awake. Why can't cats keep their sexual frustrations to themselves like we humans do? Heck, what did she care if she caterwauled all night? Cats can sleep all day.

So off to the vet she went. Since my wife's work schedule didn't correspond to the vet's, I was drafted to take the cat to the office. Having a frightened cat claw your face while you're trying to drive isn't my idea of a fun trip.

I have a hard time carrying animals. If they don't have handles, I'm at a loss as to how to lift them. I avoid holding baby anythings. I figure I'll either drop them or they'll sense my nervousness and soil the front of my shirt.

So, instead of carrying the kitty, I tucked her under my coat. She didn't seem to mind as long as she could stick her head out from the zipper.

The first thing I saw when I walked into the animal hospital was a large—make that huge—tiger cat sitting on this lady's lap.

Just lovely. One peep out of my lusty kitty and that cat will attack in an amorous frenzy, I thought.

"He's neutered," the lady said.

That was as much a relief as going into a dentist's office and learning he had gone home ill.

Joining us in the room were two Labradors, one black, one buff. It was all their owners could do to keep them apart.

There was an uneasy peace in the room. Those dogs were like two barroom brawlers just waiting for an excuse to fight. Moments later, the excuse came walking up to the door.

It was a young lady with what might have been a German shorthair. Although the dog was on a leash, she could hardly control his strength.

As is my nature, I instantly envisioned the worst.

In my mind's eye I see the woman open the door. Her huge dog bounds into the room dragging her with him. They run into the black Lab. Instantly the Lab attacks and the two dogs wrestle, the leash wrapping around their bodies, pulling the young lady into the fray.

Sensing a good fight, the buff Lab jumps on top of the other two dogs. The entangled leash continues to bind the lady to the side of her dog like Captain Ahab and Moby Dick.

Vets and nurses run from their offices to quell the riotous room full of snarling canines. Soon they become entangled in leashes and fight to free themselves before being mauled.

The tiger cat, upset by the commotion, elects to leap onto the back of one of the Labs and to dig his claws in. The dog howls in agony, rears back and rips through chairs and magazine racks trying to knock the cat off.

I see this huge churning ball of man, dog and cat coming toward me and the kitty. The yells, yowls and growls grow louder and louder. Hair, tooth and claw merge into a huge buzz saw coming closer, closer..

I shook my head to bring myself back to reality. The lady with the German shorthair had managed to get by the two Labs with only a growl or two. A receptionist was calling my name.

I don't know who suffered worse on that trip to the vet—the cat or me.

* * * * *

THE KILLER CATS

I swear my wife's cat is training to be a guerrilla.

And, I'm the target of her nightly attacks.

My wife's cat is an affectionate, quiet—well, just a friendly little cat.

But at night, she's bold, ruthless and rebellious.

Her attacks are vicious and unrelenting.

I think she's bored with being a housecat. I think she wants to be a feline mercenary fighting against impossible odds in exotic places.

I've tried to reason with her, but her attacks have only escalated. Heck, who can reason with cats? They're such snobs.

And, I can't fight back. It's not because I'm a pacifist. Heck, if I lay one hand on that cat, both it and my wife will be on my back.

Some of you might not be sympathetic with my plight. Well, for you I offer this somewhat true tale.

It was 2 a.m. I recall it was a Wednesday. I was awakened by a hungry stomach.

I got up to fix my usual midnight snack: A boiled egg, cup of strawberry yogurt, shot of Jack Daniels and can of Old Style (the egg gives me strength, the yogurt settles my stomach, the whiskey puts me to sleep and the beer gives me sweeter dreams).

I stumbled across the dark bedroom and down the hallway.

91

I was dressed in my usual sleeping attire: A well ventilated T-shirt, a-size-too-big sweat pants half falling off my hips and a pair of yellow, blue and orange argyle socks.

Only a narrow band of moonlight came through where the living room curtains parted. It was sufficient light for me to navigate around the furniture to get to the kitchen.

The instant I hit the living room, there was a violent sound of something kicking up a pile of newspapers. Suddenly a creature charged out of the darkness and leaped at my right calf.

OUCH!

I looked down and see my wife's cat hanging on my leg as if it were a tree trunk.

The cat jumped off and disappeared.

I took two more steps. Suddenly I heard claws ripping across the carpet.

"AAAAAAAAAAAGH!"

As I grabbed my aching leg, I lost my balance.

"OOOOOOOOOOOOHHH!"

My body careened off a chair, plunged through a TV table still holding the dirty dishes from supper, and landed in a pile of newspapers and magazines, my face on an empty beer can resting on the floor.

I got up, wrested the beer can from my mouth and threw it at the cat hiding somewhere in the darkness.

"BLOODY CAT!"

The can missed the cat but hit a flower vase on the living room table. A deluge of water covered the tabletop and cascaded onto the carpeting.

Out of the darkness the cat leaped again, landing on the top of my head. For a moment I looked like Davy Crockett in a coonskin cap.

The cat dug its claws into my skull, then jumped off.

"I'M GOING TO EAT YOU FOR BREAKFAST, YOU LOUSY CAT!"

I made it to the kitchen, where I forgot the egg and yogurt and doubled the beer and whiskey.

I heard the cat purring in the darkness—laughing— waiting...

I think I know what my cat's game is. I believe it is part of a grand conspiracy to suppress anti-catism in this country through violence.

* * * * *

THE COVERT CAT CAPER

Teams of cat commandoes have begun terrorist attacks on readers of anti-cat literature.

Overzealous, socially frustrated felines have turned to violence to achieve their misguided objectives.

What I'm about to reveal here I do so at great personal risk.

I may be the next victim.

From clandestine cat records I have pieced together evidence of covert cat crimes against innocent humans.

In cities having bookstores, independent five-member cat commando teams operate.

Danger and death mean nothing to these cold-blooded killers, specially trained in Catalina. These are seasoned professionals who strike silently and quickly, leaving nothing but a corpse.

I predict there will soon be reports in newspapers across the country of a rise in accidental deaths of men in their own homes.

I suspect women will not be harmed because everybody knows women are cat sympathizers.

I offer this expose of one such covert cat caper:

8:06 a.m.: Cat jumps on windowsill outside bookstore and peers inside.

He's the spotter. No one takes notice of this cat, which appears to be nothing more than a street cat looking for a place to sun himself.

9:00 a.m.: Bookstore opens. Spotter begins to watch section of store where anti-cat books are sold.

9:35 a.m.: Mr. John J. Smith enters store and purchases book "101 Uses for a Dead Cat."

As he leaves checkout counter, spotter motions to two cats across the street. They follow Smith to his car.

93

As he opens door, one cat jumps on hood to distract him. Meanwhile, other cat, called the "plant," slips unnoticed into the back seat where he will remain until Smith goes home.

5:30 p.m.: Smith arrives home.

5:45 p.m.: Smith's young daughter finds lonely, hungry-looking, lost cat on front steps and begs her father to take cat in.

6:00 p.m.: Smith relents and brings cat in. Smith unwittingly has sealed his fate.

7:00 p.m.: As family watches TV, cat pushes open back door and disappears.

7:30 p.m.: Cat rejoins commando group. He leads two black cats back to house.

8:00 p.m.: The plant cat returns to Smith's home and allows into house two Siamese assassin cats who quickly hide under furniture.

The black cats are sleek and muscular. They have cold eyes and a sinister glare. They sit perfectly still, silent.

11:00 p.m.: Family goes to bed.

3:00 a.m.: Crashing noise downstairs awakens Smith.

What he doesn't know is one of the Siamese cats has just tipped over a vase in the living room.

Smith walks to head of stairs and peers over railing.

Suddenly, from out of the darkness, second Siamese cat lunges at man's leg. Startled, man loses his balance...

AAAAAAAAGH...

3:01 a.m.: Smith lies motionless at foot of stairs. The two Siamese move silently around the body. They look at each other and utter a quiet purr. They disappear into the darkness.

3:30 a.m.: Smith is pronounced dead at scene. Coroner attributes the death to an accidental fall.

During commotion, three cats silently leave the house bound for their next assignment.

Cats are vindictive and sneaky. They will stop at nothing to destroy whomever they perceive as their enemies.

No longer can we humans trust them. And, if you see a black Siamese cat, run.

* * * * *

Non-violent Cat a Wimp with a Mouse

Next to the sea slug, my wife's cat is the most useless creature around.

You think I'm exaggerating, read this...

I was peacefully reading when I happened to glance up to see the cat acting in a bizarre manner.

I took a closer look and discovered the cat had a mouse.

Here was this little gray mouse and a whacked-out cat doing a merry minuet around my living room. The cat would pick up the mouse, carry it a few feet and drop it. The mouse would then take off running, only to be caught again by the slightly confused cat.

Well, this little game went on and on.

"Kill it, you stupid cat!" I yelled like some rabid Packer fan.

The cat paid no attention.

I was getting so mad I could have done backflips. I started pacing up and down the living room like some ranting football coach on the sidelines.

"Stop messin' around, you worthless cat. Kill that *&**!! creature!"

Why, if my wife hadn't been home, I swear I would have flung that feline through the living room window.

Hey, cats are supposed to kill mice. It's in their genes. Why else would cats need to exist?

I have a friend whose family farms. She used to tell me about their barnyard cats. Now, those were real cats. They'd take on rats the size of bulldogs and dispatch them with all the finesse of a jungle cat.

But not my wife's cat. Spiders or centipedes she'll nail in a minute, but mice she treats as sacred cows.

95

When it became apparent that airheaded cat was content to play with the trespassing rodent, I decided to take matters into my own hands.

It was 10 p.m. and no way was I going to bed with some rodent roaming about.

I started frantically looking for a weapon. You know how hard it is to find a mouse killer?

I considered bashing it with a two by four, but could just hear my wife's screams when she discovered the splattered remains on the living room carpet.

I thought about using a .22 pistol, but feared I'd be tempted to dispatch the cat as well.

Finally, I settled upon a pair of tongs which I had found in a kitchen drawer. I thought I might be able to pick up the creature and deposit him outside.

Have you ever tried to pick up a mouse with tongs? It's a challenge even when the mouse is trapped by the cat.

Well, two tries at tonging the mouse failed and the wily little critter escaped into my den. I picked up the cat, threw her into the room with it and shut the door.

"Only one of you is going to come out of there alive—you hear me, cat!"

I peeked in only to find the cat peacefully sleeping under a bookcase. I slammed the door shut and put forth a flurry of four-letter and otherwise nasty words directed at the cats and life in general.

Darn it, a cat ought to do something for the amount of time and money you spend on it. I mean, the least it should do is keep the house mouse-free, I muttered to myself.

I told my wife as gently as I could about the fugitive rodent. I even restrained my criticism of her pet.

My wife, bless her heart, sided with the cat. And, though she was not pleased with the prospect of sharing a night with a mouse, she nevertheless defended her cat's right to be nonviolent.

It was then decided to trap the mouse. I didn't have any traps at home, but luckily the all-night grocery store down the street sold them.

I returned home with four mousetraps. I booted the cat out of the den and replaced the worthless creature with what I hoped would be a more effective mouse killing machine.

Did I finally catch the critter?

Tune in next week for the exciting conclusion.

* * * * *

THERE'S A MOUSE IN THE HOUSE AGAIN

All I knew for sure was that behind the locked door of my den was a mouse.

I suspected it was alive, but hoped it had fallen victim to one of the traps I had put in the room the night before.

Someone had to go in there to find out one way or another. That someone was me.

It should have been the cat, but the worthless creature had no interest in mousing. It preferred to sleep on the couch, safe from any marauding mouse. Cats, unlike dogs, have no sense of duty.

And, the marriage contract strictly prohibits wives from participating in mouse eradication.

That left me to go one-on-one with the potentially vicious vermin.

I grabbed a length of pipe. Actually it was a bar from a bathroom towel rack. I made a couple of practice swings, bringing it toward the floor like a lumberjack wielding a large axe.

Then I took a deep breath and slowly opened the door. I watched my feet, half expecting a little gray creature to dash out from the ever-widening door.

I got the door open just enough to squeeze through and then slammed it shut. Like a cop on Hill Street Blues entering a tenement building, I held the pipe as if it were a .357 magnum Smith & Wesson and pushed my back against the wall.

97

I slowly surveyed the room for any sign of motion. My eyes glided over every book top, paused on each stack of papers and focused on the debris underneath my desk.

There was no movement.

There was no sound other than my rapid breathing. The sweat from my brow burned my eyes.

I moved sideways along the wall, always keeping that pipe in front of me, ready at an instant to bring it down upon the offensive beast.

Suddenly a hint of motion caught my eye. Something behind and left of me moved. I swung around and slammed the pipe into it and the glass of a framed picture.

A daddy longlegs succumbed among the shards of glass. It was a macabre end to an innocent creature. But, no time for remorse, I told myself, and resumed the hunt.

Step by step I approached a large bookcase against one wall. A perfect place for an ambush, I told myself.

I envisioned the mouse leaping from the third shelf and biting me right in the carotid artery of the neck. I'd be down and dead before I knew what hit me. That's how vicious mice can be.

The hair on my arms tingled from the thrill of the hunt. There wasn't much room left for him to hide. I started talking to myself. "He had to be, he has got to be, right behind this filing cabinet..."

I gasped and dropped my pipe.

There, staring up at me with those piercing, beady eyes, was the mouse, a very dead mouse. He had avoided all the baited traps only to die, I suspected, of a weak heart. The bout with the playful cat the night before was too much for his system.

I sighed, picked up my pipe and left the room. I ran to the refrigerator and broke open a bottle of beer to replace all the bodily fluids I had lost in the ten-minute ordeal.

All was well. The Oakland household was safe once again, no thanks to that conscientious objector cat... By the way, where was the cat? I opened another beer to settle my nerves.

I looked around, but still no cat. Perhaps I had shamed it into hiding. I shrugged my shoulders and headed for bed.

There, by a pile of clothes, the cat stood, its head slightly cocked. She resembled a dog on point. Oh no! I stopped cold and to my horror watched as a little tuft of fuzz shot out from the Jockey shorts.

Suddenly my mind was filled with the sound of that loud, piercing music that usually accompanies those scenes in horror movies when the mad-dog killer does in some lovely victim.

As I watched this new mouse and the cat disappear under the bed, I uttered an anguished scream.

* * * * *

Chapter Six

The Body Strikes Back

Some people have a conscience.

I don't.

Instead I have a body to keep me on the straight course to the respectable life. You see, my body rebels when I'm a bad boy.

A while back I had what is known as a good time. I drank a little, ate a little and stayed up way past my bedtime.

When I got home, which was about 1:30 a.m., I woke up my wife and her cat. My wife took her rude awakening calmly, but I thought the cat was going to give me a facial rub with her claws.

Anyway, the next morning I didn't have the hangover I expected. My stomach was fine. I was able to take solids at breakfast. My head didn't ache. I could think clearly. I even knew what time it was and the day of the week.

I went to work and was able to write, which amazed me. However, my typing floundered.

The only thing out of the ordinary was a slight stiffness in my neck and back.

By afternoon that stiffness began to throb painfully. By nightfall I could hardly move.

My body's revenge had begun.

For the next week I was in pain. I was downing aspirins as if they were candy mints.

Of course, it did little good. My body merely detoured the aspirin to parts of the body not experiencing pain.

I cuddled up to a heating pad for hours. It got to a point where I strapped the heating pad to my back, attached to it a long extension cord and wandered around the house on what appeared to be a long leash.

All this was my body's way of punishing me for one night's indiscretions.

Here's my theory.

As soon as my body realized what I had in store for it, the main nerve cell in my brain called an emergency meeting of the cellular corpus committee.

Nerve cells from all over the body—every organ, every muscle, every joint—flocked to the brain.

The chairman speaks:

"It appears Mr. Oakland is going to abuse us with alcohol and general carousing tonight. Are we going to let him get away with that?"

"NO!" scream the other cells.

"The chair will entertain suggestions from the floor."

The stomach nerve gets up.

"I could make his gut shake like Mount St. Helens and no amount of Pepto Bismol could abate it."

The frontal lobe nerve, wearing spiked mountain-climbing boots, stands up.

"See my new boots? Why, I could give him a headache from ear to ear," the cell said, jumping up and down. "I could make him feel as if his teeth would soon explode.

"We need something that will deliver a lasting impression," the chairman replies.

A group of muscle nerves rise to address the group.

"We'll go after back and neck muscles. Tie those guys up like truck springs. We'll keep pricking them until they are red and swollen. We'll waylay any drug sent to relieve their torture. For days every little movement he makes will be like a match under his spine."

"Sounds super! All in favor of hitting the back say aye," the chairman says.

"AYE!"

"Let's make him squirm!" the chairman yells. He slams the gavel down to adjourn the meeting.

And they did.

* * * * *

IT'S HERS, BUT SHE WON'T LIKE IT

Some thoughtful person gave me a cold for Christmas.

Although it is a relatively inexpensive gift, it does manage to occupy your attention for quite some time after the presents are opened. (Only recently have I had the energy to write about this.)

Unfortunately, it's a gift that cannot be returned.

Can you imagine going to a department store trying to return a cold?

"What's wrong with it?" asks the clerk.

"It's making me miserable, that's what's wrong with it," you reply sharply.

"Well, sir, that's what a cold is supposed to do," the clerk says with a sigh.

"I don't want it," you cry out as you grab for a tissue. You deliver a hefty sneeze and as you wipe your red nose you say:

"I want to return it for cash or maybe exchange it for a new shirt."

"We can exchange it, if you like," the clerk says. "But not for a shirt."

"For what, then?"

"Well, we have a nice selection of flu. I hear the Bangkok is very 'in' this season. A very fashionable disease," he says as he turns to a thick store catalog.

"Will I be in much pain?" you ask, pulling out another tissue.

The clerk guides his finger along the narrative on the catalog page.

"Well, it says here that the gastro-intestinal coefficient index on the Bangkok is a 3.8..."

"Put that in English," you demand.

"It means you'll have an upset tummy," the clerk responds haughtily. "It will be a little more upset than if you have the Singapore flu..."

"I don't want it!" you scream.

The clerk pays little attention and keeps turning the catalog pages.

"Say, here's something—the Texas flu." A smile crosses his face.

"With the country-western look in this year, why, what better than a good ol' Texas belly-buster?"

He continues reading. Then his happy expression drops.

"Oh, my! Says here symptoms are much like those one experiences after being tossed by a bull and stepped on."

"NO!"

"My, aren't we particular! With that attitude there isn't much we can do, sir," the clerk says, his voice growing more frustrated.

"Then you won't take back my cold?"

"No way," the clerk says, shaking his head and crossing his arms.

"Hmmmmmm."

You and the clerk stare at each other for a moment. Then you say:

"Tell you what, I'll pay you to take it back."

"Out of the question—totally against company policy, you know," the clerk responds.

You continue staring at him. A sneeze starts to form. You reach for a tissue only to discover you have used up the last one. You sneeze into your hands. The clerk gives you a disgusted look.

You give the clerk a desperate look.

"Tell you what, I'll order that Bangkok if you'll take back the cold. How soon can I expect delivery?"

"Oh, about ten days."

The clerk waves his arms and your cold instantly disappears. You thank him, but he passes on the handshake.

"Where shall we send it?" the clerk asks.

You pause. You begin to snicker and smile in a sly manner.

In a calm, matter-of-fact voice you give the clerk the address of your mother-in-law.

"And, that will be one Bangkok Type A?" the clerk repeats.

You shake your head.

I've changed my mind. Send a Texas flu."

* * * * *

A STRONG MIND AND A WEAK BACK

You never see a bear or beaver with back problems.

In fact, of all the creatures who walk around on four legs, very few, if any, suffer backache.

Doesn't that tell you something?

As I sit here writing, my lower back feels like a road crew of elves are laying into my muscles with pickaxes.

Every time I sit down I worry that I might never get up again. I can just see my muscles locking up, paralyzing me into a fetal-like position.

I can just see my fellow workers coming over to my desk and picking me up off the floor. Like children carrying a toy soldier they carry me out of the office.

I can see them throwing me like a bag of garbage into the trunk of someone's car because in my pretzel-like posture I won't fit through a car door.

I can see myself sitting in the emergency room of the hospital worrying that I'm going to die in that embarrassing position.

How would they ever fit me in a casket? They'd have to cut me up...

Anyway, the point of all this worrying is that I'm convinced my back is trying to tell me something:

"Superman you ain't."

"Say what?"

A sharp spear of pain crosses my lumbar region. My back begins talking.

"I'm saying you're not getting any younger and lately you've been letting the ol' body go to seed."

105

"Well, I've been busy."

"Busy sitting around drinking beer. I've talked to your digestive track. I know what junk you've been shoveling into it.

"A man has a right to his pleasures," I respond.

"I agree. But, be willing to pay the price," my back says as another sharp pain shoots up my spine, almost knocking me on my butt.

"Just look at your belly. Why, it's filling out like the delta of a river and is taking on the appearance of a water balloon about to burst."

"I'll go on a diet come fall."

"Sure you will, but in the meantime I've got to support this expanding bulk. And, trying to be macho by picking up a canoe or a sack full of heavy groceries isn't helping me any," he replies as I feel another muscular dagger.

"I'll exercise and make you strong," I say in a determined voice.

"Sure you will. I mean it took 30 years to get me in this shape. Heck, it should take only a few weeks to rectify matters with a few push ups," the back says sarcastically.

Another sharp pain scoots across my vertebrae.

"Ya know, you guys made a big mistake way back when. You should have stayed in the trees and cavorted around on all fours. Ever hear of a monkey with a slipped disc?

"But, hanging around with the rest of the animals was beneath you. You had to stand above them. So you got up on your own two legs and left them behind.

"Over the years you became smarter and did more and more things. But, you forgot that your body remained essentially the same as it was when you were amongst the lowlife."

Another sharp pain burned into my lower back.

"You take your body and back for granted because you're so busy thinking of new things to conquer. Well, I for one feel you ought to be reminded of your limitations before you kill us both," my back scolds.

Another sharp spasm nearly doubles me over.

"You made your point," I scream.

"Good. Now sit up straight, chin in, shoulders back and tuck in that gut. If we're to get along from now on, you can't sit around like some back-alley slob," my back instructs.

"Anything you say, just spare me any more pain."

For the rest of the day my back felt fine. At 4 a.m. the following day, as I was blissfully asleep, the calf of my right leg cramped into a painful charley horse. I bolted out of bed screaming.

My leg starts talking.

"Superman you ain't..."

* * * * *

SPIRIT IS WILLING BUT THE STOMACH IS WEAK

The world doesn't need any more diets.

It doesn't need any more skinny ladies bouncing about in leotards.

And it doesn't need any more weight machines.

What people really need is more mental muscle.

I'm talking willpower, boy.

You can exercise until you're red in the face, but if you don't have willpower, you'll never achieve true fitness.

What's a diet without willpower?

I don't need to diet right now. But, someday I probably will and I'll need willpower to do it. That's why I've begun an exercise program to strengthen the inner self.

How does one go about exercising the will?

You take on Grand Avenue in Wausau.

I do it about twice a week. You don't want to over-exercise the will. A sprained will is no good at all.

I have yet to complete the Grand Avenue challenge. But, that's all right. Defeat is character building.

Here's an account of one of my more recent sessions...

It's 6 p.m. and I haven't eaten supper.

I'm hungry, really hungry.

107

I stuff two $10 bills in my pocket and start walking down the avenue.

I commence deep breathing to prepare myself mentally and physically for the ordeal ahead.

Suddenly my nostrils catch the smell of hamburgers. As the winds caress my senses with the smell of french fries frying, visions of a Hardee's Bacon Burger dance in my head.

I shake myself back into self-control and walk on—right into the seductive smell of pizza. I begin to drool like a hot pup as I fight off thoughts of biting into a pan pizza overflowing with cheese. I wrestle myself away from the Pizza Hut door and continue on.

For a moment I feel good. I had just beaten that double dose of Italian-American fast food.

With great trepidation I resume walking south. Suddenly the sundae sirens beckon. My breathing becomes labored, my limbs shake as I pass within a few feet of the Dairy Queen.

There have been times I'd mug a two-year-old for his Dilly Bar.

My stomach is so hungry now it's bouncing like a pinball against the walls of my abdomen.

I look across the street and yearn for a wholesome homecooked meal at the Ponderosa. But I valiantly resist and stagger on.

With my heart racing and my breathing becoming a rapid panting, I brace for the most difficult test of all: Chicken Alley.

The Kentucky Colonel calls with all his southern hospitality. Even though I'm so hungry I could gulp down a gallon of gizzards and liver at Famous Recipe, I trudge onward.

I begin hallucinating.

A beautiful girl in a bikini tempts me with a juicy hamburger, but when I approach, her face suddenly becomes aged and she screams, "Where's the beef?" and beats me with a floppy french fry.

I scream in pain.

It becomes too much. I fall to my knees and crawl along the sidewalk. My stomach feels as if it were consuming my insides.

With one great effort I look up only to see Perkins on my right, Country Kitchen on my left and a huge American flag above. I start humming the Star Spangled Banner and fight to get back on my feet. I glance up and see golden arches on the horizon.

AAARRGH! I'm felled once more by a Mac attack.

I probably would not have lived to tell about this test of will had it not been for some kindly gentleman who rushed across the avenue with a Susie's triple-chocolate custard. A couple of spoonfuls and I was well on my way to recovery.

It was an ordeal, but every time I do it I come closer to that day when I will have that inner power to thumb my nose at McDonalds and walk on by.

* * * * *

MIGHTY OAKLAND STRIKES OUT

Baseball has begun.

Oh, big deal.

Hey, I'm sorry but I just can't get excited about it.

Every time I watch a baseball game I recall my days of anguish, or as some might say, my Little League career.

I was one of those kids who learned early on that ballplaying wasn't my destiny.

When the neighborhood kids chose up sides for pitcher's hand, it would always be me and the dog who were left. And, they'd always pick the dog first because he was a faster base runner.

Stuck with me, they'd exile me to right field because of some unwritten rule that those branded "butterfingers" should do time there.

Playing right field is like: Hey, it's the sixth inning and I've forgotten what a baseball looks like.

Usually in the last inning some jerky kid, a righthander who didn't know how to swing, would pop one right field way.

I never knew terror until I saw that hardball looping over the first baseman and bearing down on me like an errant meteor.

Yet, I also realized it was my one fleeting chance at fame, the one play Mom and Dad had been waiting all game to see.

I started running toward this fast-falling rock of fabric.

"I got it! I got it!" I cried.

Mother suddenly broke into prayer. Dad quickly covered his eyes.

WHAM!

The centerfielder knocked me to the ground and stepped on my face as he reached up his glove to snag the game-winning out. As he walked off to cheers, I chewed grass.

See, nobody figured I could handle anything that wasn't on the ground and about to roll to a dead stop.

I admit it was hard to get much practice catching fly balls.

As kids we'd play 500 on the street. At about 50, one of three things would happen: Either the ball would go through the window of a house owned by the meanest old lady on the block or it would hit a car or roll down a sewer.

I dreaded the latter.

Being the skinniest, I was always sent down to retrieve it.

To this day I hate spiders and kitty litter because of those sewer excursions.

One day I figured the only way I was going to get ahead in baseball was to form my own team. It wasn't hard. All I had to do was wait around until all the other teams were picked and draft the remnants.

I realize a team of all rightfielders wasn't too formidable, but it gave me an opportunity to debut as a pitcher.

For weeks I threw a tennis ball against the side of our house. The constant thumping sound heard within the house, I later learned, almost drove my father to trade me to another family.

My training came to an abrupt end when I tried my pitching exercise with a hardball.

Dreams of glory filled my mind as I walked to the mound. But they didn't last long. I threw four consecutive balls and listened as my teammates threatened mutiny unless I immediately retreated off the rubber.

Pitchers had little to fear from me. My parents praised me for days after every foul ball I hit. "Well, you got a piece of 'er, son, they would say.

I never was that enthusiastic about batting. I mean, it wasn't long before I realized a properly placed fastball could put me on first base in heaven.

No matter how much courage I could muster, I knew that the first inside pitch would turn me to Jell-O.

I knew then it was either get out of baseball or become a basket case every summer. I retired my glove, putting to an end my days of anguish.

* * * * *

WHAT GOES UPSIDE DOWN MUST COME DOWNSIDE UP

Know where I can get a pair of gravity boots?

They're the newest rage in exercise.

They're not exactly boots, more like metal grips that fasten around your feet and calves. Just above the heels are metal hooks. The hooks allow you to hang upside down by your feet.

Actually, you need the boots plus a contraption that looks like a chinning bar. All you've got to do is attach the hooks to the bar and let your body drop.

This outfit is supposed to be dynamite for bad backs.

And, boy, do I have a bad back.

It comes from being hunched over a video display terminal all day while editors whip me and yell, "I want that story NOW!"

Trouble is, I can only afford the boots.

I thought I had that solved until I started envisioning the consequences....

AYYYEEEE!

Slam!

The closet door vibrates on its hinges. My wife takes a step back. She shakes her head, takes a deep breath and opens the door.

"Donald, what are you doing hanging upside down next to your best blue suit? You nearly scared me to..."

"I'm exercising, dear," I reply in a mellow voice.

"In a closet—upside down?"

"It's supposed to help my back," I smile.

"It's not your back that needs help. It's that funny little round red thing between your shoulders..."

My wife continues to stare.

"Look, dear, have you ever heard of bats having back troubles?"

"Donald, I don't want to hear about it."

"I mean, bats are ugly enough, but they have good backs. Every night they allow gravity to realign their vertebrae by hanging upside down.

"You're going to hang upside down every night? I feel like writing a letter to Ann Landers."

As she walks away I hear her muttering: "Dear Ann, I have a husband who thinks he's a bat. He hasn't touched my neck since he gave me a hickey in '78..."

"Honey, come back here."

"But, he likes to hang in a closet. Should I start hanging garlic above the bed? Should I ask mother not to visit this weekend? Signed: Going Batty."

"Just a minute..." I try to reach up to unhook myself but my body gets caught up in my blue suit. "Honey, could you come here for a second?"

Silence.

"Can you hear me? Help!"

Instead of my wife, her cat walks in. She gives a peculiar stare and walks over to my inverted face. She sniffs at my cheeks and begins licking my nose.

"Scat, cat, you've got terrible breath."

The kitty purrs.

"Honey! Please call your cat."

My wife walks in, a writing tablet in her hand.

"Ahhhhh, isn't that cute," she says, looking down at the cat licking my ear.

"I swear if that cat doesn't stop messing with me, I'll feed her to the Cuisinart."

"Donald!"

"Get me down from here."

"Uh, first tell me, I mean, you're a newspaperman, what's Ann Landers' address?"

"I don't know."

112

"Too bad." My wife turns and walks out the door.

Minutes pass. I begin hearing my typewriter clicking in the other room.

I try again to reach the clothes bar, this time trying to climb, hand over hand, up my pants legs. I reach half-way. I put my hand on my knee.

Rrrrriiiiiip!

My body flies backwards like a hinge. The rack gives way and the clothes and I fall to the floor in one big heap.

I push the shirts off me and try to get up, but a sharp pain stops me.

"Honey, I can't move! I think I hurt my back!"

* * * * *

NEW TWIST ON OLD SNOW JOB

Often inspiration comes with perspiration.

I was perspiring heavily the other day as I dug my sidewalk and driveway out from under a ten ton blanket of snow. As I worked, my wife was inside the house doing aerobic exercise to some goofy record.

It doesn't make sense, I thought to myself. If she wants exercise, why isn't she out here helping me?

I mean, what better way to tone the ol' muscles, flatten the stomach and slim the thighs than shoveling snow, I said to myself as I threw a shovelful of snow to the top of a mile-high pile.

Why, I'll bet clearing a driveway provides five times more exercise than jumping around to rock songs, I grumbled.

Suddenly, as my lower back went into spasm, an idea came to me.

I threw my shovel aside and plopped down in a snowbank. In my mind the image of Don Oakland, snow-aerobics instructor, began to form...

I climb to the top of a five-foot snowbank. In front of me is a driveway and sidewalk covered with five inches of freshly fallen snow.

"OK, girls, are we ready?"

About 12 women standing along my driveway perk up. They're dressed in pink thermal sweatsuits with "I've got that healthy glow from shoveling snow" printed across the top.

I reach down and push the play button on my portable stereo cassette player. Suddenly music from "Saturday Night Fever" blares from the speakers.

"OK, girls, let's warm up..."

The women start running in place in their jogging sorrel boots.

The music switches to Joan Jett's "I Love Rock 'n' Roll."

"OK, girls, pick up your Don Oakland snow-aerobic shovels, lift them over your heads and stretch left, stretch right, stretch up, stretch down..."

Minutes pass. The music changes to Olivia Newton John's "Physical."

The women plunge their shovels into the snow.

"Keep to the beat, girls, keep to the beat!" I yell over the music. "It's one into the snow, two lift, three throw and four back to the starting position.

"Come on, ladies, faster! You're falling behind. Let me hear your body talk," I croon as I swing my hips.

The music switches to "We Got The Beat."

"OK, let's tone those arm and leg muscles. I want you to shovel and throw twice as fast. Remember, the more snow you throw, the faster you'll achieve that Jane Fonda figure..."

In five minutes the driveway is clear of snow.

"OK, girls, it's time for your warmdown—let's get in position on the sidewalk."

The women throw down their shovels and line up along the sidewalk.

"Now, we're going to bend over, with our knees slightly bent, and scoop snow with our cupped hands. Ready?"

"Ebony and Ivory" comes through the speakers.

"Bend on ebony, scoop on ivory," I instruct. Five minutes later the sidewalk is clear.

"OK, girls, that does it for today. Tomorrow we'll meet at Fred's house for a 30-minute snow-aerobic on his driveway and Thursday we'll be at George's.

"Remember, the advance class is clearing the K-Mart parking lot on Friday."

Suddenly I'm aroused from my thoughts by the sound of my wife's voice.

"Donald, will you get out of that snowbank and get in here. Supper is just about ready—look at you, you're covered with snow. I swear you're like a little kid!"

I brush the snow off my pants and look up at my sweatsuited wife.

"Say, honey," I say, "want some exercise?"

* * * * *

"DRINKERCIZE" FOR BEER LIFTERS

Medical research has finally caught up with what I've been telling people all along.

Drinking beer is good for you.

116

Recently I read that researchers at Baylor College of Medicine found beer helps the body produce high-density lipoprotein cholesterol.

I have no idea what the stuff is, but the researchers say it's good for the ol' ticker.

Now they didn't say drinking a case a day would give you the heart of a 12-year-old. However, they did imply a beer or two after work wouldn't hurt.

If beer drinking alone is good for you, drinking and exercising should be dynamite.

With that in mind, I have developed a beer drinker's 30-day exercise plan.

First you start with a warm-up.

My favorite is sitting in the sunshine, popping Old Styles and throwing the empty cans at passing joggers. This limbers you up and rids your neighborhood of those nuisance sidewalk trotters.

For beginners, three six-packs of your favorite brew is needed for the first exercise. Sorry, bottles are unacceptable.

One six-pack is for your right hand, another for your left. The third is for your thirst.

Holding both six-packs at your side, slowly raise them to shoulder height. An excellent exercise for developing the "lats."

After a half dozen reps, have a beer.

For you advanced folks, use 12-packs.

Next, let's develop the chest.

You'll need a case of cans.

Lie down on a weight bench with the case on your chest. Now benchpress the case above your head 24 times.

Have another beer, you deserve it!

Work yourself up to lifting six cases and four 12-packs.

Hotdogs can start with quarter barrels.

If you're Charles Atlas and have hernia insurance, try a half barrel.

To build up those big thighs, squat quarter barrels.

If that's too much, start with dual cases, one on each shoulder and a 12-pack balancing on your head.

Potential beer lifters should know the exercise apparatus is fairly inexpensive and is consumable.

OK, back to the mats.

Let's build up those biceps with some six-pack curls.

117

Elbow bending beer cans at the bar doesn't count because it has no aerobic value.

Forearms weak? Try can crushing. Do this once a week as you'll need a good supply of empty cans in order to get the true benefit.

A good isometric wrist exercise is taking a bottle of beer, shaking it and holding your thumb over the opening.

Agility exercise? We've got it. Take three cans and place them 50 feet apart in a field. Run to the first can and pick it up as you run by. Open it without spilling and drink it down before you reach the second can.

Weak neck?

Take two cans and tie them to either side of your head. Move your head right and left.

Weak stomach?

Grab a six-pack, put it behind your head and do 50 sit ups. Do not, repeat, do not try drinking a beer before doing this exercise.

Am I forgetting the women? No way.

Need to slim down the waist?

Drink light beer and take full beer cans in each hand, extend your arms shoulder high and twist. In three weeks you'll look like Victoria Principal.

Take a beer can, put it between your hands at chest level. Try to push the ends of the can inward. Great upper body conditioner!

So the next time one of those joggers gives you one of those self-satisfied smirks, just raise your can and give him a toast to your good health. Then throw the empty can at him.

* * * * *

GETTING FIT NEARLY FATAL

The following is an expose of the state Department of Natural Resources, so pay attention.

I have discovered, hidden away in a stand of pines on state-owned land, a DNR trail of torture. Its sole purpose is to deliver into agony all those people who have been picking on this quiet little state agency.

In the spirit of investigative journalism, I sought out this haven of horror. But I got too close and was drawn in by a force I couldn't control: My male ego.

Although I survived to file this report, the injuries and psychological pain still linger.

At Council Grounds State Park near Merrill they call it the Fitness Trail. A clever guise! DNR people are diabolical, a trait they developed after years of catching people fishing illegally.

The trail drew me in with its promise of stronger muscles and macho appearance (a seductive pledge my pot-bellied body could'nt resist.) Heck, they know I'll do anything in the name of exercise.

I ran to the first station. I call it the log. You're supposed to do push ups with your hands placed on this log embedded in the ground.

I did two push ups, then my arms collapsed, causing my face to slam into the log. I lost two teeth. One's still embedded in the log.

Next is the chinning bar. I jumped up, grabbed the uppermost bar and promptly dislocated both shoulders. In falling to the ground, I sprained my ankle.

My mouth bleeding profusely, I limped to the next station, the bunny hop: Three logs ingeniously spaced to cause the victim to trip over one and fall onto the other two.

I hopped once, hit my sprained ankle and fell on the two logs. I think that's where two of my ribs got broken.

Flying all around me were vicious biting bugs, punishing me and pushing me onward. I wanted to turn back, but the fitness fever compelled me forward.

The balance beam was next. I got to the third level before my ankle gave out. I fell backwards and landed on a large rock (marked property of the DNR).

I crawled to the next station, the sit-up bench. Somehow I managed six sit ups before sending my lower back into spasms. All sensation left my right leg.

Looking like the Hunchback of Notre Dame, I hobbled on my one good leg to the fence jump. I tried a one-legged leap, but the only thing to clear it was my chin. I left a good portion of my beard on the top of that fence.

On the jungle gym I wracked my arms until they felt like spaghetti and looked like zucchini.

The final exercise was the horizontal bar, which requires you clear it in a single bound. With all my courage I ran full speed at it. I let out a fierce scream as I leaped. But, my one good leg refused to leave the ground. I rammed into the bar, my stomach curling around it like a hand around a softball. I lost my breath and my pants.

As I lay crumbled in a bed of pine needles and ticks, I could hear someone behind the trees, in the cover of the bushes, laughing. I crawled twoard the sound. I parted the leaves and found a DNR warden rolling on the ground.

He looked my way.

"Hey, fella, if you're going to stay there overnight you'll need a sticker." I shook my head.

He picked me up like yesterday's garbage and carried me to the front gate of the park and tossed me into a pile of leaves.

"Hope you had a real good time. Ya come back now, ya hear," he said as he started laughing loudly.

* * * * *

SNOW TREK

"To explore strange new worlds; To seek out new life and new civilizations; To boldly go where no man has gone before..."

Captain's Log, Snow Date 8201.21: The Snow Trek crew is in an unchartered cross-country ski area in a remote section of Lincoln County.

I, Captain D.B. Oakland, have led my science officer, Fritz Spock, half-human, half-Norwegian, and my communications officer, better known as my wife, several hundred yards off the last known trail. We are fighting waist-deep snow.

Dissension is breaking out among the crew.

120

"Captain, we're lost," says my wife.

"Nah, the trail is right over there—well, maybe thataway," I reply. Turning to the pointy-eared Norwegian, I ask, "Spock, where the heck are we?"

"I have no idea, Captain."

"What!"

"Sir, I may have the most logical mind among us, but that doesn't preclude absentmindedness. I forgot the compass."

"We must turn back," my wife says sternly.

"No, remember our mission," I reply, digging the snow out of my knickers. "By the way, have you been able to contact snow fleet?"

"No, but I'll check again." She turns around. "CAN ANYBODY HEAR ME?"

"Captain, I'm getting a lifeform reading," Spock says. "We should have a visual—there behind that tree."

Emerging from behind a large white oak is a skier moving very fast. "Spock, that skier isn't wearing a Nordic ski sweater or hat."

"Captain, she's not wearing knickers, either!"

"Spock, she's weaaring nothing but a polka dot bikini!"

"Very strange indeed, Captain. Polka dot bikinis went out of fashion years ago."

With efficient, gliding strokes she comes down the trail and stops only a few feet in front of us.

Captain's Log, Star Date 8201.21:05: The snow trek crew has encountered a beautiful young woman dressed in only a bikini. She is tall, with blonde hair that falls below her shoulders. With her figure she should be in an ad for a Caribbean vacation, not on some desolate ski trail. We have made attempts to communicate.

"Hello," I say cautiously.

"Hi," she replies in a voice that melts icicles from my beard.

"Uh, don't you think it's a bit cold for a—uh—bathing suit?"

"Cold is relative."

"Lady, its 20 below out here."

"The aura of the pines tans my body. I think I need more lotion," she says, rubbing her well-tanned arms.

"Captain, we're not getting anywhere. I think it's time for a Norwegian mind probe," Spock says, rubbing his palms.

"You're right, Spock. I'll assist."

Suddenly there's a hand on the back of my collar pulling me backwards through the snow. "You probe her mind and I'll probe your face with my fist, Captain," my wife says angrily.

"Are there any more of you?" Spock asks the girl.

"Just my sister—and Thor."

"Thor?"

"My husband." She points down the trail.

Into view comes something resembling an overgrown Green Bay Packer tackle wearing nothing but a pair of gym shorts and skis. He has young cedar trees as ski poles.

"Captain, I think it would be logical to..."

"Well put, Spock."

"We must go, it's been a pleasure," I say to the young woman. She gives me a half-smile.

"Do you have any Coppertone?"

"Mr. Spock, warp speed."

"Right behind you, Captain."

* * * * *

BANZAI BUNNY, 1; BIKER, 0

Beware of the hare!

I was viciously attacked—nearly killed—by a bunny gone bonkers.

I tell you, the streets of Wausau are no longer safe.

They're out there, thousands of them, waiting for the right moment to maim us.

If you don't believe me, I'll show you my bruises. Well, I'll show you my bruised elbow. To show you my bruised hip would require a degree of undress which would embarrass us all.

It pains me to write about this. My right pinky finger was scraped and it hurts every time I hit the P or shift keys.

What I'm about to tell you is true. I swear it on Dan Rather's head.

It was shortly after 7 a.m. Monday, May 24. I was riding my bike to work, approaching Grand Avenue from Sturgeon Eddy Road.

Suddenly my eye caught a blur of fur just to the left of my front tire. This nondescript creature slammed into the tire, pushing it at right angles to the frame.

I went flying onto the pavement.

I couldn't believe it: A rabbit had just charged full speed across the street and thrown a body block against my bike tire.

When I got up, the rabbit was nowhere to be found. Aside from a heckuva headache, I don't think it was injured.

What irks me is every time I relate this story, the first thing people ask is if the rabbit was hurt. My body is ripped to shreds and they're worried about a dumb rabbit!

The next day I got a call from the sheriff's department saying someone wants me arrested for running down a rabbit.

And, the Wausau police called Wednesday. They might charge me with failure to report an accident and failure to yield the right of way.

At first I thought it just another weird happening, an odd variation of the car-deer accident.

It wasn't till later that morning when I saw two rabbits in a front yard that I became suspicious. Both gave me a sinister stare.

I tell you, they're out to get me.

I don't know why. Maybe it's something I wrote.

Maybe it's because I fenced off my vegetable garden.

But, rest assured, when they're finished with me, they'll be coming after you.

And we're defenseless.

You can't shoot them. What would the neighbors say? "That disgusting little man shoots little bunnies in his backyard. He ought to be put away."

Imagine trying to tell a cop: "It was either him or me. officer."

How would you like little children coming up to you and saying tearfully: "Why did you shoot the Easter Bunny, mister?"

Nature has made the rabbit a soft, furry creature with a seemingly innocuous demeanor—a perfect cover for an animal agent bent on harassing the higher forms.

Ted Kohl, chief deputy of the Marathon County Sheriff's Department, reminded me about the rabbit that tried to assassinate former President Jimmy Carter while he was fishing a couple of years back.

The incidents were too similar to be coincidental. We were both alone. In both cases the lone rabbit escaped without a trace.

Was it mere coincidence Carter lost the election soon after that incident?

. A little bunny peacefully chews on grass in front of your house until you come out the front door. Then he runs under your feet causing a fatal fall onto the sidewalk.

A little bunny waits for you at night, waits to jump on you in the darkness to scare you into an untimely end.

I give you this prophecy.

Beware of bad bunnies, else you'll be hare today and gone tomorrow.

* * * * *

DBO Presents "Jaws III"

It's a beautiful rural scene from a remote spot in Marathon County. There are green fields of alfalfa and golden rows of corn set against a fiery sunset.

Everything is peaceful. In the distance something moves along the road. It's a girl on a bike.

She is young, tall and tan. She wears a yellow bikini top and white short shorts.

125

Then, subtly at first, is heard the theme to the movie, "Jaws."
Ba dump—ba dump—ba dump...
Something moves in the bushes ahead. A large lilac bush shakes violently just ahead of the girl.
She doesn't notice the evil presence.
Suddenly a beast leaps from the bushes and lands on top of the girl. Horrible screams and cries of pain follow. The bike lies in a ditch, its front wheel slowly turning.
Donald B. Oakland Productions presents "Jaws III."
The next scene is the morning after. Marathon County sheriff's deputies have discovered the tragic scene. All that remains is a bent bicycle and a pool of blood on the pavement, a yellow bikini top in its center.
Also on the pavement are the prints of a large animal.
The county coroner arrives and makes a brief scan of the scene. He looks at the paw prints.
"Looks like a dog attack to me," he says, "but I'd like an expert's opinion."
The humane society officer is called. He takes a quick look at the prints.
"Looks like a Great White Shepherd to me..." he says.
A group of bikers pedal along Highway W north of Wausau. An insouciant bunch of biking enthusiasts, they planned to go 100 miles that day. Fate allowed them only five. Their end was bloodied bodies and bent bike metal.
Switch to a meeting of the county board. People are panicky. A large reward is offered. From the back of the room a man draws his fingernails across a blackboard.
"For $10,000 I'll get your great white..."
It's Don Oakland, a ne'er-do-well dog catcher. (It's my movie, I'll star in it!)
"My left foot is no more because I was once pedalin' and a shepherd attacked and ripped it from my leg. I've been after the big ones ever since."
It's a Wednesday morning. Oakland is pedaling his ten-speed down a country road. Strapped to his waist is a .44 magnum handgun.
He comes to a small woodlot. His senses, honed by years of experience, tell him the great white is out there.
(Jaws music returns.)

126

Suddenly the front tire of his bike blows. He loses control and tumbles to the pavement.

Ba dump—ba dump—ba dump...

A blur in the bushes. The shepherd appears 75 yards away and charges.

Oakland reaches for his gun. It isn't there. It flew out and lies ten feet away on the gravel shoulder of the road. The dog breaks into full stride.

Oakland tries to get up. He can't. His leg is broken.

He crawls toward the gun, then makes one final lunge. His fingers reach the gun's stock. Oakland turns, aims and fires. The shot misses.

The German shepherd leaps high, his bared teeth shimmering in the sunlight.

Oakland fires again and again. The bullets crash into the dog's chest, killing it. The dead dog lands on top of Oakland.

The great shepherd is dead, all 175 pounds of it—fade to music...

* * * * *

HUNT FOR BALL BEARINGS IS A WILD-GOOSE CHASE

Many a time I have refrained from repairing something for fear of finding a spring within.

Springs are sneaky, squeaky things.

Move the wrong screw just a half turn too far and suddenly another spring gains its freedom and whizzes past your eyes at the speed of light.

Yup, I thought springs were the ultimate pits until I discovered something worse: Ball bearings.

Recently I had a bad experience with ball bearings.

I was messing with the rear wheel of my bicycle when I met Mr. Ball Bearing.

I was removing the axle when suddenly all these shiny steel balls poured out. They hit the floor like raindrops and instantly disappeared.

I had no idea where they went. Hey, you try following a dozen tiny balls rolling off in a dozen different directions.

Have you ever tried to find a "few" errant ball bearings? Finding contact lenses in water is easier.

Ah, but not to worry, I said to myself. I've always had a knack for finding small insignificant things.

Examination of the other side of the wheel revealed nine ball bearings nicely packed in grease. I surmised I had nine to find.

I got down on my hands and knees and, like a hound on a rabbit's trail, I began my search through the dust, debris and sawdust.

I found two right away. Ten minutes later I found a third hiding in a small pile of sawdust. After 20 minutes I had retrieved five.

However, after 60 minutes of searching I began getting crazy. Crashing sounds filled the basement as I wildly rooted through the debris like some half-crazed warthog. Boxes, pieces of wood, tools and a host of things defying identification flew as I pursued the itty-bitty balls of steel.

Seven ball bearings had revealed themselves to me. I was convinced the remaining two didn't roll away, but flew off.

I crawled underneath the workbench only to find my wife's cat eyeing me suspiciously. I gave her a mean stare. "You *$*%&!!! cat! You ate one of those *%&**!! ball bearings, didn't you?"

The cat hissed and ran off.

I breaststroked farther beneath the table. Soon I was coughing up spider webs and staring eyeball to eyeball at the biggest daddy longlegs I had ever seen. And, underneath him was the eighth ball bearing!

Well, it looked as if the spider wasn't about to give up the ball bearing without a fight, so I grabbed a length of two by four.

"IEEEEEEEE—yah!" Down came the board with brutal force. It wasn't a pretty sight underneath it. But, right there in the center of what remained of the spider was the ball.

I concluded the ninth ball must have bounced into previously unexplored regions of the basement, an area marked by cardboard

128

boxes untouched by human hands for many years. Mounds of mold and mildew covered them.

I went upstairs for a beer—bottled courage, I called it.

I kissed my wife goodbye and with trembling hands removed the first box and crawled behind the rest.

If you can imagine crawling through a black cave populated by fruit bats, centipedes and various vermin, you'll have some idea of what I encountered.

The search didn't result in the ninth ball. It was midnight and I called it quits. I took the jar holding the balls and carefully poured them into my hand for a final counting—seven, eight—nine!! I counted again. Nine again.

In the heat of the search I had miscounted. I screamed and collapsed into a chair. The resulting impact jarred lose from my hands the nine tiny balls. I watched helplessly as they once again disappeared across the floor.

* * * * *

JOGGING SHOULD BE OUTLAWED

A lot of you aren't going to like this column.

I'm sorry, but you're going to have to be told. Jogging is an unnatural act. It should be outlawed.

When men or women run counter to the wisdom of nature, the whole cosmos is thrown out of whack. (I've been watching Carl Sagan on Channel 20.)

When that happens, things like Mount St. Helens and Los Angeles smog alerts occur.

Anyway, when we humans run counter to nature we are bound to suffer, simple as that.

How else can you explain why joggers love to tell you about their aching feet. Or, why they'll spend on funny-looking shoes enough money to purchase a week's worth of food for their family.

Why do I say jogging is running counter to nature? I ask you, on this earth how many animals that walk on two legs jog?

Remember, don't be snobbish. All we are is just another animal with an over-productive imagination.

A kangaroo, you say. A kangaroo hops.

A duck? Ducks swim or waddle. Anyway, can you picture a duck in jogging shorts? Some drunk duck hunters might.

Ducks and other birds fly, which is a lot more efficient way of getting somewhere than running.

Man's closest cousin is the ape, some say. What do apes do? They climb trees. Why? Because that's what nature tells them to do. That's what nature built them to do. And they have the good sense to listen to her wisdom.

A long time ago, Ma Nature said to us: "Just because I made you a little smarter, it doesn't mean you can leave the trees. You leave the trees and you're asking for all sorts of trouble."

But, we didn't listen. We never listen to nature. And we've had troubles ever since.

So, I submit to you that we should be climbing trees for exercise rather than running over pedestrians on sidewalks. No more bouncing down boulevards!

Fine, you say, but where is the cardiovascular benefit in shinning up a maple tree?

Well, brother, when you are 40 feet up, hanging on to a limb the size of your forearm and swaying in the breeze, your heart is a-pounding.

Look at all the additional benefits of tree climbing. Not only do you gain strong legs, but strong arms and shoulders. Also, the bark of a tree efficiently toughens the skin. And, once you get up a tree, you are afforded a marvelous view of whatever is below.

Of course, there are drawbacks. Instead of barking dogs, a climber will experience squirrels and defensive bluejays. And occasionally you might run into some dull-headed homeowner who doesn't particularly like strangers ascending his oak trees.

Tree climbing is beneficial in ways other than personal health.

If you come up against a bear in the woods, your options are darn few: Run, be eaten or climb a tree.

I contend that a man has a better chance outclimbing a bear than he has outrunning one.

And, without a doubt, man's best option when chased by an angry dog is to go up a tree. Dogs can't climb trees. (I know of only one exception over in Clintonville.)

Kids should be taught how to climb trees. Why, when I was a kid my best defense against bullies was to outclimb them.

And, the best way to elude someone is to go up a tree. You can't be tracked unless you're on the ground.

But, you say, people can fall out of trees and get hurt. Well, joggers can get hit by cars or teenagers on skateboards. There is risk in everything.

But, I have to admit, I don't know which would be worse— being run over by a jogger or flattened by some yahoo falling out of a tree.

* * * * *

STAINS BUT NO STRAIN IN INVENTIVE SPORT

I really don't think joggers get enough exercise.

Most joggers I see just plod along hogging the sidewalks.

I think they can do a lot better.

With that in mind, I introduce a new sport. I call it kiljoggering, a name with a decidedly Nordic-aerobic flavor.

I got the idea after reading about these survivalist groups who play guerrilla war. Instead of bullets, they have capsules of red dye which they insert into air guns and commence to shoot at each other.

No one ever gets hurt, just a little stained.

I thought this adult version of GI Joe might be applied to recreational running.

To get an idea how this sport works, let's imagine the first televised kiljoggering event...

"Good afternoon ladies and gentlemen, this is Howard Cosell and we're in Wausau, Wisconsin, to watch the second annual kiljoggering competition.

"Over here we have Bill, Bobby and Roy polishing up their air rifles getting ready for the competition which will commence momentarily.

"Early morning and dusk are prime times for kiljoggering, as that's when most of your sidewalk thumpers are out."

The three men pile into the back of a souped-up, big-tired four-by-four pickup. Suddenly the large truck roars off in a cloud of dust, squeals around a corner and shoots down a quiet residential street.

The truck races down street after street as the men hang on for dear life. Suddenly the truck slows.

"I think they've spotted joggers," Howard says in a hushed tone. "Yes, a man and woman are—oh, oh, they've seen the truck and have broken into a sprint."

The truck driver floors it. The three men fall backward in the box, but quickly regain their footing. Within seconds the truck is parallel to the runners.

"Looks like Billy will have the first shot..." Cosell says, his voice gaining in excitement.

Billy's M-16 air rifle makes a dull thud sound. Suddenly the male jogger jumps high, his legs in a wide split. A large red splat appears on the sidewalk.

"Excellent move by that jogger. That split really tones the thigh and groin muscles. You can tell that boy did his stretches," Howard says.

Bobby takes aim and fires just as the female runner stops. The dye-filled projectile flies in front of her and explodes against a nearby maple tree.

"That stopping really develops the quick twitch muscle reflexes of the legs. A great conditioner, but not easily learned. Ladies and gentlemen, we have a couple of real pros running here today."

Billy sets his rifle on automatic and lets loose with five quick bursts at the male runner.

But the runner instantly turns right and high jumps over a picket fence as the capsules splatter against the white-painted wood.

"What a jump! Why that required not only strong legs, but a well-conditioned upper body. Did you see how his arm and shoulder muscles strained as he lifted his body over that fence!"

Roy drops a pair of aviator sunglasses over his eyes and takes a puff on a stubby cigar hanging from his lips. With one smooth motion he raises his Winchester 94 and fires.

The woman runner goes down in a shower of red.

"A great shot by Roy; a real cool shooter, he is. He got her right on her Nike emblem. Well, ladies and gentlemen, you can send that jogging suit to the cleaners."

A loud horn sounds.

"Well, that's it, time's up. I see the men jumping off their pickup and running over to congratulate the runners. And here comes the driver with a case of Gatorade for the joggers and Miller Lite for the shooters.

"What sportsmen, what a contest!"

* * * * *

THE Y IS FOR LOVERS—OF EXERCISE

I recently read something really disturbing.

A newspaper article told how health clubs and similar bastions of self-abuse are replacing single's bars as places where swinging singles hustle members of the opposite sex.

Can't wait for this trend to hit the Wausau YMCA where I frequently go to torture my body in the name of good health.

I don't particularly relish the idea of swinging singles types parading around the exercise area in search of each other while I grunt, groan, wheeze and sweat.

The following scene comes to mind.

133

Happy Harry, perennial playboy from Poniatowski, ambles into the exercise area of the YMCA. Standing next to the universal gym in his baby blue Izod sport shirt and matching shorts, he watches the joggers on the indoor track.

His eyes alight on a curvaceous brunette bounding down one lane.

He watches her carefully as she runs by, his head nodding quickly as his eyes try to catch sight of any ring on her left hand. Seeing none, he figures her fair game.

He walks over to the running track and, as the girl passes by, he sucks in his stomach and pushes out his chest so that the top part of his shirt opens, exposing the gold chain around his neck.

After she goes by, he grimaces, realizing what he is about to put himself through for the sake of a date. He commences to jog.

He suddenly realizes that the girl of his desire is a half a lap ahead of him. He is torn between speeding up his stride to catch her or slowing down to allow her to catch up with him.

He makes the fatal macho mistake and tries to catch up with her.

"Huff—huff—huff—huff." His lungs begin to hurt. But after two laps he has overtaken the girl and now runs alongside her.

"Huff—huff—cough cough—huff—uh hi, cough wheeze cough," he says with a smile.

The girl doesn't even turn her head.

"Come here often?—huff, huff, huff, cough, huff, huff, wheeze, cough..."

"Get lost," the girl replies, without missing a beat of her steady breathing.

Happy Harry's face begins turning red, not from embarrassment but from exertion. Ten laps at a speed twice his normal and he hasn't gotten to first base.

"Say, I use the Gustav Siegfried running style, what's your style?"

"Gustav who?"

Ah ha, ol' Gustav delivers again, Happy Harry thinks.

"Well, it's—huff, huff, a style I—huff, huff—learned from—wheeze cough, wheeze cough, from Gustav himself in Geneva, Switzerland. Surely you know Gus. He's the guy who ran up the Matterhorn."

"Wow," she says as her eyes widen.

"Say, how'd you like me to show you his technique?"

"Well, I don't know."

"How about meeting me outside the locker room and we'll discuss it over dinner?"

"Not tonight, I'm busy—You going to be running tomorrow?"

A panicked look crosses Harry's face. "Sure! Heck, I run seven miles every day." If Harry runs between his bedroom and bathroom once a week it's more than normal exercise.

"See you then," the girl says, as she pulls away from Harry. After she rounds the corner, Harry collapses on the track, clutching his cramped stomach and praying that cardiac arrest doesn't occur.

Realizing the girl will soon be reappearing behind him, he crawls off the track and through the door into the locker room. He wishes tomorrow would never come.

* * * * *

"THE BALLAD OF WILMA DAY"

Seems the big fad now is for women to put on weight.

Weight as in weightlifting, barbells and Universal machines.

Some women find biceps more important than beauty secrets. Instead of reading *Cosmo*, they're thumbing through *Modern Muscle*.

According to recent issues of *Time and Life* magazines, the definition of feminine beauty in the 80's will be lean and mean.

Seems to me women have a bad case of the Charles Atlas syndrome.

Men remember Charlie.

You'd pick up a comic book and right between Superman and Superboy stories would be ol' Charlie, muscles a-bulging. He promised you a new body in something like ten days.

Real potent stuff, particularly if you had a couple of schoolyard bullies on your case or if girls seemed to think you worse than a zit.

While I haven't seen any comic book ads for women, every time I go into the bookstore it seems there's another new book on body building or, euphemistically, body shaping. Can't miss them, they're right between aerobic and jogging books.

What we need instead of more books is a ballad, a song to capture the spirit of this modern woman.

I mean, we had "I Am Woman" for the libbers, why not something for the lifters.

Recognizing this obvious oversight in pop culture, the Wildwoods music department has come up with "The Ballad of Wilma Day."

It roughly follows the melody of "When Johnny Comes Marching Home" (in the same sense Highway 51 roughly follows the Wisconsin River).

Ah-one, ah-two...

> This is a tale about a gal
> They called the shrimp.
> She was so frail, so pale and
> So meek, so weak.
> She'd go to the beach to lie in the sun
> The gals kicked sand at her for fun
> She'd have to leave in utter disgrace
> The weakling Wilma Day.
> Then one day while on her way
> To work, to work
> She found a funny kind of book
> And took a look.
> The man inside with muscles to spare
> Promised her life without despair.
> Just go to the gym and lift some weights
> You weakling, Wilma Day.
> She put down the book and ran to the Y
> To join, to join.
> She shed all her clothes and put on her tights
> To pump the iron.
> She pumped so hard her arms nearly broke
> She thought she surely suffered a stroke
> But on she pressed so never to be
> The weakling Wilma Day.

For months and months she did her weights,
The squats, the curls.
A 100, 200, 300 and more
She cleaned and jerked.
Her biceps drew taut, her thighs grew wide
She now had a physique and a lot of pride.
And the confidence she thought she never had,
The liberated Wilma Day.
She went to the beach to lie in the sun
To tan, to tan.
They called her a wimp, kicked sand in her face
Too bad for them.
She took one of the gals by the feet
Flung her over the lifeguard's seat
From that day on she ruled the beach,
The mighty Wilma Day.
She now has a body the boys do like,
So sleek, so firm.
One of them tried to make a pass,
A kiss, my dear?
Instead of a kiss she gave him a whack,
Almost broke the poor boy's back.
Ya treat me right or not at all,
Says the sexy Wilma Day.
Wilma the wimp is gone for good
Hurrah, Hurrah.
In her place a woman of strength
Right on, right on.
United we stand, divided we fall,
I'm telling you gals we can have it all.
Power is ours by pumping the weights
As Wilma goes marching on.

* * * * *

137

CHAPTER SEVEN

CLEANING REFRIG A FRIGHTENING ORDEAL

Cleaning the refrigerator is about as much fun as getting the flu.

For that reason, around the Oakland household we usually let this chore lapse until it reaches a point where it either gets cleaned or our friends turn us over to the health department.

I fear one of these days we're going to let our refrigerator go just too long...

I put down the bucket full of suds and open the refrigerator door. I stare a moment at the heaping mounds of vegetable matter which appear like fungus growing over the plastic milk cartons and bottles half-filled with pop.

Suddenly I jump back and slam the door shut.

"What's wrong, dear?" my wife asks as she puts her rubber gloves on.

"Something just growled at me."

"Huh?"

"I was just about to remove that crusted-over tub of cottage cheese when something growled at me."

"Quit your joking and get cleaning. You know I don't like this anymore than you do but, really, it's been at least a year now."

"OK, but I'm not going back in there alone."

My wife draws close as I open the door. All is quiet. I grab the cottage cheese and whip it out. It slides across the kitchen floor like a hockey puck.

I reach in again, this time to fetch a rather brown wrinkled remnant of an apple. "AAAAIIIEEEE!!" I slam the door shut again.

"Another growl, dear?"

"Something's staring at me."

"Ah, come on."

"Dear, how long have your mother's pickles been in the fridge?"

"Oh, I don't know, summer of '81 or '80."

"Well, there are two big yellow eyes staring out of that jar."

My wife gives me a disgusted look. "OK, I've had enough of your stupid excuses. I'll clean the darn thing myself." She pushes me aside, opens the door and leans inside.

"OOOOOOOOOOOOH!"

She flies backwards and slams the door.

"Donald, the pickles—they're alive."

"Oh, really?" I say with a smirk.

"What are we going to do?"

"We must assume it's hostile. I mean, anything that would choose to live in our refrigerator could not have a pleasant disposition."

I think about the situation for a moment, then suggest, "I suppose I could get my deer rifle. The only problem is the pickle jar is right next to a six-pack and I'd hate to lose any beer."

"Maybe we should..."

"I've got it, honey. We'll send the cat in after it."

"Absolutely not!"

"We'll see how much of a fighter that feline is."

"No way. I think we ought to call the police."

"What are they going to do, arrest it? Heck, they'll probably arrest us for allowing such a thing to grow."

"Well, we just can't leave it in there."

"I know, I'll just grab the jar and throw it out the kitchen door."

I open the refrigerator. "Go open the back door and stand aside."

I grab the growling jar and heave it. My wife ducks as it flies out the door and crashes on the driveway.

A green pickle suddenly sprouts legs and crawls down the driveway toward the street. We watch in horror as it attacks a curious collie and chases a little girl halfway down the block.

The pickle gives up on the girl and crawls over to a catch basin and disappears.

"Gosh, I just hope it doesn't come back like some stray cat in search of a free meal," I tell my wife.

"Say, do you hear growling?" she asks.

I return to the refrigerator and look in.

"Oh, no. Not the mayonnaise!"

* * * * *

DR. OAKLOVE'S TRASH BEARS SEEDS OF DESTRUCTION

The following column contains graphic material. Parental discretion is advised. Children should not read this unless seated with an adult. At the end of this column there will be a panel discussion of this dramatization of the ultimate disaster.

It was a quiet neighborhood on Wausau's southeast side. Children played as their parents tended to their backyard chores. Yet, beneath the apparent clam was growing tension. Ominous signs appeared that the unspeakable might soon happen.

Oakland might clean his basement.

Most people tried not to think about it. From what they heard of the clutter in his basement, the consequences of a thorough cleaning would be devastating beyond comprehension.

Yet, there were unconfirmed reports of sightings of Oakland carrying boxes into the garage. These rumors caused some to abruptly leave the neighborhood.

Then, one morning neighbors were awakened by the air raid siren sound of howling dogs.

"Good lord, he's done it!" one man screamed to his wife. He rushed to the window and looked out upon a huge trash heap on the curb in front of Oakland's house.

141

"GROSSS!" he yelled and toppled over. The sight of boxes filled with moldy, web-covered debris was too much for his heart.

Suddenly a strange odor came through the window. His wife took a quick sniff and collapsed.

Outside, people within 100 yards of the trash heap were either dead or dying. A mailman was struck down in mid-stride. A paperboy lay gasping in a pile of newspapers.

People wandered aimlessly down the streets and sidewalks. "Daddy! Daddy!" came the confused cry of a young boy.

Some tried covering their mouths and noses with damp cloths, but soon succumbed to the radiating odors.

Only spiders and millipedes seemed to thrive. One middle-aged man said to his grandson, "They always said that after Oakland cleaned out his basement, only the bugs would be left."

The neighborhood alderman, scarred and shakened, staggered down the street to his former home. Coughing from the lingering death in the air, he made his way to what was once his backyard patio. He found several strangers hunched over his barbecue.

"Get out! Get out! I say," he yelled. But they just stared blankly at him. The alderman knelt down next to his Lawn Boy. One of the strangers walked over to him and knelt with him. The two huddled together fighting for another few minutes of life.

* * *

"Hello, I'm Ted Koppel and welcome to this special edition of Viewpoint. We will begin with Mr. William F. Buckley, Jr."

"The writer of this column is playing on the emotions of the people rather than offering us an in-depth perspective on this most complicated and convoluted issue."

"Mr. Sagan."

"Thank you, Ted. The images of destruction presented here, unfortunately, are far less severe than what would actually happen. We estimate the accumulated clutter in Mr Oakland's basement to be two tons. The mold and dust would generate a cloud that would block the sun and wipe out all human life in the neighborhood for ten years."

"Mr. Kissinger."

"I have been warning people about the basement clutter problem for 20 years. But, nobody reads my books because they're too thick.

"Yet, if Mr. Oakland should reduce the amount of garbage in his basement, the threat of a total cleanup will increase. Presently, the vast amount of trash serves as a viable deterrent. It's just to much for the lazy bum."

* * * * *

FIGHTING WITH FIBERGLASS

Fiberglass insulation, only man could create such a thing.

Batts of fiberglass insulation are the devil's bedsheets. Handling it is pure hell.

I took a bath in fiberglass insulation the other day. I still haven't stopped itching.

There I was with my friend, Larry, swimming in the pink ocean of spun glass that covered my attic.

Larry knew what he was doing. I didn't. I counted on him to save my life if I should succumb with all that stuff flowing into my lungs.

The dust was terrible. Whoever insulated my house the first time used loose insulation. That stuff attracted dust like a wet car on a gravel road.

Breathing in the atmosphere in the attic was like chewing on a dust mop. I could feel my lungs giving out.

I could just see myself felled by the dust and spun glass— falling through those fluffy pink batts and through the ceiling.

I could picture myself crashing down into the kitchen and onto the table at which my wife was quietly seated.

I could see the kitchen enveloped in a cloud of white plaster dust and my wife buried in debris, a wad of fiberglass wedged in her mouth.

Getting the batts between the ceiling rafters and to the edge of the roof was no easy trick.

Larry and I had to crawl through that feather bed of old insulation. I feared other creatures might lurk in its depths.

143

Several times I went under the fluff, doing the breaststroke and clutching a batt between my legs. Insulation flowed down my shirt and crawled up my pants.

I itched where I couldn't politely scratch.

I could just see myself getting stuck between the roof and the attic.

"Well, Mrs. Oakland, your husband is wedged in there pretty good," the firefighter tells my wife.

"We have only two options," he says in a grim voice. "We can either jack up that portion of the roof, forever causing your house to tilt slightly," he says and then tries to look away.

"Or, we can wrap a heavy cable around your husband's legs and winch him out, hoping he'll stay in one piece."

"What happens if you don't get him out in one piece?" my wife asks.

The chief scratches his chin.

"We'll just have to wrap up what's left in insulation. He'll have an R-value of, oh, I'd say, nine or so..."

Many thoughts went through my mind as I coughed up insulation.

It's all the fault of the state Public Service Commission. In their wisdom, they made a rule that before you could get a new furnace you had to insulate your home to a certain R-value.

I bet they never had to put in insulation. They're probably rich enough to have it done by others.

Only man would torture himself this way. Animals are smart. They burrow into the ground, using it as natural insulation. We are just catching on to that idea.

Most animals carry their insulation on their backs. It's called fur or feathers. Man has neither, thanks to Schick and other razors.

It's typical of man to purposely evolve himself into a fleshy state and then have to spend hundreds of dollars for insulation and thousands of dollars for fuel just to keep himself warm.

Things like that don't make sense when you've got fiberglass between your teeth.

* * * * *

144

HAPPINESS IS NEVER HAVING TO RAISE YOUR HAND

Some people dream of owning the perfect home.

I don't. I dream of one day being able to afford the perfect bathroom.

I've already got it drawn out on paper. Heck, one of these days my number has got to come up in the Reader's Digest sweepstakes.

You know, bathrooms are the most underrated rooms in a house. Women talk about their kitchens. Men talk about their dens or workshops. Bachelors talk about bedrooms.

Nobody ever talks about their bathroom with any semblance of pride or affection. In fact, the only time you ever hear anybody mention the bathroom is to ask where the homeowner has hidden it.

I think our lack of respect for the bathroom stems from our childhoods.

How many of you had to go through the ordeal in school of asking permission to go to the bathroom. I mean, in front of the entire class you had to admit to a most intimate problem. It was embarrassing to reveal your lack of planning or that you drank too much milk during break time.

Come to think of it, the bathroom is the only room anywhere that you have to ask permission to visit.

I absolutely hate it when I visit the home of a friend or acquaintance and have to interrupt the conversation with: "May I use your bathroom?"

Heck, I'm embarrassed to even ask. I usually say something like: "May I use your facilities?" or "Where's the little boy's room?"

Another reason I suspect we dislike bathrooms is remembrances of our worst experiences with the evils of alcohol. Many an evening of overindulgence has ended rather ignobly in the bathroom.

Well, I happen to like bathrooms despite numerous run-ins with fiesty toilets which either refuse to flush or play Mount St. Helens.

I like the bathroom because it is one of the few convenient places where I can get away from it all.

Do you realize the bathroom is the only room in the entire house you can lock?

And, I never share a bathroom. To me a bathroom is a temple of solitude.

I do my most creative thinking in bathrooms.

Why, the original ideas for at least half these weekly columns came to me while I was meditating in the men's room, so to speak.

My perfect bathroom would be about the size of a moderately spacious kitchen. It, of course, would have your traditional tub and sink, although the toilet would include such extras as a fur-lined, foam-padded and electrically heated seat.

There is nothing worse than sitting on a cold seat first thing in the morning.

I'd also have the flusher electronically linked to a Dolby stereo system within the room. I hate that repulsively raucous "whoosh." I'd much prefer hearing the "1812 Overture" or Olivia Newton-John when I flush.

In front of the toilet would be a large wood paneled wall which would house a remote-controlled big-screen television and the stereo.

There would also be a fold-down table holding an electric typewriter upon which I could record the products of the meditations.

Instead of a bathtub I'd have a hot tub complete with water jets.

I often wonder what would happen if you put bubble bath in a hot tub. I mean, with that air jet agitation, you'd produce bubbles to the ceiling.

Can you imagine drowning in wall to wall bubbles?

On the opposite side of the room, I'd have one of those environmental modules. You just lay in there and by merely pushing buttons create sea breezes, Wisconsin in July or some tropical island.

Heck, I could just see myself coming in after battling a ton of snow and 50 below zero winds and sitting down in the midst of an artificial Caribbean Isle.

Just mix up a few pina coladas and wake me up Tuesday, Jose!

* * * * *

146

CLEANLINESS CAN BECOME TOO CLOSE TO GODLINESS

I'm afraid to go into my bathroom.

Recently I read about a Michigan State University researcher finding more than 100 strains of bacteria, yeast and fungi living on bar soap.

He called typical bar soap "a reservoir for germs."

Apparently Ivory soap is no longer 99/100 percent pure, as the television commercials used to tell us.

I have visions of all sorts of terror by toiletries.

"Donald, our soap—it's green," my wife yells from the bathtub.

"Honey, it's Irish Spring, they make it that way."

"But, Donald, the green is growing!"

She jumps out of the shower, wraps herself in a towel and takes off for the bedroom.

I peek in the bathroom door and to my horror see a giant toadstool rising from the bar of soap in the dish.

Green slime oozes like so much suds. It clings and spreads across the shower walls and spills onto the floor.

I slam the bathroom door shut.

"Honey, where's the kitty?"

"Why?" my wife asks from her hiding place under the bedcovers.

"Well, I figured I'd throw him into the shower to see if that green stuff is toxic. I mean, if it eats the cat, no great loss."

"DONALD!"

"OK, OK, the cat lives," I concede. "But, no way am I going in there."

Suddenly the bathroom door bulges as if being pushed by a great hand on the other side. The wood begins splitting and tiny droplets of green appear on the surface.

"WE'RE DOOMED!" I cry as green slime begins crawling up my pants.

I can see soap being at the bottom of some foul play.

NEWS ITEM: Phineas T., 52, noted Wausau industrialist, died suddenly Wednesday morning. It is reported his entire $5.2 million estate was left to his 21-year-old wife. Police are at a loss to explain the death as Phineas was reported in good health at the time.

"Forensics says he died of a strange infection," the chief detective tells his assistant.

"Poisoned?"

"Perhaps, but our lab people have analyzed everything he ate or drank. Nothing was out of the ordinary except for one thing."

"What?"

"He seemed to take a lot of showers," the detective said, turning to the grieving widow.

"Oh, I insisted Phineas always be clean. I dislike men who are, uh, soiled."

"Strange that a man would always use Dove," the detective said with a puzzled look.

"Gee, I never noticed."

"That's odd, he had a closet shelf filled with unwrapped bars. Of course, you used..."

"No, I preferred Dial."

"Did the deceased take a shower with Dove prior to his last supper?" he asked the widow in a stern voice.

"Why, yes, I think he did."

The detective turned to his assistant. "Arrest her for the death of Phineas T."

"Are you mad?" the wife protested.

"No, you are. It was you who bought those bars of soap and it was you who every night sprinkled deadly viruses on them, knowing full well they would thrive. You knew every time Phineas took a shower millions of those bugs were being absorbed into his body and that it was only a matter of time before he'd succumb— and, without a trace of the culprit."

"Yes, I'm afraid Dove was the bird of death for poor Phineas."

* * * * *

148

A CLOGGED DRAIN IS A ROYAL PAIN

When you begin taking a shower and end up taking a bath, you know it's time to clean out the bathtub drain.

I hate the job.

When my bathtub drain plugs, no amount of liquid drain opener fazes the clog. It must be surgically removed.

I remember the last time I had to unclog it...

Down into the basement I went, searching for the elusive trap. After crawling through curtains of cobwebs, I found it suspended just below a couple of floor joists. I had to get a ladder to reach it.

Ever try to open a trap? It's as if the plug is held with Superglue. Even with a large pipe wrench I nearly put myself in traction trying to get the blasted plug to loosen.

I wrestled with it for the better part of 15 minutes before it finally yielded. As I turned the cap, water gradually started dripping from the exposed threads.

I gave it another turn.

WHOOSH!

It was as if I had just opened the floodgates of Hoover Dam. A virtual Niagra Falls of vile, black, molasses-thick goo poured down. Within seconds I looked like some tall, irregular licorice stick.

"GRRR—ROSS!" I screamed.

My wife's cat, who had been watching me with its usual curiosity, suddenly arched its back, hissed at me and ran full-tilt up the stairs.

Even the spiders dangling from the webs surrounding the trap couldn't stand the sight of me. They all shot back into their holes.

149

I looked as if I just had an unnatural encounter with a tar wagon and smelled as though I had just spent a week camping on a mountain of old kitty litter, but I couldn't stop my quest for the clog.

The drain could humiliate me, but it couldn't stop me.

I stared up into the darkness of the trap. I knew somewhere inside resided a great biomass hardened to the consistency of concrete.

I reached up and put my hand inside the trap. Although it barely fit, I managed to turn and twist my fingers and grab a fist-sized ball of fiber.

Unbeknown to me, the liquid grime was forming a slick coating over the basement floor. Suddenly the ladder slid down and across the floor, leaving me dangling like some great black ape by my one hand wedged into the trap.

Trapped by the trap!

I did my melody of every curse known to civilized man, but to no avail.

I was hanging there trying to figure out how to free myself when I heard my wife come in the front door. I heard her footsteps go into the bedroom and a short time later go into the bathroom.

"WOMAN, DON'T USE THE...

I heard a faucet turn on.

Instantly a river of water gushed down my arm into my face.

"$%*&*##*&*% (gurgle gurgle, cough, spit) TURN OFF THAT %&%&*$F#!! FAUCET!"

Well, she didn't hear me until after she had taken her ten-minute, very hot shower. The basement was a veritable lake. A flotilla of wood from the workbench passed beneath me.

My persistent cries finally brought wife to the rescue—with a jar of Vaseline and a crowbar.

Out with my swollen hand came a softball-size wad. The drain was unclogged.

I had won, but the battle scars would remain forever.

* * * * *

THE TOILET PAPER CAPER

Do you realize that man is the only creature on this earth who uses toilet paper?

Oh, no, Oakland is going to write another one of those distasteful columns, I can hear you say.

Not so. This column is not about toilet paper or its proper use, but about consumerism and saving a buck.

I got to thinking about the sociological ramifications of toilet paper after I had made a major toilet paper splurge at Dale's Supermarket.

You see, I'm a compulsive coupon clipper. When Wednesday's Herald comes around, I tear into it like a kid unwrapping a Christmas present.

Anyway, on a recent Wednesday I noticed Dale's was having a sale on a certain brand of toilet paper or, as they say in polite society, bathroom tissue.

I remembered that I had recently clipped a couple of coupons for that product.

Not only did I have coupons, I had enough money to buy as much tissue as would be required to meet the provisions of the coupon.

You see, the coupons would give me one free four-pack of tissue for every three four-packs I bought at the price marked. Because the price marked was about 20 cents off the regular price, I figured to make quite a killing.

Armed with my coupons, I went right to the display and took eight four-packs of pink tissue. Why pink?

Well, once I brought home an armful of green toilet paper and my wife screamed. Apparently, green clashes with the decor of our bathroom. Henceforth, only white or pink would be acceptable, she informed me sternly.

Feeling a bit conspicuous with a cart full of toilet paper, I purchased two grapefruit, a package of carrots, a six-pack of Pepsi and two cans of tuna fish (for which I had ten-cents-off coupons) just to disguise the true intentions of my visit to the store.

I will confess that I felt a bit nervous checking out with 32 rolls of toilet paper. I tried not to look at the checkout girl's initial expression.

The only drawback of my purchase was that I was forced to buy one-ply tissue.

I'm a two-ply man myself. I haven't done a detailed analysis of the cost effectiveness of a two-ply roll over a one-ply roll. I haven't the money to afford consultants to help me figure it out.

But this toilet paper caper wasn't my biggest coupon coup. My grandest was at a discount grocery store in Clintonville when I walked out with four four-packs of toilet paper, four rolls of paper toweling (I had coupons for both products) and two cases of Old Style, which was selling at a ridiculously low price.

The checkout girl there must have thought I was heading for some really bizarre party.

I've been stockpiling toilet paper for quite some time. At this moment, I have 106 rolls in a closet in my basement.

Now, I don't think that's strange. Heck, toilet paper has an unlimited shelf life and there will never be a time when I won't need it. And, it's saving me money which can be spent on more important things, like beer.

And, if the world should end tomorrow—well, I shudder to think of those poor people who don't have toilet paper reserves.

* * * * *

A GOOD WINTER'S SLEEP IS IN THE BAG

I swear, when women were created, somebody set their thermostats too low.

My wife is always colder than I am.

That causes a continual battle over heating the house in the winter. I mean, we don't have a thermostat for the furnace, we've got a yo-yo.

She turns it up; I turn it down. She yells about catching cold; I scream about heating bills.

The temperature fluctuates so much the stupid cat doesn't know if it should shed or not.

I don't think I should have to strip to T-shirt and shorts just to stay comfortable in winter.

But, my wife is not pleased having to wear three sweaters, wool pants and long underwear and sit under a stadium blanket just to watch television.

Then there is the problem of the bed. When she is comfortably warm, I feel like a chicken in a roaster.

We thought we solved the problem by buying a twin-size electric blanket for our queen-size bed. She had the electric blanket on her half and I had plain blankets on my side.

Well, that didn't quite work out.

Because one side of my blankets had nothing to anchor on, they kept sliding off the edge of the bed. I'd find myself shivering under a sheet in the middle of the night.

Rather than get up and pick up the blankets, I'd try to mooch off my wife's electric blanket. Cold men are desperate men.

That only succeeded in starting Wife War III.

Ever resourceful, I decided to abandon the blankets and put a sleeping bag on my half of the bed. Peace returned to our home.

I'm quite happy in my bag.

My feet no longer pop out from under the covers and my wife can no longer steal my blankets. Even if I should fall out of bed, I'd still be warm.

Honestly, I can't see why more people don't use sleeping bags on their beds.

Why, in college I slept in a sleeping bag my last three years. I found it quite handy.

In the dormitory where I stayed, guys would get up at 6 a.m. for an 8 a.m. class. They'd shower, shave, dress and spend a good 15 to 20 minutes neatly making their beds.

Heck, I'd get up at 7:45.

I'd jump out of my bag, roll it up and tuck it away in the closet. I'd jump into my jeans, shirt and shoes and turn on the coffee pot as I left for class.

After my first class, I'd rush back to the dorm room for a cup of caffeine while sitting on a bare mattress covered with a cotton sheet.

By not making a bed every morning I'd conserve sufficient energy to make it through my first hour class—well, most of the time.

First hour geology was an exception. Rocks put me to sleep. A friend from the dorm and I would alternate sleeping through class.

On Mondays I'd sleep and he'd take notes and on Wednesdays he'd be like moss on granite and I'd take notes. If the geology teacher happened to say something particularly illuminating, a quick poke to the ribs aroused whoever was sleeping.

On Fridays we usually both slept because of indiscretions the night before.

I've always had an aversion to bed making. I could never see the point in trying to make my bed look like something out of *Better Homes and Gardens* when it would be messed up the following night.

I get suspicious of people who try to impress you with how neatly the corners of their bedsheets are tucked in.

No sir, a bed is a bed and not a statement of character. And, a bag is better for a blissful winter snooze.

* * * * *

BOUT WITH SOCKS A MISMATCH

My socks are promiscuous.

They sock swap.

Over the years, I have accumulated dozens of pairs of socks. I just can't throw them away, even when there are holes where the toes go.

But, try to find a matching pair among them.

I don't know where their mates have gone.

I have a sock drawer that looks like a snake pit with a huge ball of innertwined creatures. Yet, few match.

The mate to one of my blue socks has long since disappeared, run off like some errant spouse.

It seems that socks stay together about six months, then split.

I have visions of a blue sock running off with a green sock in the middle of the night, leaving behind two orphaned and mismatched socks.

Maybe the washing machine eats them.

Throw in a dozen pairs and the machine consumes two socks as dues.

It's really getting bad.

The other morning I was rushing because I was ten minutes behind schedule. I was going great until it came time to find my socks.

I couldn't find a blue pair to go with my blue pants and black shoes.

I ripped through the socks drawer.

I found plenty of blue socks, but none the same shade or style.

155

The clock was ticking and I was getting more desperate. It reached the point where either I grabbed a pair of white sweat socks or got to work late.

I went with the white.

Luckily, I have a pair of six-inch tall boots. I figured the boots would hide this indiscretion.

I mean, do you know what it's like to wear a sport coat, tie, slacks and sweat socks?

It's worse than wearing dress socks of two different shades.

Freaked out Hollywood stars could get away with it. Woody Allen could. Punk rockers, sans the sport coat, could.

But, reporters? No way.

It's like you're talking with somebody, somebody really important, and all of a sudden you notice their eyes drop down and their eyebrows raise up.

It's most uncomfortable talking with someone who is staring at your feet and trying to hold back a laugh.

I suppose you could make up some lame excuse.

"Gee, funniest thing happened at the Y. Someone broke into my locker and stole my socks. Had to put these smelly old things on."

Or, "My wife sent all my socks to the dry cleaners. I ask you, what's a guy to do?"

Or, you could use the old tried and true: "You see, I get dressed in the dark and my crazy wife accidentally put sweat socks in my dress sock drawer."

In Southern California you could just put tennis shoes on and pretend you're laid-back mellow. "The three-piece suit I'm wearing is for business, the tennies are me, for sure," you'd say.

If you tried that in Wisconsin, you'd need the tennies to cushion your fall as they threw you out the door.

Actually, I wish American fashion would just standardize the sock.

All socks would be the same style.

A person would then select one color of socks and he would wear that pair regardless of the shoes or clothes worn.

That goes for athletic socks.

You know, I could never figure out why athletic socks, which get the dirtiest, smelliest and foulest of any sock, are white. Black would seem more appropriate.

And, why they have those colored bands on the top of sweat socks stumps me. I have as much trouble matching those as I do dress socks.

So, let's make life easier for ourselves and move to identical socks.

Then let's do away with striped ties and colored belts.

* * * * *

There's Suspense in Suspenders

I've been accused of trying to look preppy.

You see, I've started wearing suspenders and people have told me suspenders are very preppy.

Look, I wear suspenders to keep my pants up, not to look preppy.

My lifestyle can't tolerate preppy.

Let's face it, the preppy look doesn't go well with a beer belly.

I wear suspenders because I'm sick and tired of running around with my pants at half-mast.

People were continually hassling me because my shirttails popped out all the time. It was like being surrounded by 1,001 mothers: "Donald, tuck in your shirt!"

Doggone it, just because your shirttail hangs out doesn't mean you're some kind of derelict.

To solve the problem would require either tighter pants or suspenders and I refuse to wear pants that would require me to grease my hips to get them on.

I can't understand it. Women hate girdles, yet will buy stretch jeans having twice the compressive strength.

Anyway, I was buying loose fitting pants and using a belt to hold them up.

Then I lost a little weight and my belted pants looked like the top of a gunny sack.

Not desiring to purchase new pants or alter the ones I own, I decided to buy suspenders.

Wearing suspenders makes sense.

I tend to put a lot of things on my belt and in my pockets which makes my pants rather heavy. I feel like I'm lifting weights when I put my pants on in the morning.

The suspenders transfer that weight from my hips to my shoulders. If men's hips were designed to carry loads, we'd all be sporting saddles and walking on all fours.

I've got to think wearing suspenders will improve my upper body physique. They're putting isometric tension on the ol' deltoids and pectorals while relieving the gluteus maximus.

Heck, if I wear suspenders every day, by the time I'm 40 I'll look like Arnold Schwarzenegger.

That or my back will collapse.

I have to be honest about this and relate three drawbacks to suspender-wearing.

First, they tend to slip off the shoulders while the wearer is seated. It's a terrible nuisance.

I can now sympathize with women who have to wear underwear with straps.

Second, there is a certain kind of deviant personality that enjoys snapping suspenders.

These people should be put away.

After a day of dealing with these jokers, your back looks like some one-eyed barbarian has whipped you with a cat-o'-nine-tails.

Third, suspenders tend to hike up your pants, causing them to ride slightly above your shoes.

You end up looking like a kid who just inherited the pants of his older but shorter brother.

You aren't "dressing for success" when your socks show.

Anyway, the only way to solve this is to counterweight the pants. I keep putting junk in my pockets until the weight pulls the suspenders and pants down to the proper position.

It's sort of like ballast for a hot air balloon.

The only trouble is when one of my pockets rips. The avalanche of stuff down my pants leg is most unnerving. And, the lack of weight on one side causes my pants to hang cockeyed.

I'm also terribly fearful of my suspenders breaking.

I could just see one of those babies snapping and sending one of the little metal clamps shooting into my mouth, KO'ing a tooth.

Hey, wearing suspenders is risky business. Suspenders aren't for sissies.

* * * * *

MONDAY MOURNINGS

The following three part essay was written after a particular Monday morning.

The Awakening

I'm alone on a secluded tropical beach. I'm lying on a beach towel and watching the sea winds whip through the palms.

I sense a presence other than my own. I turn my head to discover a beautiful young woman running toward me.

It's Bo Derek.

She's wearing a sleek and sexy bathing suit. Her long blonde hair floats in the wind.

Her eyes are fixed on mine. In a moment she's within my reach. I get up to embrace her. She smiles. Her lips draw close to mine...

Buzzzzzzzzz, hisssssssss...

"This is the Equity Cooperative with your morning farm market report."

"Bo?" I say groggily. I glare at the clock radio on the dresser.

"The hog market around the state was 50 cents to a dollar lower..."

I lift myself from the covers and place my feet on the cold floor. In two steps, I'm on top of the clock radio.

159

"Shaddup!" I growl, slamming my fist on the off button. Two steps later I'm back in the warmth of the covers.

Maybe if I can get back to sleep quickly enough, Bo will return. I shake my head. With my luck I'll probably find Dudley Moore.

The Forced March

I feel a foot in the small of my back. It's pushing me toward the edge of the bed.

"Donald, it's time to get up."

"Just a minute," I grumble.

I feel the growing pressure of her foot.

"GET OUT!"

"AAAAAAAGH!" Thud!

I look up at the foot that just pushed me from the covers. I glance at the cat who was sleeping near where my body landed.

The cat hisses. I growl. My wife pulls the covers over her head.

"Stop picking on the cat and get into the bathroom. I don't want to be late for work," she says sternly.

I crawl toward the light switch. I miss it and slam my head into the wall. I back up and try for the doorway. On all fours, I enter the hallway.

The cat jumps on my back and digs her claws into my spine. She leaps off and disappears in the darkness.

I collapse to a spread-eagle position as I curse the invisible cat.

"Can't you be more quiet!" my wife says angrily.

The Lament

I crawl into the bathroom, stand up and flick on the light. I stare into the mirror at the red-eyed abomination staring back at me.

I turn on what I think is the cold water faucet and place my hand in scalding hot water.

My screams bring another stern rebuke from my resting wife.

I face the creature in the mirror once more and begin talking to it.

"I suppose I should be thankful to be awake. The alternative is not that appealing.

"But, should that happen, I wouldn't care. At the time, I couldn't care, could I?

"My wife would care, I suppose. Maybe not. I mean, it would give her a clear shot at the bathroom if I weren't there...

"The cat wouldn't care.

"Oh, why can't getting up be as gentle as falling asleep?

"Why can't I learn to like getting up?

"Other animals seem to awaken so naturally and peacefully. Of course, they don't have Mondays."

"Who are you talking to?" My wife calls out.

"Nobody."

"Well, tell nobody you don't have time for conversation. I'm giving you two minutes to get out of that shower and start breakfast."

I turn to the creature in the mirror.

"Tell you what, I'll take a shower, you start breakfast. Deal?"

I nod. The creature nods.

"See ya tomorrow."

* * * * *

CHAPTER EIGHT

INCENTIVE PLANS FOR THE WEAK-WILLED

Because of the overwhelming success of Oakland's Rent-A-Dog Program for Lackadaisical Runners, Wildwoods Enterprises is offering two new services.

Wildwood Enterprises—an organization dedicated to bettering the self-concept of animals by offering them alternative lifestyles—announces Oakland's Cat Attack Plan for Breaking the Cigarette Habit and Oakland's Rent-A-Dog Diet Plan.

Both programs operate on the premise that what willpower you lack, some dog or cat can graciously provide.

Some of you who want to quit smoking just seem to lack sufficient motivation.

We have a special breed of cats, a cross between Siamese and puma, which have been trained to stalk smokers.

Say you want to get your wife to quit puffing on the Virginia weed. All you have to do is rent one of our cats for a week and pretend you are giving it to her as a gift.

Initially her cat will be friendly, very affectionate.

But, watch what happens when your wife lights up. Watch the cat give her an icy stare. Note the panic in your wife's eyes as she watches this archbacked, hissing creature stare up at her.

"Darling, is something wrong with the cat?" she'll ask.

To which you will reply: "She doesn't care for smoke."

"Well, too bad," your wife will say.

At that point our cat will leap. As it flies by her face it will pluck the cigarette from her mouth using its two-inch long front claws.

No matter where in the house your wife might try to sneak a puff, our cat will be silently stalking her.

Our service will also eliminate that uncomfortable task of asking people not to smoke while visiting.

"Ah, I don't mind if you smoke," you say nonchalantly. "But, our cat thinks it's the pits." Then watch them put away their packs as our kitten looks at them as if they were hostile dogs.

Says Mrs. T.C., an advertising executive from the Gold Coast of Lake Wausau:

"For 20 years I smoked and for years I tried to quit, but just couldn't. Then my husband put an attack cat, 'Vein Slasher,' in our home. Within a week I stopped smoking for good."

"Every time I see a cigarette now, I think of those yellow eyes staring at me in the darkness and those gleeming incisors glistening in telltale light."

Oakland's Rent-A-Dog Diet Plan allows you to rent one of our elite corps of Russian German shepherds fresh off duty along the Berlin wall.

Our doggies are docile and affectionate at all times except meal time. That's when they assume guard duty at the dinner table.

The dog has been trained to allow you to eat for one minute and 30 seconds. You can consume all the food you want, but at 91 seconds the dog will jump onto the table, bare his impressive teeth like some horror movie werewolf and gobble up whatever is left on your plate.

If you so much as try to pick up a fork he'll give you a growl that will be guaranteed to take five pounds off your backside.

And, should you be a midnight snacker, don't even think about trying to get to the refrigerator. You'd never live to see the other side of the bedroom door. Look, we didn't pick Berlin wall dogs for nothing!

We guarantee you will lose 15 pounds in a week, ten from lack of eating, five from canine-induced anxiety.

Listen to J.P. from Slab City, Wisconsin: "Thanks to my shepherd, 'Blood Lust,' I can now enjoy life 50 pounds lighter."

* * * * *

MAN'S BEST FRIEND IS—DID YOU SAY BAT?

You remember how bad the bugs were last summer?

There certainly seemed to be a lot of them flying about. And, they all seemed to be in your backyard, didn't they?

You tried spraying. You wore yourself out swatting. You may even have purchased one of those electric bug zappers.

But, none of them worked, did they? Every time you had a picnic with a few friends, an air force of flying critters would come to call.

Well, next summer bugs won't drive you bonkers if you take advantage of Wildwoods Enterprises "Bats on Bugs" service.

For $29.99 we'll send you a family of 24 cuddly and bug-hungry American brown bats to rid your life of pesky insects.

Bats! I know, just the thought of a bat makes you shudder. Buy a bunch of bats, no way!

But, these are no ordinary bats. These are specially trained, housebroken and exquisitely groomed bats.

Remember you're dealing with Wildwoods Enterprises, whose slogan is: Dedicated to finding alternative lifestyles for our fellow animals so that they may enjoy a more fulfilling life.

Before your first bat arrives, one of our counselors will come to your home and hold a frank discussion with you about batdom. He will attempt to break down some of the unfounded bat biases you might have.

Why, I bet you didn't know that a bat will eat 500 insects an hour.

I defy any bug zapper to equal that kill rate. And, a bat will do that without expending one cent of electricity. Nor will he pollute the air as do spray insecticides.

He's silent, clean and death on bugs.

But bats are ugly, you say. They're nothing but flying mice!

Not our bats. Our bats are bred from the finest stock. And, when our bats are a year old, our specially trained plastic surgeons give each of them a new face. Some people say our bats have an amiable, teddy bear look to them.

But, bats will attack you, they'll pull your hair out and drink your blood, you protest.

Nonsense! Why our bats are really very affectionate, as lovable as any puppy. They love nothing more than being petted as they hang upside down from your outstretched arm or your nose.

And, our bats are fun-loving. They'll be the life of any cocktail party with their aerial aerobatics. And, it's great fun watching your guests dive for the floor as our bats playfully buzz their faces.

We teach our bats a really neat trick that will surely impress your guests. All you do is stretch out both arms, whistle and all 24 bats will fly to you and perch upside down on your arms.

We also have on hand our protector bats. These South American fruit bats are about the size of a small cat. They have been specially trained to fly silently around your home at night to protect it from all intruders.

Pity the poor burglar who comes up against one of our bats. He'll think Dracula is after him.

Around family members, our fruit bats are as harmless as kittens. They love to have their tummies tickled.

For $13.95 we'll send you a two-story dollhouse custom made for bats. It has perches for 50 bats, central heating and stereo radio. Bats love country music.

And, don't worry about feeding them. Insects are all they eat. However, our Wisconsin-bred bats do enjoy an occasional beer.

So be the first on your block to have bats.

Why, you'll be the toast of the neighborhood as you walk down the street with one of our protector bats flying alongside in his designer leather bat collar and leash.

* * * * *

DIPLOMAT NEEDED FOR DOG DAYS

Do dogs intimidate you?
Does every pooch seem to want you for its lunch?
Do you just plain dislike the creatures?
Then you need a Doggy Diplomat.

Wildwoods Enterprises proudly announces this new service in keeping with its tradition of finding alternative lifestyles for our animal brothers.

Too often man-dog conflicts stem from misunderstandings which could easily be avoided by face to fang negotiation. Unfortunately, very few of us are versed in the verbal or gestural language of dogs.

Because of this inability to properly communicate, negotiations often break down, leading to unnecessary bloodbaths.

Our Doggy Diplomats can solve this problem by mediating your disputes with the four-legged set.

From the time they are pups, our dogs are trained to be conciliatory instead of protective, nonviolent instead of vicious, caring instead of killing.

Our dogs receive nine months of intensive "I'm OK—You're OK" training. Our dogs don't go through tedious sit and heel training, but gather around the kennel for group discussion about feeling good about yourself and your canine brothers.

Our dogs attend various seminars where they learn to break down biases they may have about man.

Because one often has to be forceful in negotiations, our dogs receive a specially adapted assertiveness training.

From time to time they also attend canine adapted lectures on Positive Mental Attitude and Parent Effectiveness Training. When our dogs graduate, they feel good about life.

167

So, how can they help you?

Suppose you're jogging and suddenly a vicious dog comes charging after you. Unless you find a tree quickly, he'll probably nail you.

Such a grim encounter wouldn't have happened had you had a Doggy Diplomat along.

He would have run to intercept the charging canine and attempted to sit down with him to rap.

Maybe the offended dog didn't like you jogging across his turf.

"Hey, I can relate to that. I see where you're coming from because, hey, I've been there myself. Territoriality is a heavy trip," our dog says in a calm bark.

"Get outta my way, canine, lunch is getting away," the aggressive dog growls.

"Really, those hostile feelings toward humans are just creating a lot of negative energy. Lighten up, old boy. Get rid of that fear of humans," our dog says.

"Fear humans? Hah!"

"Hey, you can level with me. You had a bad experience with a human when you were a puppy. By chewing on joggers, you're merely acting out deep-seated frustrations with an inability to come to terms with humans. Your mad dog routine is just a guilt trip."

Of course, our trainers realize there are occasions when being positive won't change the mindset of some mongrel miscreant.

That's why only wolf-sized shepherds are accepted into our program and given rigorous physical fitness and combat training. Our dogs are both articulate and, if need be, physically assertive.

"Outta my way, bowzer, my jogger is getting away," the offended mutt snarls.

"Look, biscuit breath—you take one step and you're Gainsburger!" Our dog growls as his chest muscles bulge and his two-inch fangs flash.

"Uh, what were you saying about pent-up hostilities?" the other dog asks meekly.

Don't be down on dogs any longer. Adopt one of our Doggy Diplomats today.

* * * * *

DOGGED RUNNERS GET ON TRACK

The joggers are out in force again.

But, I've noticed a lot of you runners are just plodding along, just kind of shuffling by. You seem to lack the necessary enthusiasm.

Well, ladies and gentlemen, the Wildwoods is ready to give you that needed inspiration.

So, without further ado, let me introduce Oakland's Rent-A-Dog Program of Lackadaisical Runners.

We have a kennel of specially trained German Shepherds who are eager to assist joggers to run farther, faster.

Bred from guard dog stock, these vicious looking—but wouldn't harm a flea—shepherds can be rented out by the hour by anyone interested in achieving true aerobic exercise.

Here's how it works.

You tell us when you plan to jog and your anticipated route. Then we'll take one of our dogs and park him between two houses along the way.

As you run by, we will release the dog and he'll come after you as if you just killed his mother.

If the sight of a 150-pound German Shepherd with teeth like bear claws doesn't get your little legs moving, well, I'm afraid nothing will.

Although it will appear that the dog wants to wrap his fangs around your thigh like a Vise Grip pliers, he won't touch you. But he will bark, growl and nip just inches from your flesh.

He'll keep after you until you finish the distance you told us you desired to achieve. When you have reached that point, our man will whistle and the dog will retreat.

We had one poor runner who inadvertently left his assigned course and ran out of our man's whistle range. Three days later we caught up with him somewhere between Stanley and Withee, the dog still at his heels.

But, we have many satisfied customers. Take for instance Diana M., downtown Poniatowski:

"I lacked the desire to run. One of Oakland's Dogs, called Meateater, gave me instant inspiration. Why, I ran so fast I nearly took the treads off my tennies."

Or Annie O., a housewife in a suburb of Bevent:

"Until I rented a dog, I was unable to go faster than a nine-minute mile. Now, thanks to Oakland's Rent-A-Dog, I'm under the four-minute mark."

Or Felix F., certified public accountant from the upper east side of Nutterville:

"Feeling like a shepherd's next meal gives me the strength to do that extra mile. When I began jogging I could hardly make it down the block. Now I'm running from Nutterville to Hogarty and back before breakfast."

Or. L.J., a Rozellville condominium owner:

"I'm 66 years old. Doctors said I didn't have much longer to live because my heart was all plugged up.

"Well, I said nuts to them, became a vegetarian and started jogging. But, it wasn't until I rented a dog that my condition improved. Just the sound of that hound cleaned out my cardiovascular plumbing.

"After three weeks of being chased by a dog called 'Slow Death,' my heart is like a teenager's."

D.J., Miami Beach:

"We had the same idea down in Florida, but we couldn't figure out how to make an alligator run. Oakland's dogs are the rage down here now."

The Oakland Rent-A-Dog Program for Lackadaisical Runners will soon announce a new service. We call it the Oakland Canine Wake Up Plan.

Every morning, instead of an alarm clock waking you, we'll put a Russian wolfhound in bed with you.

If you don't get up to run, well, as Belker says on Hill Street Blues, "You're dog meat."

* * * * *

170

MISSION: IDENTIFY VIDEO ALIEN INTERFERENCE

Here at the Wildwoods we try to solve problems before they exist.

Satellite television poses one such potential problem.

Receiving television signals from orbiting satellites is becoming really popular. You see these huge dish antennas all over the place.

But, what bothers me is the potential to receive more than you bargained for.

I mean, there's no law that says your antenna can't pick up any other signal that might be bouncing around the cosmos.

And, as we all know, but never admit, we're not alone.

You could be sitting right in your own living room watching Fraggle Rock on HBO when suddenly something other than a Fraggle flashes onto the screen—something on the order of a patron from that bar in the first Star Wars movie.

What would you do?

What would you do if Dan Rather suddenly becomes a Martian Roger Mudd?

Call the sheriff?

You gotta be crazy!

"Hello, officer, this is Fred Smith. I was sitting here watching 'Laverne and Shirley' reruns when all of a sudden the screen went purple and there appeared this creature with the face of an overly ripe peach."

"What do you mean bad acid will do that to you?

"You gotta believe me, I'm looking at this thing that looks and moves like a break-dancing barbecued chicken. And, it's talking with this other creature that looks like a hairless rat..."

"No, I don't need Orkin..."

171

Five minutes later there is a knocking at your door and behind it are men in white suits waiting to greet you with nervous smiles.

As an alternative, we suggest you call the Wildwoods ET-TV Investigation Service.

For a nominal fee we will come to your home and watch your television for evidence of extraterrestrials.

With our spohisticated equipment, like Uncle Floyd's video cassette recorder, we will document any alien programming and subject it to our Alien Profile and Evaluation, APE for short.

First, we will determine if what you are watching is indeed alien. Hey, sometimes satellite television owners latch onto the wrong satellite and get some pretty weird stuff. I remember this Swedish X-rated movie channel once, but that's another story.

Second, we will attempt to determine if the creature you are seeing is potentially harmful. Does it have teeth? Does it have legs? Hey, if it has teeth but no legs, no sweat, right?

Third, we will try to determine if the transmission carries a message and who might be receiving it. I mean, if this dude is talking to someone on earth we are in big trouble.

If we think the transmission is being directed toward earth, we'll check out your neighbors. Our research shows most aliens living on earth take the form of young women living alone. Therefore, any neighbor matching that description will be thoroughly examined by myself.

Finally, with our portable dish antenna we will attempt to beam a message to whatever is on your TV.

Who knows, we might be able to arrange a close encounter of the third kind right in your backyard. Why, media rights to that would net you millions.

However, the possibility also exists that the aliens might get ticked off at our eavesdropping and send a mother ship to zap your home into something resembling burned bacon.

We might also determine whether what you are witnessing is a television signal or a transporter beam. You wouldn't want a Yoda to suddenly appear on your coffee table, eat your dog and leave.

Hey, this is the real world, buddy! Not all aliens are as lovable as Steven Spielberg would lead you to believe.

* * * * *

LEARNING TO BLEND INTO THE WOODWORK

The Wildwoods Academy of Liberal Arts and Shop proudly announces a new course: Survival Skills for the Self-Conscious.

This is a nine-week course in how to be inconspicuous.

It is being offered by the social skills department of the academy. The academy, you may recall, stresses the practical aspects of living. It was founded on the premise that a degree in liberal arts isn't worth Charmin if your toilet backs up.

Often we suffer through embarrassing situations because we think they are unavoidable. We live knowing our moment of weakness is someone's gossip.

Ever get a speeding ticket?

It's embarrassing—makes you slouch down in your seat so you can't be seen by the hundreds of gawking motorists passing by. It's sort of like being a kid again and your father spanking you in front of all your friends.

And, you know your friends will be among those motorists passing by. They'll take pleasure in your indiscretion and tell everybody, happily adding all sorts of wicked embellishments.

Well, Survival Skills for the Self-Conscious will teach you techniques to avoid such embarrassment.

After taking this course, the next time you're stopped for speeding you'll get out of your car, walk to the trunk, get out the jack and pretend you are fixing a flat tire.

Some of our students prefer to raise the hood.

Either way you'll turn a potentially embarrassing situation into an inconspicuous disabled auto.

Ever go into a restaurant alone and have to wait for a table or wait for your carryout?

173

For the self-conscious, that's really uncomfortable. They get the feeling everybody is staring at them because they seem to be out of place, sort of like a flower in a bathroom.

Our experienced professors will teach you never to go into a restaurant without a magazine in your back pocket. With your face buried in a magazine, you'll never be recognized.

Or, you'll learn the bathroom retreat trick. When informed there will be a slight wait, you say to the waitress: "Could you direct me to the restroom, please. I'll just be a moment."

Stay there ten minutes and reappear just in time to be seated.

Ever go to a party, only to discover you are the only person dressed in a suit and tie or a nice evening dress?

For the self-conscious, that's a sure-fire way to kill an evening. Why, the anxiety alone will take years off their life.

Well, our course will teach you how to dress for all occasions at the same time.

For example, when our students arrive at the party in a suit instead of shorts and a T-shirt they merely tell their host:

"I'm terribly sorry. I had an important meeting and couldn't change. But, just give me a minute."

Our students have been taught to wear underneath their business suit Bermuda shorts and a T-shirt with "It's Miller Time" emblazoned across its front. Their specially designed ties become natty scarves. In 30 seconds they're real cool, casual and they fit right in.

You'll even learn how to carry tennis shoes in the inside pockets of your suit.

We'll teach you how to handle a sneeze when you don't have a handkerchief. We'll show you the Heinrich Maneuver for correcting meandering pants zippers.

You'll learn how to enter a room filled with strangers and be unnoticed.

Sign up today by mail. We know how you hate to stand in line.

* * * * *

THE MEDIA—MAYHEM AND MAALOX

The Wildwoods column which normally appears here has been pre-empted this week to bring you this transcript of an important lecture on the media.

Recently Phineas Artemus, professor emeritus at prestigious Wildwoods Academy, delivered this lecture as part of his series titled "The Media: Mayhem, Madness and Maalox."

We feel periodically the readers of the Wildwoods column should be exposed to serious academic thought on terrestrial issues.

And, now Professor Artemus...

Dan Rather has hemorrhoids!

Hemorrhoid advertisements right there with his evening news!

How can we be informed citizens of the world when we have to sit and watch some gal talking about hemorrhoid relief?

Every night Dan Rather presents us with the suffering of humanity and the chaos in our political and economic institutions, then follows it with a dose of Preparation H.

But, that's not the worst of it.

I recently completed an exhaustive, in-depth, scholarly analysis of two of these half-hour news programs and found scandalously subliminal forrays into our subconscious.

There is a subtle relationship between Rather's rather innocuous commentary and the commercials which periodically interrupt him.

They're foolin' with our psyches, boys and girls.

Case in point: A recent program began with a report on warfare in Lebanon. It dramatically, and I say deliberately, showed rising TENSION in the Middle East.

175

What was the first commercial shown after that? Sanka coffee, which has no caffeine because, here it comes, caffeine makes you TENSE. "I love coffee, but too much coffee makes me TENSE," says some burly deep sea diver.

The viewer's subconscious becomes tense.

The next commercial shows George Burns (picked to arouse age anxiety) with a bunch of beautiful women (selected to arouse a certain type of tension in men and anxiety in women who wish they could look like that) talking about a device to clean the air.

Is my air dirty? You give a nervous sniff.

Then comes a segment on the TENSE political situation in Poland, suspiciously followed by a commercial on Sominex.

Here are two people who can't sleep because, you guessed it, TENSION.

You're tense. The news is depressing. The commercials tell you that you drink the wrong coffee, you breathe smelly air, you're unattractive and have trouble going to sleep.

But, do the media masters relent? No way, Jose.

They run a segment on a tragic car accident followed by a commercial on life insurance.

Your subconscience is crying out with worry.

They've got you now and are ready to finish you off with...

A right to the chin: A commercial about denture cream. Buddy, your teeth are falling out! A left to the midsection: Arthritis pain acting up? Feel tense and aching? Take Anacin.

Between Dan Rather's rather sly commentary and Madison Avenue's guile, you walk away from that half hour show feeling lousy and worrying if your life insurance is paid up.

And, I'll wager you'll have trouble falling asleep that night and next morning will feel guilty about having that first cup of coffee.

Be warned. They are out after your mind.

Read a newspaper instead.

The preceding lecture by Phineas Artemus has been brought to you as a public service by Wildwoods Academy and this column.

* * * * *

176

THE SWEET SMELL OF TRANSGRESSION

I was at the Mead Wildlife Area the other morning when this skunk came ambling my way.

I immediately jumped into the front seat of my car, rolled up all the windows and prayed that I wouldn't be sprayed.

The skunk continued on, paying absolutely no attention to me. b

It was at that moment, cowering on the floorboards of the car, that a great thought struck. I had, just then, discovered the solution to street crime in America.

If we humans could be given the defense mechanism of a skunk, why...

Well, I jumped out of the car and took after the skunk. I thought sure he'd be more than happy to tell me what makes a skunk stink.

I imagine it was the way I posed the question that made him do what he did. But, it's a reporter's lot to suffer such indignities in search of truth, justice and the American way.

But, think of it! If we could arm everybody with a vial of skunk scent, who would be dumb enough to attack us?

Why, I remember the crazy Labrador I had as a kid. While he was helping us hunt pheasant, he suddenly came upon a skunk. Not knowing exactly what a pheasant was and possessing a lot of dumb curiosity, the dog decided to strike up an acquaintance with the black and white creature.

He soon discovered skunks have little regard for dogs and are not shy about spraying so (terrible pun intended).

You should have seen that dog run with his tail between his legs and howl as if somebody had put a hive of bees on his hindquarters.

I suspect the skunk's defense would have a similar effect on humans.

177

Imagine you're a little old lady walking down a street and this huge thug grabs you. Instead of screaming you just pull out your vial of skunk scent and crash it over his head.

"Yeeech!" the assailant cries as he stumbles away. With his clothes saturated with essence of skunk, he has no choice but to begin ripping the wet clothes from his body. While he's busy disrobing, you walk away.

A little while later, you encounter a policeman. You tell him you've been mugged and the location. The police merely go to that spot and with their noses follow the trail of the thug. In a short time, they find a naked hoodlum trying to take a bath in vinegar and tomato juice.

Imagine you're a teenage girl with a guy who's coming on a bit strong. As he gets fresh, you merely reach into your purse and say:

"How about a little aftershave, chump?" Then just smear essence of skunk on his cheeks as you give him a couple of hefty slaps.

I guarantee that boy will not get another date from you or any other girl for a long, long time.

And, when that guy gets home, his parents are bound to smell the essence of skunk. They will immediately know their son is either a street thief or a Lothario.

As soon as I get some time, I'm going to the Marathon County Library and find every book I can on skunks. I suspect there aren't that many, considering the foul disposition of the skunk toward inquiries about its private life.

However, somebody somewhere, perhaps a scientist with sinus troubles, must have come upon the chemistry of the skunk's potent present to the curious.

If I can find the right ingredients, I can make a million. Why, I'll put "Mace" right out of business.

* * * * *

178

GETTING UP WON'T GET YOU DOWN

Do you have trouble waking up in the morning?

Do you feel harrassed and intimidated by alarm clocks?

Sure you do. Face it, mornings are real downers.

Well, folks, waking up can be an extraordinary experience with the Wildwoods Wake Up Wonder.

Yes sir, this sophisticated product of modern technology guarantees to get you hopping on the right track morning in, morning out.

It will add years to your life, make you a more pleasant person and improve your work efficiency.

More importantly, it will eliminate all those negative aspects of getting up: No more alarms or forced marches to the bathroom.

The Wildwoods Wake Up Wonder is a multi-faceted, completely automated arousal system. It's as reliable as a Big Ben, but as gentle as a mother.

Here's how it works.

The night before, you set a clock to the time you want to get up. An optional feature allows you to set the time you'd like to have breakfast, something no alarm clock can offer.

At that time, the Wildwoods Wake Up Wonder activates a hydraulic lift underneath the mattress. This lifts you off the bed onto a padded board sitting on a conveyor belt.

You're not awakened.

The conveyor silently guides you into a chamber heated to precisely the temperature of a womb.

The moment you enter the chamber, a switch is automatically thrown which triggers a stereo tape player. Suddenly the chamber is filled with the sound of your heart beat.

Then comes the sound of a baby crying and next the patient voice of a young mother saying, "Time to get up, you've got to get to school..."

As the tape brings you up to adulthood, you reach the point of consciousness. The chamber is filled with relaxing music. Meanwhile, another set of timers have just activated the coffee maker and any other appliance needed in the preparation of your breakfast.

You and the chamber begin moving toward the bathroom. As you move, rollers underneath the platform begin massaging your back. Mechanical fingers remove your bedclothes. A gentle mist of water falls over your body. Jets shoot fragrances of roses and daffodils

The light in the chamber increases as gently as a summer's sunrise.

The soft music fades. Beginning very quietly and gradually increasing in intensity comes invigorating music like the "Theme from Rocky."

Dubbed over the music is a confident voice:

"Good morning, today is Monday, June 21. It's a great day! You're great! You feel fine! You look fine! Really impressive! You're loved and respected."

Suddenly the chamber begins to get cold as the temperature of the mist drops. It reaches a point you almost get chilled.

Splash! The conveyor drops you into a hot tub or shower (your choice).

All you have to do is wash, get dressed and walk to the kitchen.

The Wildwoods Wake Up Wonder will be available as soon as some of the bugs are worked out.

The other day the tape got stuck on the infant mode and our test sleeper went to work wearing only a diaper. However, none of his coworkers noticed a drop in his work efficiency.

During another test, our man ended up face down on the platform. He awakened rather abruptly when he found his nose being massaged at right angles to his face.

I tell you this will be the product of the 80's. We've tolerated morning too long. It's time morning becomes an experience not a drudgery.

* * * * *

CHAPTER NINE

FOOD MAY BE HAZARDOUS TO YOUR HEALTH.

When it comes time to clean out the ol' refrigerator, I invite friends over for Oakland's famous omelet.

I know of no better way to get rid of old and forgotten food than by putting it inside a big juicy omelet.

Hey, my omelets are renowned for their distinctive flavor.

Making an Oakland omelet goes something like this...

Friends arrive and are escorted to the living room where they are served the best $4.95 a gallon wine available. When half the bottle of wine is gone, I announce it is time for me to disappear into the kitchen to prepare the omelet de extraordinaire.

As my wife keeps the conversation and wine flowing, I enter the kitchen and bolt the door behind me. Can't have the squeamish wandering about the kitchen when such a delicate dish is being masterfully prepared.

I begin with a dozen eggs, smashed and beaten into submission. Then I place the Cuisinart next to the refrigerator and turn on the oven to 500 degrees.

The hot oven is critical to the success of the omelet and the health of those eating it. Ten minutes in that oven and anything is edible!

My philosophy of cooking is kill it before it kills you.

I don my rubber gloves and venture into the refrigerator on a search and destroy mission.

A block of moldy cheese hidden behind a half-dozen beer bottles; some very flat 7-UP and year-old pickle relish all find their way into the Cuisinart.

Some cottage cheese about to walk out of its container and an apple that looks like a prune are given a five-minute spin in the chopping machine.

Sour cream that has an extraterrestrial appearance; ketchup so hard you could pave a road with it; spaghetti looking like something out of the Exorcist—all are fodder for my hard working food processor.

When the mixture reaches a brown-gray color, I add something that had been living in a plastic container at the bottom of the refrigerator. I tentatively identify the stringy mass as long-forgotten French style beans. Being French, they add an international character to the omelet.

Brown lettuce and a scoop of mayonnaise top off the filling.

I do not use any of the green vine-like stuff growing on the refrigerator shelves. You have to draw the line somewhere.

I pour or scrape the contents onto a cutting board and whack it with a butcher knife just to intimidate anything living within. Then this omelet filling goes into a hot oven.

While it dies—uh, cooks, I make the massive omelet. It's got to be thick, else the filling will eat through it.

Just before filling goes into omelet, I utter a loud war hoot signaling to my wife that it is time to seat the guests. It also signals her to begin her spiel about this recipe being handed down for generations of the Oakland family.

When everybody is seated at the table, my wife dims the lights and lights candles. It gives such a romantic atmosphere and prevents close scrutiny of the meal.

I bring the omelet out on a silver platter, place it in the center of the table, pour 151 proof rum over it and touch a match to it. Such a dramatic presentation also burns off any errant omelet gases.

"What is that unusual—tangy—uh, fruity taste?" a friend exclaims. "I have never tasted anything like it. I must have your recipe!"

"Oh, I can't reveal my secrets," I smile as I offer a second helping.

* * * * *

184

YOGURT-MAKING PUTS REFRIGERATOR IN DEEP FREEZE

It's a quiet Saturday morning. I step outside the front door to fetch the morning paper.

Suddenly the sound of sirens fills the air. Army-green cars squeal around the corners on both ends of the block. Men pour out of utility trucks and set up barricades at the intersections.

The cars pull up in front of my house and men with automatic rifles pile out. They stand on the sidewalk staring at me through aviator glasses. I check to see if my bathrobe is open.

"I give!" I scream.

A limo rounds the corner and skids to a halt in front of me. Several three-piece-suit types wearing earphones roll out.

A gray-haired, distinguished looking man gets out and walks up to me. "Mr. Oakland," he says solemnly.

"Yeah."

"Do you recognize this?" he asks, pulling a small jar from his pocket. Inside is a puddle of white something. I give it a close look.

"Doesn't look like much to me, mister."

His stern expression doesn't change. He removes the lid. "Smell it."

I take a whiff.

"Smells like yogurt. Hey, that isn't some of my homemade yogurt is it?"

"Seize him!"

Two of the gunmen rush up and handcuff me. "Bring him inside," the man in white says.

"Mr. Oakland, are you aware genetic engineering is illegal in the United States?"

"Genetic engineering!"

"Don't play stupid with us. We have evidence you have been creating life here."

"I have not. Ask my wife. All I ever create is a mess."

The man in white holds the jar up to the sunlight coming in the window. He carefully studies the white glob inside.

"You might think this is ordinary yogurt with bacteria feeding on the milk sugars and replicating like crazy."

"Yeah, that's what yogurt does," I interrupt.

The man gives me a nasty look.

"Yes, but inside this jar are bacteria the likes of which man has never seen. You have created new life, sir."

"Oh, wow! Hey, what should we name it? What's Latin for Oakland?"

The man in white rolls his eyes upward. "Mr. Oakland, I don't think you realize the significance of what you have done."

"Hey, how'd you get my yogurt, anyway?"

"Two weeks ago Friday, you forgot to eat the yogurt you had taken to work. On Saturday, the security guard called police to report something was consuming the insides of the employee refrigerator.

"The police managed to kill it with a fire extinguisher. However, they were able to put a sample of the stuff in an empty beer bottle.

"Eventually, the stuff came our way because nobody could identify it. Heck, the state Department of Natural Resource boys were actually afraid of it."

"Gee, vicious stuff."

The white-suited man shakes his head. "We don't know what it is. For all we know, it might be intelligent."

"Chip off the ol' block," I say. "This stuff ought to make me millions!"

"I doubt it, Mr. Oakland. We destroyed all of it except that which remains in this baby jar as classified material."

"Hey, give me back my yogurt. You have no right!" The man in white smiles as other men carry off my refrigerator and all my yogurt-making equipment. "The government will replace your refrigerator, but I'm afraid your yogurt-making days are through, Mr. Oakland."

"How come?" I cry.

"Your government doesn't want anybody playing God, Mr. Oakland. Not anybody but the government."

186

*****

WHEN THE WIFE'S AWAY, THE WOLF WILL BAY

Whenever my wife leaves me alone in the house, it's like a full moon rising over a werewolf's head.

I begin to change.

The minute she hits the city limits, an evil metamorphosis begins within me and I become—a bachelor again.

It's not a pretty sight.

I begin thinking and acting as I did in prehistoric times when I was young and living alone.

Just recently my wife left me for a couple of days to visit her parents. Suddenly I found myself reliving old habits.

Take for instance the ten-minute supper.

When my wife is around, preparing supper takes 30 minutes on up. But, when I'm alone, I fix and feast in 15 minutes.

Don't believe me? Here's how you do it.

First you make sure that before the wife leaves she cooks enough chicken to provide leftovers for several days.

You begin by grabbing a can of veggies and dumping them in a saucepan. I prefer canned veggies because they'll take a lot of abuse while cooking and still taste the same.

Next hit the refrigerator for a couple of carrots and the chicken.

Time elapsed: Two minutes max.

Throw chicken in microwave, set on reheat for three minutes.

You know, the microwave oven must have been developed by a bachelor. I mean, only a bachelor would have seen the worth of an oven that allows you to heat food in its wrapping.

See, you want to leave the Saran Wrap on because when the chicken is done, you can eat it off the wrapping instead of dirtying a plate. When I'm batching it, I'd rather die than do dishes.

187

Anyway, back to the dinner.

Peel the carrots and begin eating them. That's your salad.

Here's a helpful hint. Stir the canned veggies with one of your carrots. It works as well as a spoon and when you're done you eat it rather than wash it.

By the time you finish with the carrots, your chicken is done. It takes about three minutes to consume two pieces of chicken using a fork.

Thus far, ten minutes has elapsed.

When you finish with the chicken, the veggies are done. Eating them right out of the pan not only saves time, but reduces dishwashing chores considerably.

Two minutes to eat the veggies, three minutes for dessert and—boom—you're out of the kitchen and relaxing in front of the television with a cold beer.

Take note, the above supper dirtied only one pan and a fork. Once you learn to drink milk out of the jug, you'll never need to worry about glasses.

Despite these efficiencies, dirty dishes do accumulate over a period of time. However, if you confine them to the sink, all is manageable.

You know, it is amazing what beautiful things you can grow on dirty dishes. At times my sink rivals a professionally managed floral rock garden.

What about bugs, you ask?

Heck, any bugs appear, I just sic the cat on them. The cat finds great sport in tracking them down.

With the wife gone, clothes become troublesome because eventually you have to wash them.

However, that can be avoided by careful dressing.

Instead of wearing a clean shirt every day, I wear one every other day. I mean, what's the big deal about wearing the same shirt twice. Heck, you wear a different tie with it, nobody will know the difference.

But, it's dirty, you say. Come on, I'm a reporter, not an auto mechanic. How dirty can you get sitting in front of a typewriter all day!

Any odor problems are easily solved by shooting a bit of anti-perspirant under the shoulders of the shirt. Hey, you wear a little extra cologne, nobody is going to smell anything disagleeable.

By taking these steps, a husband turned bachelor can survive and leave most of the household chores for the little woman when she returns.

* * * * *

HAPPINESS IS BOWL OF NON-AGGRESSIVE JELL-O

You know you're in trouble when you find bliss in a bowl of Jell-O.

I hadn't eaten Jell-O in years. Oh, I've had Jell-O salads, but that isn't the same as pure, virgin Jell-O.

Recently my wife made a batch of orange Jell-O for our kid, who at the time was experiencing intestinal distress. Jell-O, we were told, would soothe the troubled tummy.

Unfortunately, the kid would have nothing to do with it.

I have no idea what brought about her intense dislike for this gelatin dessert. I mean, the kid isn't old enough to make judgments about food based on personal experience.

I concluded her aversion must be genetic in nature. I'm also convinced whatever she inherited didn't come from my side of the family.

Anyway, her refusal to eat left us with an entire bowl of Jell-O. Since everyone in the household, including my wife's stupid cat, was ignoring the stuff, I was elected, by default, to eat it.

There I sat, spoon in hand, contemplating the first taste. I cut through the gelatinous mass and with a slight twist of the wrist lifted up a sliver of Jell-O.

For a moment I stared down into the bowl. Gosh it was neat how the spoon cut through and left a mark resembling chipped glass.

I made a couple more slices with the spoon, each time cutting away little canyons and cliffs from the otherwise smooth and unblemished Jell-O.

My motions became more deliberate as I carved out fancy French curves.

My wife walked in with kid in tow. She gave me a funny look, then swept the kid into her arms and carried her off into another room. I could hear her talking to the little one: "Mommy doesn't want you to go into the kitchen right now. Daddy is being weird again."

Have you ever noticed that when you cut through virgin Jell-O the edges of the cut come together so perfectly that you cannot see the cut except for a hairline mark on the surface.

I found that fascinating.

Jell-O is such a nice food. It makes no demands on you. You don't have to chew it. All you have to do is put it in your mouth and let it slide down.

Jell-O is so nonaggressive.

And, it wiggles. What other food looks like it is having so much fun being what it is?

I began carving out something resembling the coast of California in the orange gel. I suddenly realized how peaceful things had become. All was quiet. Jell-O makes no noise. I like that in a food.

I felt so content interacting with my Jell-O that I set my mind free.

I shouldn't be a writer in Wausau, but a sculptor in Venice, California.

I should be sitting on a condo balcony overlooking the Pacific beach, carefully sculpting a four-foot mound of Jell-O and Epoxy into statues of the gods who pump iron on the beach and the goddesses listening to mellow rock in their stereo headphones as they float by on roller skates.

Dressed in a white-striped tank top and faded blue jeans, I sit pondering my work as I toy with a long silk scarf wrapped around my well-tanned neck. With a glass of fine Chablis at my side, I listen to my wind chime choir and watch the sunshine filter through dozens of window crystals. Seagulls fall from the sky and alight on the balcony railing. They sit begging for a few morsels from the bowl of pickled herring, caviar and Saltines on the plexiglass table by my suede leather director's chair.

At the door a young woman appears. She has the face of Christie Brinkley, the body of Jacqueline Bisset and the toes of Brooke

Shields. Instead of giving me the kiss I expect, she starts squeezing my right shoulder.

"Donald, will you please stop playing with your food and take out the garbage!" my wife yells.

'Tis a pity, dreams and Jell-O are so easily consumed.

* * * * *

THE GALUMPHING GOURMET STRIKES AGAIN

A while back, the Herald sponsored a cooking contest and I was really hurt. They didn't ask me to submit a recipe.

I mean, my Wildwoods Whole Wheat Stress Bread surely would have taken a prize.

Well, I thought rather than wait for another cooking contest, I'd share the recipe with readers of this column.

It's an old family recipe that I made up about eight years ago when I was a bachelor in Clintonville.

It was during that period of my life that I concluded either I had to learn to cook or face starvation.

I had it in my head that in these liberated times finding a woman who was a good cook was about as likely as Christie Brinkley asking me for a date.

I was also into health foods and beer drinking.

All this led one day to an overwhelming desire to make whole wheat bread—nothing fancy, just your b asic wheat, water, yeast mix.

But in making it I discovered it's not what you put into bread that makes it special, it's how you make it. And, that's how Stress Bread was born.

Here's how it goes.

Dump a package of yeast into a bowl of tepid water. Throw in some sugar and white flour and let the yeast do its thing for about 10 minutes. Dump in several cups of whole wheat flour and mix thoroughly.

Normally the next step would be kneading the dough, but with Stress Bread you strangle it.

Pretend the dough is your worst enemy and gouge, squeeze, rip, poke, choke, turn, twist and trounce it. Squash it into submission.

Do this for about 12 minutes. I guarantee it will give you that great feeling of vengence. Let the animal within you spring from your gripping hands dripping dough.

Throw the glob of dough into a bowl, set in a warm place and take a breather. Have a can of beer. Take a walk around the block. Have a Popsicle. Do anything to relax the rage within you.

About an hour later, take the puffed-up heap of dough and throw it on a wooden cutting board. And I mean, throw it! Show that bread who's boss.

Once again pretend that dough is somebody you dislike intensely. Maybe it's your boss. Maybe it's the governor or Howard Cosell. Visualize him in the dough.

Now make a fist and fire it right in to the middle of that mass. Make a fist with your other hand and do likewise.

Lately I've been perfecting an Oriental approach. I take my shoes off and flour my feet. Then I roll the dough into a ball and toss it straight up. As it falls I give a yell and whack the wheat out of it with a karate kick.

Hammering the dough really works the tension from your body. It beats aerobic exercise hands down.

Finally, pick up that dough in both hands, raise it above your head and—with a defiant yell—slam it down on the board.

Scrape the dough into a bowl and put it in a warm place.

Now take a rest, you've earned it. Take a hot bath. You have released all the tensions of the day or week into that wheat. Savor the moment.

About an hour later, take a knife and butcher the dough into two loaves. Then follow the standard baking procedure.

The bread will taste great. You'll feel relaxed and fit.

It's a nutritious feast for both mind and body.

One warning: Bread abuse is illegal in some areas. Don't make Stress Bread in the presence of others.

* * * * *

AN APPLE JUICE A DAY...

What I'm about to write, I do so at great risk. Once people read this, they'll be laying for me.

So far this season I have yet to catch a cold. I'm going to tell you why. After doing this, I'll probably catch a cold and everyone will pounce on me: "And you think you're so smart..."

With complete disregard for the abuse this may bring, I offer to you my answer to the common cold.

Apple juice.

I drink apple juice every day. Not apple cider or apple jack. Apple juice.

In deference to personal privacy I will not reveal to what degree I spike the juice.

On those days that I partake of the red orb's juice, I suffer not.

Why? (When I have to wrestle with a "why" question I retreat to the woods, there to contemplate the possibilities under some aging oak. It usually takes an afternoon and a nap before things are resolved.)

Apple juice works because it's got discreet cells.

There are two ways to get rid of cold viruses.

One way is to eliminate carriers of the virus. This could be easily facilitated by shooting dead the first person suffering from a cold you come upon.

The second way, which I assume a majority of you would agree it s bit more palatable, is to usher into one's body some element that will usher out invading cold germs.

When a cold germ enters the body, all hell breaks loose. The body's defense cells arise.

"Hey, man, there's a lousy cold cell. Let's get him, boys."

And, there ensues a rumble that results in numerous injured to be carried off the field. Man conveniently accomplishes this task by sneezing and hacking.

Apple juice cells don't work that way.

After you drink a glass of apple juice, billions of apple juice cells enter your bloodstream. There they float about until your body assigns them a task—like becoming caloric energy or fat.

Being natural, apple juice cells are mellow sorts. They have no biases. They are satisfied to do their thing and help out when needed.

Up the old schnozzola comes this cold cell. Now, the cold has no ax to grind with human cells. He was sort of blown into the situation when some jerk sneezed.

So, the cold cell is wandering about your bloodstream trying to find a way out. All these other cells are giving him the evil eye (No, I don't know if cells have eyes...ask Carl Sagan, not me).

Along comes this apple juice cell. He notices the cold cell because it seems out of place.

"You lost, man?" the apple juice cell says.

"Yeah," replies a very nervous cold cell.

"Well, you better get your nucleus outta here because there are some bad dudes about that would like nothing better than to pound the protein outta you," the apple juice cell says.

"Yeah??"

The apple juice cell smiles and says, "Here, let me show you the way out."

The apple juice cell then guides the cold cell through the bloodstream, past the nasty defense cells man cherishes so, and out the ol' bladder.

No rumble, no cold.

Because an apple juice cell begrudges no other cell, and I assume though I have yet to prove, that it would treat a flu cell no differently.

194

Would eating apples have the same effect? I don't' know. Eating apples gives me rumbles in the stomach.

* * * * *

SNOW TIME FOR ICE CREAM

I think it's ridiculous that we limit ice cream cone consumption to summer.

Seems to be the best time to have a cone is when it's 20 below outside.

Look, one thing an ice cream come won't do in winter is melt. And, if there is anything a man with a beard loathes, it's eating a quickly melting ice cream cone.

I mean, your beard turns into a gooey ball in two seconds flat. When you try to wipe it off with a napkin, the paper sticks to your whiskers.

Summer's heat forces you to gobble down your cone before it flows over your hands, down your sleeves, across your shirt and down your pants.

Ever try to eat ice cream fast?

It isn't pleasant. Take a couple of quick big bites and it feels like you have a hornet's nest in your sinuses.

And, it seems patently ridiculous to suffer frostbite on the tongue in the middle of July.

But, ice cream is something you can savor in subzero weather. You can spend all day at nibbling away at it.

Heck, if you tried that with a six-pack of beer, you'd end up with beer-cicles in nothing flat. And, sandwiches turn to leather in seconds in January.

As you regular readers know, I always stand ready to back up my words. So awhile back I went to the ice cream shop downtown and ordered a double-dip,. chocolate mint cone.

Had I don't that in summer, I would have taken a bath in a cone like that.

But, not in winter.

That double decker hunk of ice cream held firm, didn't drip once on my hand or in my beard. For once I didn't feel compelled to chomp into the cone like some hunger-crazed animal.

So what if it was minus 10 outside. I was relaxed and content with my cone.

Anyway, the colder it is outside the better.

Look, ice cream is frozen at something less than 32 degrees. I suspect it's around zero.

Say it's 20 below outside. That ice cream at zero will actually be 20 degrees warmer than the air. I admit it isn't hot chocolate, but it shouldn't make you any colder.

Now, I realize some of you have psychological aversions to winter. For you people I recommend Arizona or Fort Lauderdale. I mean either you can handle winter or you can't.

Eating an ice cream cone in January is to laugh at winter! Never let winter intimidate you!

I would also like to point out that ice cream is loaded with calories, the fuel for the human body. In winter your body needs those calories to stay warm, so what could be better than a double-dip vanilla fudge.

Anyway, ice cream is out of character in summer.

How much ice do you find in August in Wisconsin. Except the cubes floating in your cocktail, very little.

Well, in February ice is everywhere. Winter is a natural for ice cream. Fits right in. Walking down the street in subzero weather with a strawberry ripple cone in your hand is being one with nature.

I think it's time to have ice cream/ice skating socials.

"Mommy, Mommy, here comes the Good Humor Man," the little girl yells as she points to the man in white riding across the lawn on his snowmobile.

Now, I'm not recommending milk shakes and malts in mid-winter.

I mean, you'd never get the ice cream up the straw without adding some sort of antifreeze like 151 proof rum or Southern Comfort.

On the other hand, such a combination has possibilities.

* * * * *

THE GRAPES OF GAFFE

How can one politely eat grapes that aren't seedless?

I mean, you can't just go "ppphtt" and spit the little devils across the table.

Cover your mouth, spit the three or four seeds into your palm and then dispose of them in an inconspicuous manner, you say.

Ha! How, may I ask, do you inconspicuously cover your moth, spit and lower your hand containing some rather slimy seeds. And what, pray tell, do you do with the seeds once in hand?

Drop them on your plate?

Then you end up with a plate full of seeds, not a very appetizing sight for others seated at your table. And, what if they stick to your hand as you try to drop them?

Use the tablecloth to scrape them off? A knife perhaps?

Sure, slash the palm of your hand attempting to extricate the little gems from your sweaty grasp.

Of course, there is the every popular put-it-under-the-table strategy. Those who implement this approach generally hold the philosophy: out of sight, out of mind.

But, this approach seems ignorant of the fact the seeds might be discovered prior to your leaving the table.

I can see someone bending down to pick up an errant fork and declaring: "Uh, Mr. Oakland, there seems to be a pile of seeds covering your shoes."

I suppose fair play would require that you pick up the seeds at you feet, an exercise that would certainly ruin the evening.

If you're a macho type, you could swallow the seeds. I suspect this ploy, while convenient initially, would in time cause other inconveniences.

I suppose that ingestion of seeds would not contribute to one's caloric intake. Dieters would find that encouraging.

Anyway, another seed disposal strategy is to gently push the seeds between your upper gum and lip, using your tongue. This requires a degree of dexterity beyond some of us.

Once you get a dozen or so seeds lodged up there, you excuse yourself from the table, walk to the front door, open it, stick your head out and, in machine gun fashion, expel the nuisances.

There are several disadvantages to this approach.

Your frequent trips from the table may cause concern on the part of the host, especially if he or she prepared the meal.

Also, if one is required to speak while engaging in this seed storage, the result may prove unpleasant to yourself and to those who must watch.

Also, should anyone witness you dislodging the seeds from your mouth, it would create a lot of idle talk about your grip on life.

Also, if one indulges in this activity with any regularity, one might find one's facial appearance resembling that of a chipmunk.

I suspect a solution to this seedy situation is beyond my reach. More innovative thinking is required, I fear.

For example, smokers have a unique means to deal with this problem.

All a smoker has to do is after every grape is take a puff on his cigarette. As he puffs, he pushes the seeds into the back of the cigarette—hollow filters work best.

When he puts the cigarette back on the ashtray, he inconspicuously picks the seeds from the filter.

Aside from filling the room with smoke and possibly harming one's health, this exercise has some potential.

198

It is my humble opinion that social norms should be amended to include a provision for the grape eater.

I think polite society should adopt an etiquette in which each person at a table eating seed-filled grapes be provided with a small spittoon. During that portion of the meal when grapes are normally served, rules against spitting are temporarily suspended.

If one is to have a pleasurable dining experience, one mustn't be inconvenienced.

Now that I've got that settled, how does one type a column while eating seedy grapes?

* * * * *

IF LIFE HANDS YOU A GRAPEFRUIT, DUCK!

We ought to outlaw oranges.

Oranges exhibit definite anti-social behavior while being eaten.

Grapefruit should also be banned.

I always thought little kids with squirt guns should be shackled and tossed into bedroom closets. Put them in solitary for a couple of hours—then see if they want to play Public Enemy Number One.

But kids have nothing on grapefruit.

A grapefruit can hit an eye at 25 paces.

Every morning I endure this mischievous fruit. I innocently plunge my spoon into a grapefruit half and am duly annointed. What a way to start a day, humiliated by a fruit!

Did you ever notice that the more grapefruit you eat, the more juice is produced?

By the end of the meal you're staring at an ocean of grapefruit juice with these funny looking seeds floating around.

Now the grapefruit presents you with a challenge: Getting that juice out of the rind.

If you are of a certain economic class, say you earn more than $40,000 a year, you'll probably take a spoon and sort of squeeze and ladle the liquid.

But, if you're like me, 20 minutes behind schedule in the morning, there just isn't time for such indulgence.

For people like me there is only one approach. Pick the thing up, tip it over a gaping mouth and pour.

Invariably, a certain portion of the contents miss the mouth and end up on : A) my tie; B) my shirt; C) my lap. In all cases, a complete change of clothing is required or else one could be accused of sloppiness or worse.

Like a pastor's friend, grapefruit always leaves something on the plate.

I'm of the tip-and-sip school. I love challenges of this sort. Real high stakes stuff. One slip of the sip, one too-loose lip and the whole thing goes cascading down the front of your shirt and right into your lap.

Besides being a really delightful sensation, cold grapefruit juice in the lap really enlivens table talk when you get up. I mean, there is absolutely no way to hide your accident short of crawling under the table, which would, I suspect, create a new set of problems.

Whereas grapefruit mainly perpetrates crimes upon the eater, oranges malevolently lash out at those seated with the eater.

You're seated at the lunchroom table. A half dozen of your co-workers are with you. You're engaged in small talk as you deftly peel your orange.

Without a care, you take the peeled orange in both hands and attempt to divide it in half. The orange divides easily.

Then you watch in horror as a stream of orange juice shoots from the center core, flies over the table and lands on the blouse of the gal across from you. The blouse she just blew her paycheck buying. The designer blouse that can only be dry cleaned.

There's a moment of silence.

Did she notice? She did. Will she ignore it? She won't. What can I say so she won't stick me with the dry cleaning bill?

If you can solve that delicate social problem, the orange immediately presents you with another. The second you bite into an orange slice, juice spews out with the force of water from a firefighter's hose.

Where does it go? Well, I can tell you with assurance it never hits the floor. It hits eyes, clothes, the food of others, windows, tablecloths.

With all the passion I can muster, I recommend oranges not be sold without a warning label and an accompanying splash screen.

* * * * *

THE GREAT GRINDING REVIVAL

Hey, can you freeze chicken salad?

The reason I ask is that I've got several pounds of the stuff and I'm not too keen on eating it every day for the next three weeks.

You see, ever since I bought this meat grinder, I'm really into making chicken salad. Actually, I'm into grinding.

I love to take something, push it into the grinder and turn the handle. It gives me a sense of power to see things become pulp by my own hand.

You might ask what recipe I follow.

Well, I start with cooked chicken. Then I take the meat off the bone. I have been thinking about grinding the meat and bone, but ground bone might be too chewy, me thinks.

Anyway, after I grind the meat, I add to it anything to make it palatable.

First time I made chicken salad I ground up a whole chicken. You know how much chopped chicken that makes? It's mind-boggling.

I added to this mountain of chicken some mayo. Then I dumped in some pickle relish, chewed-up celery and carrots and mixed the whole works into a delectable mass.

I kept adding mayonnaise until the mixture took on the appearance of a slimy paste.

201

My wife tasted the batch and, while picking the celery strings from her teeth, informed me rather sternly that I must scrape the celery prior to grinding it.

This meat grinder is the best kitchen appliance I've purchased in a long time.

It's going to save me loads of money—money better spent on more important things such as beer.

There are other benefits.

Ever since I've had this grinder, my wife's cat has treated me with more respect. Perhaps it's the way I smile at her when I'm grinding.

Man, just think of all the leftovers I'll be able to recycle with my grinder.

I'll just take whatever is hanging around the fridge, throw it into the grinder, add a little mayo, lots of pickle relish, a bit of chicken stock and voila!—chicken salad.

Liver, beef, pizza, potatoes, meatloaf—whatever, just grind it up and call it chicken salad.

If the color's wrong, I'll call it ham salad.

Heck, if it looks like chicken salad and you say it's chicken salad, it'll be chicken salad to anyone eating it.

Then there's all the exercise I get cranking.

The possibilities for aerobic exercise while grinding are exciting.

I could put on a sweatsuit and tennies and jog in place as I grind.

Or, I could just grind. I'd begin slowly and then progress to faster and faster cranking speeds. Then I'd throw into the grinder stuff like bones, rocks or lumber to add more resistance.

I bet after daily doses of grinding I'd develop strong arms and massive shoulders. I'd have the looks of a weightlifter and something for tomorrow's sandwich, too.

You know, I can envision the day where I don't have to throw anything away. Just grind it up and call it sausage.

I could eventually write a cookbook.

"Oakland's Orgy of Great Grinding."

I see a great and glorious revival of grinding. I see those snobs with their Cuisinarts and other electric food mashers banished from the kitchens of America.

America was built on the blood and sweat of pioneer labor. I think that tradition should not be lost in the kitchen. A little blood, a little sweat and a lot of grinding will return to our daily lives meals that made America famous.

Postscript: I have it on good authority that you can't freeze chicken salad. Nuts!

* * * * *

LONELY LITTLE LEFTOVER MAKES ITS OWN FUN

I have this penchant for turning food into fungi.

Hey, some of my leftovers are lethal.

I swear I've got Amanitas growing on the carrots in the veggie hamper of the refrigerator.

You see, I hate throwing out food. But, I'm also terribly absent minded.

When I make too much for supper, I just wrap the excess in a a little Glad Wrap and figure I'll have it for the next day's supper.

The trouble is, when the next day's supper comes, I have completely forgotten about what I had saved.

The result is a lonely leftover relegated to the back of the refrigerator to succumb to slow decay.

Eventually I'll discover the neglected leftover, usually when looking for something else.

"Dear, do you know what's in this Tupperware?"

"What Tupperware?"

"This red-topped jobber sitting next to the green mayonnaise."

"I have no idea. You'll just have to open it," she says.

I gasp and hold the container up to the light, hoping for some hint as to the identity of that within.

"Look, if it's spoiled we'll just throw it out. It's no big deal."

"That's easy for you to say, you're not holding death in your hands," I reply in a quavering voice. Against my better judgment I pop the lid.

A footlong toadstool pops up like a jack-in-the-box. It uncurls like a party favor to a length of nearly a foot.

"AAAAAAARRRRGH!"

I throw the container skyward and run out of the room. My wife shrieks and dives out the back door.

The container spills vile black mold all over the floor. Spores fly out from the toadstool's umbrella top, filling the house with a putrid green cloud.

The cat and I escape out a bedroom window.

An acrid stench pours from the house like smoke.

"Good lord, what's the awful smell," a neighbor yells as he runs out his front door.

"Leftover macaroni salad, I think," I reply.

Soon all the neighbors have left their homes and are wandering about their yards sniffing the air.

"What died?" one lady says disgustedly.

"Maybe a septic tank truck rolled over," her neighbor replies.

A white stepvan squeals around the corner and stops in front of my house. It's followed by two fire trucks, three squad cars and two Department of Natural Resources pickups.

Out from the van jump a half dozen men wearing what appear to be spacesuits.

"Hazardous waste detail! Your house?" one of them barks at me through the glass portal of his helmet.

I nod meekly.

"You're under arrest," he says as two of his cohorts pull me into the van.

One of the neighbors suddenly breaks into a run. "Love Canal! Love Canal!" he screams to the shocked homeowners he passes.

Soon the quiet street is plugged with cars and people trying to get out. The entire neighborhood becomes gridlocked.

The men in the spacesuits surround the house with machines with strange whirling heads, dials and digital readouts.

A team of men enter the house and minutes later carry out the refrigerator like pallbearers carrying a casket. They disappear into the van, which drives off across front lawns, screaming police cars in full escort.

Days later, Environment Protection Agency officials from Washington still can't persuade the neighbors to return home. "It's all right," they say reassuringly. "The blue grass is only temporary and the leaves will return to the trees next year!"

204

THE JAPANESE DO IT BETTER

I'm afraid to say it, but I think the Japanese have another better idea.

Awhile back, my wife and I found ourselves in a Japanese steakhouse where they prepare your food at the table.

Aside from the trauma of using toothpicks—uh, chopsticks—everything was really impressive.

I don't have the digital dexterity for chopsticks, evidenced by the wads of rice I dropped into my lap or sent flying into my neighbor's eye.

Anyway, we're sitting there when this Japanese cook walks into the center of our horseshoe-shaped table. He flicks on a grill that is a part of the table, waits a few minutes and then starts throwing things on it.

Soon he's got bean sprouts, shrimp, steak, zucchini, lobster and lord-knows-what sizzling.

From a sheath on his belt he pulls out a huge butcher knife and begins deftly chopping everything in sight. Then he grabs two dumbbell-shaped salt and pepper shakers and juggles them as he seasons the food.

Everything tasted super.

But, at this restaurant you wouldn't see me complain about the food. No way. I mean, here's this dude a foot from me wielding a butcher knife like a Zen warrior.

Hey, I was ready to double the tip if he'd put his knife away.

I began to envy this multi-talented cook and started thinking about what it would be like to cook like that in my home.

"Welcome to my humble home," I say in my best Charlie Chan accent.

My wife seats the guests around the table.

"AAAAAAARGH!"

"Not wise to touch middle of table," I admonish a guest with fingers in his mouth.

I throw a steak on the grill and it begins sizzling and spitting grease. Suddenly my guests begin waving their arms as if batting flies.

"Don't worry, the grease stains will come out with a little soap and water."

I grab the handle of a large knife in a scabbard on my belt. "AAAAAAyyee!" I yell as the knife leaves the sheath, leaves my greasy fingers and flies upward, knocking out the light and embedding itself in the ceiling.

"Uh, this part is better in the dark anyway," I say dramatically. I grab a bottle of saki, take a swig and pour the rest over the steak.

WHAAAABOOOOM!

"Honey, where's the first aid kit?"

My wife and guests reappear from underneath the table. She grabs a flashlight and shines it on my once-bearded face.

I take a few more swigs from the charred bottle to settle my coughing. My wife brings in a couple of floor lamps from the living room.

"We'll just get rid of this piece of charcoal and..."

"That's our steak, dear," my wife says sympathetically.

I grab a spatula and give the shrunken steak a shove.

"AAAAAAAAIIIIEEEE!"

"Omigosh! I didn't mean to put it in her lap. Honey, go catch Miss Jones before she upsets the neighbors." My wife takes off after the woman last seen running full tilt out the front door.

"Anybody for bean sprouts?"

"You mean those things that look like dead worms," my remaining guest says of the stringy brown-black mass.

"Little well done, I'd say." I take another swig of saki. "Hey, give me a minute and I'll make sukiyaki..."

I look up and he is gone.

"Guess he couldn't take the excitement of Oriental cuisine."

I grab what I think is the saki bottle. A low groan from under the table is heard as the cook realizes he's just downed half a bottle of soy sauce.

* * * * *

A BURGER AND FRIES, S'IL VOUS PLAIT

Thank goodness there are no French restaurants in the Wildwoods.

For some of us raised on the haute cuisine of McDonald's, a French restaurant can be intimidating.

First off, the menu is incomprehensible. Heck, even if there are English subtitles, you still don't know what you're ordering.

If you don't believe me, try to find a plain steak on a French menu.

When given a French menu, I first try to determine if everything is a la carte. If it is, it means that I'm going to pay far more than I intended for the meal or else starve.

Family style is not in the French dining vocabulary.

"I think I'll have a crepe," my wife said to me as we sat down at a fancy French restaurant in Washington, D.C.

"Ah, isn't that something you hang in gymnasiums during proms?" I asked.

"No, silly. It's like a pancake."

"A stack of flapjacks for supper. I really don't think that will sit very well before bedtime," I advised.

My wife looked around to see if anyone was paying attention to our conversation. Satisfied we had not aroused anybody's curiosity, she said in a whisper:

"Will you keep your voice down? You'll get us thrown out." After glaring at me for a moment, she continued:

"It's not a pancake. It's LIKE a pancake, one pancake folded over a meat or vegetable filling. My crepe will have a creme of spinach filling."

"You eat that and you'll have bad dreams," I said sternly. "Such a combination is unnatural."

She shook her head and resumed looking at her menu.

"Anything resembling a Big Mac and fries on this menu?"

"NO," she fired back in a voice loud enough to draw the attention of nearby diners. Her face turned the color of French red wine.

"Well, I'd try this beef dish, but it says here it's covered with red wine and almonds. Heck, why can't those French leave a good piece of meat alone," I said to my wife who had her head buried in her menu.

Then the waiter came.

"And what would madam like?"

"I'll have the salmon."

"And monsieur?"

"I'll take a number six."

"Would you care for some wine?"

"Got a bottle of Gallo Brothers?" I asked confidently.

My wife's eyes grew as big as soup spoons. The waiter stared at me quizzically.

Sensing a blunder, I quickly grabbed the wine list.

I instantly discovered the place had none of the wines I was used to drinking. Whatever they were, they were sure expensive. I decided to ignore the names of the wines and just find the cheapest. "Give me a bottle of, er, number 12."

The waiter smirked.

"Is that a good wine?" I asked.

"It iz an excellent wine," he responded.

I got the feeling he'd say that even if it had been a half-consumed bottle of three-day-old muscatel snatched from the arms of a back alley bum.

From the expression on the waiter's face, I got the distinct impression we were more of an inconvenience than patrons to be served. And there was a touch of arrogance in his voice.

I remembered the words of Sydney Harris, the noted columnist: "The most gracious thing a Frenchman imagines he can do is to forgive you for not being one."

What bothered me even more was that our waiter didn't deliver our food. Some other waiter did. I was supposed to handsomely tip a guy who just took our order?

My wife thoroughly enjoyed her meal. I ate slowly, fearing my next bite would be my last. I was relieved when I managed to get through it without stomach cramps. I survived!

Postscript: The above story is a slight exaggeration of an actual dinner at the La Nicoise in Georgetown. I'm indebted to my sister and brother-in-law, who had been to this restaurant before and knew how and what to order. I'm especially grateful to my brother-in-law, who knew what wine to order. Also, I'm appreciative of the efforts of my wife, Kathy, in trying to broaden my meat and potatoes philosophy of dining.

* * * * *

SEED CATALOGS: THE PLAYBOY OF MULCH LOVERS

Every May I get the hots for horticulture.

I start re-reading all those home gardening books. I go through seed catalogs with all the fervor of a teenager perusing his first Playboy.

As soon as the frost leaves, I'm in my postage-stamp-size garden moving dirt and mapping out future seeding.

Finding room for all my seeds is an annual problem. See, I'm sort of an impulse seed buyer.

It's nothing for me to order sufficient seeds, not only to fill every square inch of my garden plot, but cover the lawns of neighbors on both sides of me.

About this time of year, you'll find me in front of the television anytime one of those gardening programs comes on.

I really don't know why I watch them. They only frustrate me.

What irks me is the vegetables on TV are always growing so well, while mine are valiantly fighting for life.

I can't figure out how these TV gardeners do it.

Heck, you never see them work.

Oh, he might put in a plant or two and spade up a token clump of dirt. But, all he really does is just lean against his hoe and yak.

But, come next week, the plot he planted is lush with growth.

It's like: "Whoa, boy, don't get too close to that lettuce. You fall in, they'll never find ya."

Or, "Back off, man, those squash vines are like squid. Oops, see ya got one around your ankle already. Well, we'll just take this machete and whack 'er off before it cuts off your circulation."

Once I thought I had his secret figured out.

His garden is all plastic plants.

I figured that off camera was a virtual army of little Chinese women expertly fashioning flowers. Next to them would be some spaced-out graduate ag student blowing up fake cucumbers with a bicycle pump.

It made sense to me. I mean, how many times have you actually seen the dude eat anything from his garden?

Later, I discovered his real secret: Money.

Of course, his garden grows, the darn thing is subsidized by the likes of Exxon, IBM and every seed company this side of California.

Heck, if he needs fertilizer he orders it by the truckload and has migrant labor spread it. I cringe every time I've got to buy a bag of weed and feed.

Maybe I should ask Wausau Papers or Wausau Insurance Companies to help support my garden...

"Sir, I wonder if your company would be willing to underwrite my vegetable garden in 1984?"

The chairman of the board gives me a mean look and then glances at his richly carpeted floor.

"Gosh, I'm sorry. I guess I should have wiped my shoes. I came right from the garden. Spreading manure today."

The head of the company growls as only chief executives can.

"All I need is $10,000," I say matter of factly.

"Ten thousand dollars!"

"Heck, that amounts to only $52.52 per plant, assuming a normal harvest. However, if we get some good rains, I'd get that down to $32.98 per plant."

"You're out of your..."

"You see, it's the backhoe that costs the big bucks. And, of course, there's the expense of trucking in that black dirt from

Lousiana delta country. Like to return a little of that Wisconsin top soil the Mississippi stole."

The chief exec flinches.

"Tell you what. For your investment I'll give half my tomato crop and maybe some carrots. Haven't had much luck with carrots, but after five years without a harvest, my time is

I don't think this plan would work. I envision being thrown out after proposing the overhead irrigation system.

But, gosh, with just a few bucks I bet my garden would rival anything PBS could muster.

* * * * *

GIVE ME A L-E-T-T-U-C-E

There I was, sitting on the compost heap crying.

Something which didn't go unnoticed by the neighbors, who sat by their windows staring, or my wife, who came bounding out the back door.

"Will you please shut up!"

"But, dear, my..."

"Donald, I don't want to hear about it," she says, shaking her head.

"But, dear..."

"Don't you think what you're doing might be interpreted by a reasonable person as somewhat strange?" she asks.

"But, dear..."

"Look, Donald, normal people don't pick compost heaps to cry on," she says as she tries to pull me off the odious mass. Unfortunately, she loses her balance and falls face first into the heap.

As I wipe the foodstuffs and dirt off her brow, I try to explain.

"My veggies aren't growing. Look, that lettuce has laid back leaves. I've never seen such a bunch of bummed out beans."

"Yeeeeyuck!" she replies as she removes a melon rind from her head.

"I tried everything, watering, feeding..."

"Have you tried talking to them?" my wife asks.

"Talking???"

"Sure, you've heard of people talking to houseplants. Well, why wouldn't it work for..."

"By gosh, you're right..."

"Donald, I was just kidding."

"No, you're absolutely right. What my veggies need is a little POT—positive organic thinking."

"I'm getting out of here," my wife says.

I take a long look at my veggies and with the most confident voice I can muster begin...

"All right guys, we know the weather has been the pits this year: Too cool in June, not enough rain in July—but that's passed us now.

"Hey guys, you've got the potential to be a great garden this year. I know you have it in ya."

I turn to the lettuce.

"Lettuce, you're a born leader. You're up early raring to grow. You set the pace for the whole garden."

I stand up and begin chanting, "Let's grow lettuce—Let's grow lettuce."

I grab two large bunches of carrot tops from the heap and begin shaking them over my head like pompons. Suddenly I find myself singing "On Wisconsin," but with slightly different lyrics:

"On you onions, on you onions

Make those big bulbs grow...

Rah Rah Rah Rah!

Come on carrots, come on cukes,

Fill my basket full.

Rah Rah Rah Rah!

Fall's upon us, frost is near us...

It's now or never guys.

So, push those roots down, spread those leaves out.

I need my greens right now. Rah Rah Rah..."

Suddenly I hear a shriek from inside the house. The next thing I know my wife is running toward me with a big blanket in her arms.

"Will you PLEASE shut UP" she yells as he throws the blanket over my head. Meanwhile the neighbors have congregated by the fence. They're clapping and singing "On Wisconsin."

I toss the blanket aside and look down at my greens.

I see a pea pod burst and send a half dozen peas crashing to the ground.

"It's working, it's working," I yell.

"Shussh!" my wife says frantically.

I turn to the neighbors. Come on people—to the tune of "America the Beautiful..."

"My garden tis of thee

Sweet corn and big-pod peas..."

I grab an oak branch and begin directing the neighbors as if they were a huge chorus...

214

"It's the Morman Tuber-nacle Choir, yeah," I yell as the neighbors begin singing in rounds:
"Hoe, hoe, hoe your row, gently round the peas..."

* * * * *

"HI-YO, GLADBAG, AWAAAAY!'

It's 6 a.m. An odd noise has awakened Mrs. Smith and drawn her to the window.

"Frank," she says with whispered alarm. "There's a strange man in our yard."

The old man rolls out of bed and stumbles to the window.

"Wilma, will you look at that! He's got a big plastic bag and he's going around picking up clumps of cut grass.

"Better call the police," he says as he jerks open the window. "HEY, YOU!"

"Me?"

"What do you think you're doing?"

"Taking your grass."

"Well, put it back!"

"Why? You don't need it. You'll just let it lie around until it turns yellow."

"Well, its mine and you can't have it."

The strange man puts down his bag and walks toward the open window.

"You see, I live down the street and, well, I'm sort of an amateur gardener. And, I was reading how compost is great for gardens and how grass clippings make great compost.

"Well, I don't have a big yard like you do, so I don't have that many clippings. I figured I'd just go around the neighborhood shopping for piles of grass."

The old man's face turns red.

"Look, sonny, this is America and Americans don't steal other people's grass. Remember the range wars were fought over grass..."

"Sir, Wausau is hardly the Old West. And, I believe the range wars involved cattle, not compost."

"Don't get smart with me, boy. And, put that grass back!"

"I can't. See, this bag contains grass from nine different lawns. I don't know which grass is yours."

A squad car pulls up, two officers jump out with their guns drawn.

"FREEZE, mister."

"Hey, Floyd, we've got ourselves an early morning window peeker," one officer says to the other.

"No, no, officers, you've got it all wrong. I just have this bag of grass..."

"Well, what do you know, Floyd. We've got ourselves a pot smoker. You'd better call for a back up.

"Will you look at the size of that bag of canabis illegalis?"

"Officer, I'm just collecting lawn clippings for my compost pile..."

"Oh, it's you again. Floyd, hold off. It's our fearless composter again."

The officer turns to the man in the window.

"Don't worry, sir, this guy's harmless. Every morning he's out with his bags picking grass off people's lawns. I tell you, he's a better grazer than a goat..."

"Well, arrest him, he's stealing my grass!"

"Nothing illegal about stealing grass—just smoking it," the officer says with a laugh.

The strange bearded man, who looks amazingly like a certain columnist for the Daily Herald, clears his throat.

"Gentlemen, a lawn is not just a cover of grass, but a verdant field of food for starving squash, pitiful potatoes, malnourished melons, languid lettuce.

"We are all part of an ecological tapestry, each dependent on the other. We are all brothers of the Earth, from the lowliest blade of grass to the mightiest of beasts.

"We need each other to survive. Remember, the compost heap you help today will be the better beet tomorrow."

The old man shakes his head.

216

"Well, you put it that way, I guess it's the least I can do for the environment. Go take your grass."

The strange man picks up his bulging bag and puts it over one shoulder. As he walks away, Smith turns to the police officer.

"Who was that, anyway?"

The officer smiles.

"That, sir, was the Lone Composter."

* * * * *

218

CHAPTER TEN

WHO SAID THAT?

I heard something ominous on the radio the other day.

It was a report about Westinghouse developing a talking elevator that utilizes a mechanical voice synthesizer. It was uncanny how human sounding the elevator was as it rattled off "Second Floor," "Watch Your Step" and "Have a Nice Day."

When an elevator starts wishing me a nice day, I know the end of the world is near.

I mean, once you give a machine a voice, it's not too distant a leap to machines voicing opinions and developing personalities.

I can envision the following encounters:

Man walks into the elevator. From a speaker comes: "What floor, please?"

"Thirteenth," the man says.

"No way, man. This elevator doesn't stop at any 13th floor. It's a jinx, man."

"What?"

"If you want to go to the 13th floor, try the third elevator down the hall. But, the way he goes up and down, I wouldn't guarantee your arrival."

The radio report indicated that Westinghouse was on the verge of applying this electronic voice technology to appliances.

Can you imagine an ice box with a voice box?

"Hey, whatcha doing?"

"I'm making myself a late night snack," the man replies.

"Uh, huh. Remember the ol' battle of the bulge, fatso. You don't need those calories. Have a glass of water and a cracker and then go to bed, you blimp!"

Or, how about a talking alarm clock.

"RISE AND SHINE, STUPID," the clock blares at 6 a.m.

A startled sleeper bolts from the covers.

"You've got 15 minutes, buddy, or it's no breakfast for you," the clock commands.

"It's Sunday!" the man screams as he comes to his senses.

"RISE AND SHINE, YOU SINNER," the clock replies.

The sleeper falls back onto the bed and begins to cry.

The radio reporter even suggested that in the not too distant future such voice synthesizers could be installed in the dashboards of cars.

When that happens, I'm giving up driving.

Here's what could happen:

"Speed 55, oil pressure okay, engine temperature normal, battery okay," the dashboard reports.

The driver pushes down on the accelerator.

"Speed 65 and rising. Warning, you are now exceeding speed limit by 10 miles..."

"Hey, I'm in a hurry, forget it."

"You jerk, you want to get us both killed. Slow down. Mario Andretti you ain't."

"Shaddup."

"You're going to get a ticket. My sensors feel radar impulses."

The driver looks into his rearview mirror and sees only flashing red lights. He pulls over.

The officer walks up to the car and begins writing the ticket.

"Gee, officer, I was only going 60..."

"He was going 70 and not a mile per hour under," the dashboard interrupts.

"Shaddup!" the driver screams.

"Sir, does your dashboard always laugh like that?" the officer says.

"Sometimes. It laughs a lot when my wife drives," the driver says with a smirk as the officer hands him the ticket. The driver tries to restart his car. It won't start.

The dashboard laughs even harder, its various dials and lights flashing furiously.

* * * * *

THAT'S REALLY TOOTING YOUR OWN HORN

I think American car manufacturers can regain their dignity and beat those darn Japanese by making talking cars.

The other day my wife and I took her car to a service center because she thought the transmission was acting up and the engine idled too fast.

We told the head mechanic what we thought was wrong with it. He got behind the wheel, turned on the ignition and...

Everything was just fine.

"Transmission is good, ma'am," he said. "And it's idling fine."

I thought my wife was going to kill the poor guy.

She wasn't crazy. The car had been idling fast and the transmission had been making funny noises. It just wasn't doing it now.

How much easier this encounter would have been if the car could have done the talking instead of my wife and me, both mechanical klutzes when it comes to automobiles.

I can picture the scene.

My wife drives into the service center. The service manager strolls up to the window.

"What's wrong, ma'am?"

With a smile, my wife flicks a switch underneath the steering column and suddenly a voice comes through the front grille.

"Hello, I'm Kathy Oakland's car and I'm not feeling well today. Let me tell you a little about myself."

The voice talks about its make, model and year; type of engine and where it was made; mileage and gasoline consumption. The mechanic copies down the information on his service form.

Then the voice pauses.

"My transmission fluid is low and I suspect there's a developing problem with the clutch linkage... Also, my choke has been sticking, causing my rpms..."

After the car is finished giving a detailed diagnosis of itself, the mechanic smiles and turns to my wife.

"Ma'am, we just have some minor maintenance here and it shouldn't take but an hour. Based on what your car has told me, the bill shouldn't be more than $30."

"Fine, I'll be back this afternoon."

To me that would be a more meaningful and pleasant way to handle car repairs than to have a mechanically illiterate driver try to explain a problem to a service manager who has no idea what he's talking about.

I mean, when you go to the doctor do you bring someone along to tell the physician what's wrong with you?

Of course, with every great idea there are always drawbacks. I could see myself getting a talking Detroit lemon...

"Hey, you creep, I'm getting low on oil," the car's voice says sharply.

"I just gave you a quart yesterday," I reply.

"Look, if you'd just fix that gasket..."

"I can't afford to."

"Sure, you really don't care about me. You always take me for granted. What have I ever done to you to deserve such treatment? Huh? Haven't I started every morning?"

"I do care about you, really. It's just that money is tight right now."

"Don't you think I know that?" the voice begins to whimper. "I see you eyeing those other cars, those sleek new sports cars. It's just a matter of time before you trade me in, sell me to a junk yard like yesterday's trash."

"Ah, I wouldn't do that. You're a fine car, first class. Why, with a good wax job, I'll have you looking like new."

"Really?"

"Sure, I'll give you the once-over Sunday."

"Gosh." Suddenly the horn starts honking and the headlights begin dripping coolant.

"There, there, dry your headlights. I wouldn't want my baby getting rusty bumpers."

* * * * *

WHERE ARE WE NOW? DON'T EVEN ASK

The next car I get is going to have navigation.

It will be a car with a brain, a vehicle that knows where it's going.

For years, planes, boats—even trains—have had built-in navigational systems. Well, finally somebody has figured out a way to put a similar system to use in the family automobile.

I just hope American auto makers don't get beaten by the Japanese on this one. Hey, maybe they haven't thought of it yet. I mean, how lost can a driver get on an island the size of Japan? A wrong turn, you're either in the Pacific Ocean or Tokyo.

Anyway, if car makers succeed in this technological pursuit, then it will be goodbye to asking strangers for directions on how to get out of the middle of nowhere to somewhere halfway habitable.

Goodbye to finding oneself in a dead end alley in the middle of some big city battlezone with tough-looking men with crowbars in their hands approaching your car.

Goodbye to trying to read an AAA Triptik while whizzing down a two-lane highway at 55 mph.

Or trying to find the Minneapolis map in a glove box crammed full with Wisconsin and Illinois maps dating back to the age of 29-cent-a-gallon gasoline.

Yup, satellite-to-car navigating is just the ticket.

I can't wait.

Just think, toolin' down the highway knowing that by simply punching a few buttons you can learn precisely where you are.

223

The systems I've read about would equip the car with an on-board computer and video screen.

All the driver would have to do is punch his destination into the computer. Whenever he wants to know where he is, he just punches a few buttons, the computer receives homing signals from a satellite and translates that into a map which appears on the screen. A flashing dot indicates the car's position.

Of course, as with any new gizmo, there might be a bug or two...

Like where the heck are you going to put the antenna? We're not talking about a little telescoping antenna here. Only satellite receiving antenna I've seen are six-foot dishes.

I mean, a dish mounted on the hood certainly wouldn't add anything to the car's appearance. It would screw up aerodynamics something fierce and be a welcome target for vandals.

"Dear, we've been driving for two hours and I have yet to see a sign for the Grand Canyon," my wife says with a worried tone.

"Fear not, my dear, I will tell you precisely where we are," I reply confidently.

I reach down to the console next to the gear shift and flip a black toggle switch. Suddenly a plastic cover disappears into the console to reveal a small television screen.

I flick another switch.

The screen turns green, flashes a series of numbers and suddenly produces a map of the United States.

I flick a third switch.

Onto the screen flashes the city map of Moscow.

"We seem to have a bit of a malfunctrion here," I say with a half smile. I give the computer a rap on its side. The computer starts computing again. "Not to worry," I say confidently.

A map of the seven best beaches in Jamaica appears.

I begin flipping switches madly, forgetting for the moment that I'm still driving.

"Donald! Look out!" my wife yells as I swerve to avoid an oncoming semi.

I look down on the computer screen. A map showing the craters of the moon shines brightly.

I pull off the road and ask a man coming out of a cafe for directions.

"Grand Canyon, just head west and turn right at Illinois."

Okay, maybe the computer might not be all that great. But, if I can pull in HBO on that bitty screen it would be well worth the relief from certain out-of-state radio stations.

* * * * *

THE VENDORS STRIKE BACK

The other day I wanted an ice cream bar in the worst way.

But the machine wouldn't give it to me.

It sat there silently and stubbornly refusing to acknowledge all my pleadings, threats and laments.

I gave it 50 cents for a 25-cent bar, but it didn't faze it.

I could have put $100 in its coin changer and it wouldn't have cared.

I walked away and spent the entire afternoon licking my bruised ego instead of ice cream.

Ice cream vending machines are among man's most masochistic creations.

I've seen petite young women lay a forearm into a vending machine that would dazzle Sugar Ray Leonard.

I've seen otherwise mild-mannered men curse, punch and pound these mechanical merchants.

Yet, I've never seen a vending machine relent.

They may not be the smartest machines around, but they sure are tough. Heck, you blink at a computer, it'll go into a frenzy. You bump a toaster, it'll give you burnt offerings.

I should think with the extent of man's technological advances, we could come up with a better vending machine.

But, with electronics people trying to design variations on a Pac Man theme, I bet they haven't given vending machines a thought.

I mean, electronic wizards are probably too engrossed in micro chips to hit a vending machine for some corn chips.

I offer these suggestions from a vending machine victim.

First, install a voice synthesizer. I hate dealing with something that won't answer.

Next, install sensors at key points of operation and attach them to the synthesizer.

When your quarter doesn't produce results, you get an answer:
"BEEP...This is Victor the Vendor, your quarter is stuck in my coin separation unit, please give a mild tap two and a half inches below coin slot. This should dislodge coin and facilitate product delivery...BEEP."

Or, how about a vending machine that offers sales.

"BEEP...This is Victoria the Vendoress. Before you pull that lever I'd like to call your attention to the Milk Duds. We are running a special today...a nickel off."

But, I'm dreaming. If they came up with a talking vending machine, the following would probably happen...

Clink, clunk, and I pull the lever for ice cream bar.

Nothing.

"Hey, you blasted machine, give me my ice cream.

"I did."

"You didn't."

"I did too."

"Thief!"

"Liar!"

I give the machine a rabbit punch near its coin box.

"OUCH!"

"Serves you right. Now give me my ice cream bar."

"Okay, okay, take your ice cream bar."

I reach for the door.

ZZZZZAAAAAP!

The electrical shock knocks me to the floor.

"Take that, scum breath!"

I get up and charge the machine. My shoulder goes deep into its midsection.

ZZZZZZAAAAP

"Nice shock, Henry," the ice cream machine calls out to the snack machine.

I go spinning across the room and land on the Coke machine. Suddenly I feel ice cold Coke spilling onto my pants leg.

ZZZZZZAAAP

I cartwheel over a table and land headfirst in a wastepaper can.

"Well, boys, we certainly showed him," the ice cream machine says to the other machines.

"It felt good," the Coke machine replies.

228

"Yeah," yells the snack machine. "Today this lunchroom...tomorrow the WORLD!"

* * * * *

'SMART' PHONES OUTWIT PEOPLE

When you traipse into the wildwoods, one of the many things you leave behind is the telephone.

At least, where I camp, I haven't noticed any telephone booths.

I haven't noticed any telephone lines leaving bird nests, bear dens, or beaver huts, either.

There's a reason for that. Nature doesn't need phones. Communication is limited to how far you can cry, crow or screech. Anything beyond that range isn't worth communicating with.

Man, on the other hand, doesn't feel fulfilled unless he can talk to some stranger halfway around the globe.

He doesn't feel smart unless he can memeorize dozens of seven-digit numbers.

He doesn't feel modern unless he has a computer phone which does everything except reduce the phone bill.

At work, I have one of those 'smart phones' that you can program to automatically dial numbers.

For it to dial, I must push four buttons. To do it myself I must push eight buttons.

Tha 50 percent savings means, oh, maybe three seconds less effort. Now I realize I don't feel as tired after work as I used to.

This technology is nice until you unexpectedly run into another human, an operator.

"Number dialing, please," she says in a rather mechanical tone.

"Huh??"

"Number dialing, PLEASE."

"I don't know." I grimace knowing how ridiculous that must seem.

"You see, the phone dialed it...I mean, it's one of those phones that...let me see if I can find the number."

I grab for the phone book and tip over my full coffee cup.

"Number you're dialing FROM."

Suddenly I realize that is what she originally had said. Feeling doubly stupid I get ready to give her the office number when I realize I have forgotten it.

"It's aaaaaaah 842 something..." I hang up. I wipe the sweat from my brow.

I didn't make another call that morning.

I seems that phones multiply like rabbits in an office. The more phones, the greater the chance of getting someone else's call.

Then you play dialer's roulette, or, in more polite circles, transferring a call.

In order to transfer a call you must put the caller on hold. That's akin to banishing someone to oblivion.

Once you've dispatched the caller to limbo, you must push a series of buttons or dial without losing whatever tenuous link you have.

"Uh, you have the wrong extension, I'll transfer you," I tell the caller confidently.

I push the hold button and tap, tap, tapedity, tap-tap out the numbers...Voila:

"Vhat you vant?" a husky voice says.

"Uh, is this you, George?"

"No George here. Vhy you call Kremlin."

"Uh???"

"Uh, this is Don from Wausau."

"Warsaw?"

"WAUSAU!"

"Polish people not suppose to call Kremlin. We send tanks to blow up your house."

"I'm not from Poland, I'm an American!"

"American!" Hushed voices are heard on the other end. "How American know secret Kremlin phone number?"

"I was just trying to transfer a call to George."

"No George here. Must be spy. We go find him..." CLICK.

Apprehensively, I try transferring the call again.

"George?"

"Who??"

I slam the phone down. The caller disappears into hold heaven, like a man on a mountainside whose safety rope has been cut.

"Heck, if it was important, he'll call back," I say to myself. I just pray I don't get the call.

* * * * *

TECHNOLOGY SOMETIMES TRYING

Technology sometimes get the better of me.

I'll give you one personal example and another that involved an acquaintance.

The other day I experienced my first conference call. A conference call is a phone conversation in which there are two or more persons on the other end.

It was really neat. I was talking to one gentleman while another listened and occasionally added his own comments.

I can really see why this improvement on Alexander Graham Bell's gadget is loved by businessmen. It saves the need for making two or more separate calls; it promotes a fuller dialogue and it lessens the possibility of misunderstandings.

But, with any new technological advance, there is the fatal flaw—sort of the flea on the dog's back.

With the conference call, the flaw is simply saying goodbye.

To get the full impact and feel for what I'm about to write, take a deep breath and read the follwoing out loud while employing three separate tones of voice (denoted A, B, an dC).

Ready?

This is how a conference call ends.

"(A) Bye Don."

"(B) Bye Roger."

"(B) Bye Bob."

"(C) Bye Roger, Bye Don."

"(B) Huh???"

"(A) Bye Bob."

"(B) Bye, bye...bye bye birdie..."

I'll have you know it took me an hour and a half to figure out how to translate that goodbye into words on a page.

It boggles my mind to think how one would say goodbye to a conference call involving four or more persons. Maybe: "All those in favor of saying goodbye, say aya."

The second example involves the police, birds of prey and the laws of nature.

The other day an acquaintance got caught speeding on a residential street. This person was going 38 mph in a 25 mph zone.

I could have been me. I traveled down that same road and went by that same policeman. I saw him pointing that hand held radar device at me. I must have been going under the speed limit, for the officer paid little attention to me. However, no way could I tell you at what speed I was travelling.

When I'm driving home from work, I'm zonked. My body does the driving while my mind wanders from the grim to the bizarre. I'm oblivious to such things as speed, time or space.

Luckily my involuntary bodily functions recognize red lights, stop signs and occasionally traffic lanes.

Anyway, the point is that neither my acquaintance nor I had any warning that we were being electronically violated, that some invisible, but nevertheless hostile, thing was trespassing upon our private space.

With radar you haven't a chance. Long before you see the police car hidden on a side street, the officer has your speed clocked a dozen times. He's just waiting patiently for you to reach that magic number on the unit's digital display.

Such things go beyond the laws of nature.

In nature, there is something called a warning. When a field mouse is attacked by a hawk, the mouse usually has a few moments warning: a shadow, a telltale screech, a fluttering of wings.

Nature always gives the fly or the mosquito warning of an approaching hand. That's why there are so many of those pesky creatures about.

Nature gives them all a chance, albeit a slim one, to escape.

232

Not so with radar. No warning, no shadow, just invisible technology waiting to gobble you up.

* * * * *

A BEEP IN TIME...

I wish I had one of those beepers on my belt.

You know, those cigarette pack-size gizmos that hang silently and suddenly go beepeeee beep.

And, when one of these things does its thing, the wearer jumps up and rushes to the nearest phone.

Although people often look embarrassed when they get a beep, deep down they love it. Getting beeped means only one thing: You're important.

Somebody, somewhere, needs the wearer of the beeper. He doesn't need him tomorrow; he needs him now, this instant, right away.

Heck, nobody ever needs me right away. Tomorrow will do. Maybe next week.

But, if I had a beeper, well, I'd be important, vital—a spoke in the wheel of society rather than a stone picked up in the tire tread.

Now, I could go out and buy a beeper and fasten it to my belt.

Of course, it would never go off! As I mentioned before, most people can do without me. A silent beeper is as good as no beeper at all.

No one ever notices a sleeper beeper.

The other day, I was in the tavern feeling down and beeperless. I was downing my third beer when I came upon a wonderful idea.

Rent-a-beeper!

This service would provide you with a beeper and, for a small fee, would beep you periodically.

The fee, would depend on what type of message you would like to receive.

Take the $5 Basic Beep:

"Beep, beep...Mr. Oakland, please call your answering service immediately."

Or, how about the $8.50 Doctor Beep, a neat beep to use at posh restaurants where no one knows you:

"Beep, beep...Dr. Oakland, please call the hospital immediately."

It helps in getting a table when you don't have a reservation.

"Golly, can I get served right away? I have to get to the hospital. My patient just suffered a myocaridourinary distraction of the left clavical..."

For those want to project a manly image, or maybe try to impress a new date, there's the $15 Macho Beep:

"Beep, beep...Emergency, Code Red, go to airport immediately. Join helicopter crew for air rescue of man hanging upside down on the top of the Rib Mountain observation tower. Chief says you're the only one who can do it..."

For $10 more you could rent out the Playboy Beep:

"Beep, beep...(a woman with a deep, sexy voice) Don, Mary just called and you're to call back. I also have calls from Diane, Debbie, Susie, and Victoria says bring champagne..."

Those would be the middle income services. Rent-a-beep would also provide a premier series for those who want to appear really important.

First there would be the $100 Financier Beep.

"Beep, beep...Mr. Oakland, E.F. Hutton wants to know if you want to sell off those half million shares of African Diamond Mines Inc.to provide capital for that Pacific coast condominium project."

Or, the $125 Political Beep:

"Beep, beep...Mr. Oakland, Senator Proxmire's on the phone, wants your input before he votes on the Senate appropriations bill."

Finally, what service would be complete without the Get-Even Beep. For a mere $35.75, you could arrange to have the following message beeped to someone more status-conscious than yourself.

"Beep, beep...Mr. Moneybucks, the bank called, your checks bounced again. And your attourney called; that Chicago woman is still pressing her paternity suit..."

* * * * *

KEYING IN AND CHIPPING OUT

I love to read stuff I don't understand.

The other day Dave, one of the more technically minded on the Herald staff, gave me a copy of Electronics magazine. He thought I might be interested in an article about researchers putting computers on Antarctic seals.

Hey, what consenting adult seals do with computers is their business.

Anyway, I had a lot of fun paging through the rest of the magazine, reading everything and understanding absolutely nothing.

* * *

You know I'd love to be able to talk computer. Betcha, I could wow the girls with a little dose of candid computer talk...

"What do you do for a living," she asks.

"I'm currently working on a one-chip, frequency-shift-keying modem for teletex and videotex," I reply with a husky voice.

"Why, you're the most intelligent, sexiest man I've ever met," she says, melting into my arms and kissing my cheeks.

"Yeah, baby, it's a silicongate complementary MOS device in a 16-pin dual in-line plastic package," I whisper in her ear.

* * *

235

There was an article that told about the need for an "electronically steerable phased-array radar" for U.S. surveillance aircraft.

It's lighter and more shapely, the article says. Sounds like Cheryl Tiegs.

There was mention of a Yagi antenna and its four parasitic beams. Can just imagine a frantic co-pilot rushing over to a member of the ground crew.

"Have you see the pilot?"

"Yup. The yagi got him. He got too close, and it just et him."

* * *

Here's a short conversation based on an article about supercomputers in Hollywood:

"I tell you Steven, this baby is capable of the several hundred million mathematical computations per second you need to compute 6,000 by 4,500 pixels on your 70-millimeter film..."

"Yeah, but will E.T. like it?"

* * *

Reading one article I learned that some dudes in Paris were studying low pressure organometalic vapor-phase epitaxy.

Hey, can't they get arrested for that?

Who are the scientists, Cheech and Chong?

* * *

I love the headlines in the magazine:

"Thermistor gives thermocouple cold"

Well, if it'd cover its transistors when it sneezes...

"Pulse-width discriminator eliminates unwanted pulses"

Word on the street is the Mafia did it.

"Relational DBMS runs on 32-bit supermini-computer

Does GM know about this?

Hey, when will they come out with the 16-bit economy model?

"Monolithic C-MOS amplifier boasts a noise figure of 0.7 uv from dc to 10Hz"

I know. It's hard to be humble.

"Fan pumps lots of air with little noise."

Sounds like some politicians I know.

"$1,785 buys complete computer includes software"

You heard right. That's Don's Competent Computers, corner of Fifth and Main. $500 down 90 days free financing and service backed by Don and his staff of two genuine Japanese technicians. We will not be undersold, no way...so come on down...that's Fifth and Main under the big Light Emitting Diode sign...or call Wausau 38..24..35...sorry no COD orders, please!

* * *

Hewlett-Packard has a "fast number crunching computer." Nobody's buying it, though. Sounds like a 7-year-old devouring a box of Cracker Jacks, has bad breath and scares the secretaries.

Some company had one of these things and it crunched so hard it chipped its chips on a series of fives to the sixth power.

* * * * *

LOCO REPLACES MURPHY'S LAWS

For anyone who works with computers or is thinking about working with computers, I offer the Wildwood's Laws of Computer Operation, otherwise known as: LOCO.

These laws are based on my more or less intimate relationship with the Daily Herald's computer.

The first two LOCOs are:

Any computer with a memory possesses the ability to forget.

An ailing computer forgets.

Or, put another way: You'll never know a computer is ailing until it forgets something valuable.

Perhaps the most important LOCO law is the third:

Never, under any circumstances, trust a computer.

Computers might be bright and calculate at the speed of light, but their silicon chips are without compassion. A computer will forsake you without ever blinking a diode.

I once thought that if you gave a computer some information you could trust it to keep it until you wanted it back.

I realized how naive I was when the Daily Herald's computer one day blew into electron heaven every story I had written over the previous five days.

Do you think it was the last bit remorseful about losing those valuable stories I had worked so hard to write? Heck no. It just went on as if nothing out of the ordinary had happened.

I mean, after losing thousands of words the least it could have done was flash on its screen: "Gee, I'm really sorry about that."

LOCO law number four: When a computer forgets, what it forgets is gone forever.

If a human forgets something, chances are he'll remember it later on. It might be in the middle of the night, but eventually it will come back to him.

But, a computer blows data into never-never land.

Sometimes I'll ask the computer to retrieve a story I wrote the week before and onto the screen will flash: "Take number non-existent."

"Whatdaya mean, non-existent!" I scream as I slam my fists on the keyboard.

"Take number non-existent," it flashes.

What a cop out!

We couldn't get away with an answer like that.

Picture your neighbor coming over to ask if he could have back the hammer he let you borrow.

"Hammer non-existent," you reply.

I'm sure the resulting conversation would be less than cordial.

LOCO rule number five: Ranting and raving doesn't faze computers.

I have on occasion sworn, cussed, hurled a litany of nasty insults at my computer terminal with absolutely no effect other than raising my blood pressure.

Loco rule number six: Computers hold no loyalties. There isn't a computer made that isn't a tattletale.

All you have to do is ask a computer something in the right way and it will spill everything it knows, no matter how embarrassing it might be.

Just recently the government was embarrassed by its computers blabbing sensitive information to a bunch of kids in Milwaukee.

LOCO rule number seven: Under no circumstances ever ask a computer technician what's wrong with the darn thing.

You really don't want to know because: A) It's going to cost thousands of dollars to fix; B) the parts needed are on a slow boat from Japan; or C) he has no idea what's wrong and needs a company representative from Tokyo flown in immediately.

To some questions, the answers are best not known.

* * * * *

THE SAD STORY OF MY GAL, "CAL"

This is the tragic tale of a calculator that broke my heart. So get your hanky ready.

Earlier this year the newsroom got a new calculator.

Right away you could tell it was a cut above the ordinary desk calculator. It had more than the usual number of keys and a sleek and sophisticated appearance.

We later discovered it could take data and fashion it into various graphs and charts.

This was one sharp calculator.

I admit I was attracted to it, seduced by its sophistication.

I guess that's what made me ask to take it home one weekend. Maybe I was wrong. Maybe we should have kept our relationship confined to the office.

At first it was kind of awkward. With instruction book in hand, I tried to establish a dialogue, but I kept hitting the wrong keys. I guess its good looks just made me nervous.

But, later it learned to trust my touch and I became more at ease tapping its keys. Soon we were spending hours together making graph after graph.

By the end of the weekend I thought we had established a rapport, a special relationship which gave me great pleasure.

All that was shattered recently as I paged through the June issue of *Playboy* magazine. There, on page 263, was my calculator uncovered. It even listed its real name, EL7050.

I was emotionally devastated.

How could such a nice calculator expose itself like that, allow itself to be gawked at by strangers.

Oh, sure the photo was well-done. Its pose was in good taste, not like the sleazy pictures you see in some office products catalogs. The lighting was expertly done to show its best features. The photo was even airbrushed to hide blemishes on its keys.

Call me old-fashioned, but I don't think it's right for a calculator so young to be in such a publication. My gosh, what would her manufacturers think if they knew. It would break their hearts.

I can understand how *Playboy* 1 editors were impressed with its features. I imagine it was easy for those slick editors to convince a gullible small-town calculator to commit itself to pose uncovered.

Oh, what impetuous notion lay in its circuits to make it want to give up its good name for such an immodest display.

I guess we'll have to get rid of it now. Can't see the Herald allowing a calculator of that type to hang around the office. What would people say?

Visitors would come into the office and see it on a desk and give it salacious leers.

Its presence would be an affront to the high moral integrity of the Herald's newsroom.

But I guess things will work out for our little calculator.

I suppose some rich executive-type will see the picture and come buy our calculator. He'll take it to the big city and it will be producing graphs for national publications or big corporate reports.

But, it will find calculating in the fast lane is not all glittering silicon chips. It won't find the satisfying and lasting relationship it might have had at the Daily Herald.

It will be just another pretty calculator in a room of mini-computers.

When it gets older, its keys a little less attractive, it will realize what it gave up in its youth,

I guess I'll just go back to my old 20-key pocket calculator with its sticky percent button and faltering battery.

But, I'll always remember EL7050.

I'll always hold in my heart our moments together that fateful weekend and the beautiful graphs we made.

* * * * *

WRITER HAS A "FIX"ATION

We've got several guys in our office who can fix just about anything, from a squeaky chair to a cantankerous computer.

I really envy them.

The other day while one of them was repairing my computer terminal, healing an electronic wound caused by my gonzo typing, I was thinking how I should have gone into repair work rather than writing.

As a kid I should have spent my time with a screwdriver instead of a pencil. I should have been reading schematics instead of making up stories.

I should have taken industrial arts, electronics and woodworking courses instead of driving English teachers up the wall with my attempts to put words together which neither offended good taste nor the rules of grammar and spelling.

Really, you don't get the satisfaction repairing a sentence that you do fixing a toaster.

Gee, when I try to fix a toaster the thing looks up at me and says: "Try it, fella, and make your wife a widow."

241

People really don't need writers. You don't call a writer when your car stalls.

If your toilet backs up you don't immediately cry out to your spouse, "Honey, quick, call a writer."

Gosh, I wasted my youth writing.

If I had asked for the tool box instead of box of pencils that Christmas 25 years ago, life would have been far different.

Heck, I probably wouldn't have gotten beaten up so much. Sitting by a tree while writing about spaceships was just asking for it. A bunch of toughs would come by, take one look at me and yell, "Kill the wimp!"

But, if I could have fixed things, I could have negotiated. "Hey, fellas, tell you what, you don't pound the brains out of my skull and I'll fix your Harleys."

They probably would have made me a charter member of their gang.

And, teachers would have loved instead of dreaded me. I could have fixed their movie projectors on the spot.

I bet my social life in high school would have been better. In my day if girls had a choice between dating an introspective aspiring writer or a football star it was no contest.

But, a football star couldn't fix a cheerleader's record player when it went on the fritz. Or, get her father's car running after it stalled at the outdoor. Yup, ol' Don would have been in demand.

At college I probably would have been a big man on campus.

I can just see myself sitting in class overhearing a conversation between two luscious coeds. "Marge, I don't know what to do, my drain is all plugged up and I'm afraid to call the landlord."

"Excuse me, I think I can be of help," I smile as I pull a pipe wrench from my back pocket.

Well, not only would that give me an instant invite over to her apartment, but I'd work it so I'd finish just about supper time and she'd be so appreciative, well...

You don't realize how hard it was for a journalism student like me to get a date in college. "Oh, you're one of those people who write those boring articles in the school newspaper," they'd say. Or I'd get gals who wanted to do nothing but argue politics.

How nice it would be to get through life without fear of springs, belts and bolts. It would be great to lift the hood of the car and not break into a sweat and begin whimpering.

242

I envy Mr. Fixits. People see them coming and yell, "Thank god you're here!" People see me coming, they grumble, "Oh, what's he want?"

* * * * *

THE CHEVY CAR CONSPIRACY CAPER

I think my car was trying to tell me something.

In fact, I think it was conspiring with my wife's compact car to humiliate me.

They're both malevolent machines on wheels.

It all started a couple of weeks ago. I was in a bookstore when I happened upon a book on auto repair.

It was a well-illustrated, fairly understandable guide to the automobile. I impulsively bought it.

My mistake was not putting it in a plain brown wrapper.

When I got to my car, I just threw the book on the seat. I'm convinced my car saw it and got upset.

I can just imagine the conversation my car had with my wife's car when I got home.

"Guess what?" my car says.

"What?" asks the little Chevy.

"My driver just bought a book on car repair, heh heh. I think he's got it in his mind that he's going to try to repair us, heh heh."

"Oh, he does, does he!" the little car says sharply.

"Don't worry..."

"Sure, sure. Hey, I don't want that klutz adjusting my carburetor. The fool would foul my plugs for sure.

"Remember the last time that jerk tried to change my oil. He forgot the gasket, I sprayed oil all over myself. I was so mad I nearly popped a piston.

243

"No sir! No way do I ever want HIM manhandling my manifold!"

"Hey, I feel the same way. But, don't worry, nothing's going to happen," the big car says. "We'll just discourage him a bit."

"Discourage him?"

"Yeah. Tell you what I want you to do," the big Chevy whispers to the little Chevy.

A few days later my wife notices the brakes on her car becoming soft. Knowing precious little about brakes and the book sounding mighty complicated, I'm forced to take it into the garage.

All four brakes have to be replaced, the man says.

A couple of days later I discover the little Chevy's tires are going bald.

Back to the shop it went.

Next it was the big car's turn. But, he was more insidious. He figured to give me a problem I would believe I could handle.

He gave me bad shocks.

Ah ha! Finally something I could fix, I said to myself as I whipped out my book. I had the tools to do it, plus assistance from a brother-in-law who's a machinist.

We couldn't get the first shock off. The blasted car refused to release the bolts holding it. We tried socket wrenches, Vice-grips, crescent wrenches, box wrenches, pliers—everything short of dynamite.

It took a trip to the auto shop and a mechanic with an air chisel to free them.

I could almost hear my car laughing under its horn.

Then the compact got into the act again.

It's starter didn't start.

My handy dandy $23 car care book was of no help. It indicated repairing starters was something for pros to mess with. I didn't need a book to tell me that. I realized it when I found the starter was half hidden by the engine block.

Back to the shop went the car.

"He's weakening," my car said to the little Chevy. "Now to finish him off."

On vacation, 400 miles from home, my car starts klunking every time I turn. Every time I brake, he grinds.

I was without my book, without tools and without hope. Luckily, I was visiting a friend who was a good mechanic.

My car had blown its brake shoes.

Returning home was a study in automotive paranoia. I figured at any moment a wheel would fall off.

"You win, car!" I yelled. "Never again will I lift a wrench against you."

* * * * *

SILENCE SOOTHES SAVAGE LISTENER

"DOC, YOU'VE GOT TO HELP ME."

"Mr. Oakland, there's no need to shout."

"WHAT???"

The doctor puts his hands over both ears and makes a motion as though he's taking off earmuffs.

I give him a nervous smile and take the mini-cassette headphones off my head. I click off the tape player on my belt.

"That's better, Mr. Oakland. However, I think it would be better if we could dispense with that," he said, pointing to the portable stereo boom box blaring next to the couch.

"Sure, doc, anything you say." I punch a button putting an end to Olivia Newton-John in concert.

The doctor smiles and pulls out a notebook.

"Now what seems to be the trouble?"

I give the doctor an anxious glance.

"Doc, I'm a cassette-alcoholic," I whisper.

"A what?"

"I'm a chain cassette listener. Tape after tape, I can't function without listening to a tape."

"I see, you have this compulsive behavior involving the playing of cassette tapes," he says matter of factly. He jots down something in his book.

245

"Compulsive! My wife is threatening to leave me if I listen to my cassette player at the dinner table one more time."

The doctor grimaces as he shakes his head.

"My wife doesn't complain about my snoring at night, but she does yell about the heavy metal coming from the headphones under my pillow."

He gives me a curious look.

"Doc, I'm surrounded by tape players. Like I have this belt unit and my boom box. There is also the tape player that is part of my home stereo system. And, there's the in-dash player in my car.

"One day my car player ate one of my Jethro Tull tapes. I wept as I pulled that mangled mass of plastic ribbon into a big ball in the palms of my hands. It was as if my favorite dog had just died in my arms.

"The next day I took it in the backyard and buried it."

"Were you listening to a cassette at the time?"

"Yeah, I was listening to a recording of the funeral march. I thought it was the appropriate thing to do."

I sniff and wipe tears from my eyes.

"I think it all began in high school. That's when I got my first reel-to-reel tape player.

"In college I switched to records. Instead of studying for tests, I'd sit in the window of the dorm and listen to Iron Butterfly at full blast."

I start humming, "In-a-gadda-da-vida."

"In recent years, it just seemed that I've gotten hooked on cassettes. I mean some people carry cigarettes in their shirt pockets. I carry cassettes.

"I visit someone and the first thing I ask is, 'Hey, man, got any tapes?'"

The doctor smiles knowingly and sets aside his notebook. He takes a long drag on his pipe and watches the smoke weave upward.

"Your case is not unusual, Mr. Oakland. Our progress as a society has been measured by the amount of noise we can produce.

"Trapped in such an environment, we try to suppress noise with music, something more compatible to our personal preferences."

I make a move to push on my boom box, but the doctor grabs my hand.

"No more boom box for you, baby! We're going to re-introduce you to the pleasures of silence.

246

"As a first step, whenever you get the urge to play a cassette, play this one," he says, handing me an unmarked cassette box. "Eventually you'll get the message."

"Great, what's on the cassette, anyway?"

"Simon and Garfunkel's 'Sounds of Silence.'"

* * * * *

CHECKING OUT AT THE BANK

I don't mind the little challenges of life.

But, there's one challenge that comes at me like a barnyard dog: Balancing my checkbook.

Every month the bank sends me a statement and all my checks. When I get a certain masochistic urge, I check their statement against my checkbook.

My problem is that I don't get that urge often enough. I just can't seem to keep my checkbook current and that gets me into all sorts of trouble.

A while back, I decided to update the balance on my check stubs after two weeks of neglect. I discovered I was $796 overdrawn, a new personal record!

Checks bounced like Fourth of July fireworks.

I put off balancing my checkbook because the bank and I never agree. And, as many times as I have prayed, the bank has never been wrong.

Now, there are a lot of well-adjusted, financially solvent people who don't give two hoots if they're off $1.

But, not me. I won't stop torturing myself until things equal out.

After the first run through, I'm usually off by some exotic amount, like $234.99.

After a mile of adding machine tape and a medley of curses, I get the difference down to less than $5. It takes the rest of the night and two cans of beer to whittle that down.

It's when the bank and I are a penny off that I come perilously close to going off the deep end.

At that point my mind wanders from the endless column of numbers...

A man in a banker's grey suit bursts into the office of the president of my local bank.

"Sir, there's a man atop our building and he's threatening to jump."

"Ignore him. He'll go away."

"Sir, we can't leave him up there. It's bad public relations. What if he falls? I can just see maintenance up and quitting on the spot. What if he hits the sculpture..."

"OK, what are his demands?"

"All he wants is for someone to balance his checkbook."

"Is that all? Heck, our bookkeepers can handle that."

"Well, they've been working on it for over two hours and two of our top bookkeepers are threatening to resign."

The two men go outside. The president lifts a bullhorn to his mouth.

"Mr. Oakland, please come down."

"Not until my bank and I come to terms."

"We're working on it. We have four bookkeepers, two Certified Public Accountants, a computer programmer and the FBI trying to balance your book."

"I can't stand it anymore!" I scream. "When your checkbook is worse than Rubik's Cube, your life suddenly becomes meaningless."

"There are people who can help you," the president responds.

"Really?"

"Through behavior modification/shock treatment techniques you'll learn to record your checks immediately after writing them. By sitting in on second grade arithmetic classes you'll learn how to add, subtract and keep running balances..."

"Wow!"

"And, after a few sessions with a psycho-financialist, you'll actually smile when your statements come."

"Gosh! How can I sign up? I feel like a new man already."

The bank president turns to a television camera:

"You, too, can feel like a new man, possessing the respect and integrity and sense of macho that comes with knowing you can balance your checkbook.

"Call today for a free no-obligation evaluation with one of our trained consultants."

The president smiles broadly. "Remember, you can't go through life unbalanced."

* * * * *

THE OL' BANK-BOOK JUGGLE

One thing I envy about animals of the wildwoods is they don't need bankers.

They don't need checkbooks, savings accounts, NOW accounts, certificates of deposit and they don't get overdraft notices.

I've got nothing against bankers. They are fine, upstanding, community-minded individuals who wear three-piece suits.

Writers, on the other hand, are slovenly, hunched over (typewriter tilt) and have minds far removed from their community. They don't own a three-piece suit and have one tie for use at weddings and funerals.

Animals don't have money so they don't need bankers. They seem to get along all right without either.

Men have money and the seemingly innate need to covet it. In order to have bucks to covet, man needs to manage his money. That's where bankers come in to play. And, that's what this is all about.

I'm getting downright embarrassed every time I go to the bank—and it's all because of money management.

You see, I developed this money management system which I dubbed fund accounting. It's a very simple system.

When I get a paycheck (bucks to covet) I take it to the bank and divide it into various accounts.

Some goes into a checking account to cover the mortgage payment, grocery bills and utility expenses.

Some goes into a savings account to cover future known expenses, such as insurance premiums.

Some goes into a savings account to serve as the family nest egg, also known as the emergency fund.

What's left over is for wine, women and related sin. In my case, it's wife, car and related bills.

A nice, neat and practical system, right?

Only on paper. It fails to take into account my weak will and insatiable desire to spend. It also neglects something called a credit card.

Here's what inevitably happens.

Halfway through the week, I spend all my wine, women and related sin money. That forces me to borrow from the checking account or charge everything. I end up doing both.

Next paycheck I'll pay it all back, I say to myself.

Well, by the time the next paycheck comes around, the mortgage comes due. And, as a result of my earlier excesses, there are insufficient funds in the checking account to cover the mortgage payment.

Now it's time for the ol' bank-book juggle.

While the poor bank teller watches, I begin juggling.

I take money from the family nest egg to cover the deficit in the checkbook.

But, that leaves too little in the savings account to qualify for free checking. So I transfer funds from the future expenses savings account to push the nest egg account above the free checking minimum.

Then I begin dividing my paycheck, but since I have a charge card bill due, I have to put what normally goes into the family nest egg account into checking.

Then I've got to put a portion of my wine, women and sin money in future expenses savings to repay the amount transferred out of the nest egg account.

However, I can't completely cover the nest egg account transfer with my wine, women and related sin money because, if I did, I wouldn't have any wine, women and sin money to use on my wife, car and related bills.

As I do all this, I think about my wife yelling at me for never taking her out.

And, I think how my car is low on gas and how my refrigerator is low on beer.

All this ponderous thinking causes me to lose what miniscule ability I have at adding and subtracting numbers.

Instead of depositing $105 in savings, I deposit my account number.

While I struggle, a line of people forms behind me, a long line of grumbling customers who are probably double-parked in front of the bank.

Yup, I certainly do envy the animals who are so dumb as not to have any money.

* * * * *

ROBOT ETIQUETTE: NEVER OFFER IT A BEER

You may not be aware of this, but robots are misunderstood.

Yup. It's hard to believe, but true.

The other day I got this newsletter in the mail from the Wisconsin Council of Safety Division and in it was an ad for a videotape called "Working Safely with Robots—explore the misunderstood realm of robots."

Heck, if the darn tape wasn't $440 I'd have ordered one right away.

This tape "destroys myths" and "deals with the most hazardous aspect of the robot's personality," which happens to be something called "dwell time."

Hey, this is hard-core stuff, I said to myself. It's sort of the Swedish Erotica for those who lust over mechanical engineering manuals.

251

Then I got to thinking. Maybe robots do have feelings. Maybe it's time we become more sensitive toward our mechanical friends.

I think it's about time we have a robot relations guide, something like "How to Win Friends and Influence Robots."

Here's a few suggestions from this proposed machine relations guide:

1. Never tell robot jokes in the company of robots. Robots have little tolerance for hydraulic humor. They tend to react by blowing hose couplings.

Case in point: A worker in a Detroit car plant told a joke that began, "How many robots does it take to screw in a lightbulb..." Well, the punch line caused robots along the body assembly line to shut down for a week.

2. Never make derisive remarks about the Japanese when near a robot, even if it's an American-built robot.

You never know where in the world their parts were made.

3. You can swear all you want at a robot, but never ever hit it. Remember, robots are not vending machines. A Coke machine passively takes the abuse. Robots kill.

Case in point: A mechanical engineer for a Detroit car maker, upset because a robot arm was moving left when it should have been moving right, kicked the machine below the on-off switch.

The robot suddenly swung its arm around, grabbed the hapless engineer and proceeded to weld him to the inside door of a Buick.

4. You can talk sex in front of a robot, but you may find yourself on thin ice if you begin talking about the merits of automobiles or home appliances.

Robots are machines and have a certain kinship with other mechanical devices. They are likely to take offense if you begin bad-mouthing your toaster or lawn mower.

5. Robots usually are driven by computers. Humans should realize not all robot problems are the fault of the mechanics. Quite often it's the result of the computer.

However, don't beat on the computer. It might be in cahoots with the robot and send commands to the mechanical arms to trash you.

6. Human workers occasionally like a beer after work. Robots are no different. Between shifts, give your robot a shot or two of WD-40 and it will boost its morale tremendously.

Under no circumstances should you attempt to give your robot a beer.

7. When a new robot is introduced into a plant, make sure the human workers are made sensitive to potential insecurities felt by the other robots.

I mean, nobody, man or machine, likes to be replaced or feel likely to be replaced.

In times of technological transitions, we ought to be particularly tolerant of malfunctions in automated systems.

8. Robots like to have nicknames. Make sure the nicknames reflect their positive attributes and aren't demeaning.

A Harvard study showed poorly named robots blew out electronics 40 percent more often than robots with positive sounding names.

* * * * *

CODE PROTECTS HOME, NOT THE OWNER

Electronic home security systems make me insecure.

Recently I was a guest in a home protected by such a system. Because the family lived near a not-so-nice neighborhood, they installed the rather elaborate system.

Operating it is relatively simple.

Every time you leave the home you must punch in a numbered code on a keyboard mounted on the wall. Upon your return you punch in another numbered code to disarm the system.

Simple or not, the thing had me absolutely paranoid.

The problem was if these codes weren't entered within 30 seconds, sirens would wail and an army of police would come a-charging.

All I could think about was what would happen if I didn't make the 30-second deadline. Just thinking about it made me sweat.

253

A day later I got my first opportunity to arm the security system. I recalled my host's instructions:

"Now, all you have to do is punch in a number, open the door, get out and close the door tightly within 30 seconds."

I told my wife to go outside and stand back.

I hit the number on the wall-mounted keyboard, raced outside, slammed the door and locked it all within five seconds.

Then for the next 25 seconds I waited in agony for the potential calamity. I died about four times as I waited for that piercing siren that could be heard for miles.

It didn't come.

I plopped my sweat-soaked body into the car and drove off. All I could think about was the inevitable ordeal of disarming the blasted thing.

Upon my return I nervously unlocked the door. I felt like a novice member of a bomb squad.

I flung open the door, leaped for the keyboard and frantically punched in the code.

Nothing happened.

"Oh Lordy!" I screamed.

I punched in the numbers again.

A green light flashed on. Safe! I collapsed from nervous exhaustion.

When my host arrived home, I told him about my ordeal.

"Did it make a noise when you walked in?" he asked.

"Uh, no."

"Well, it wasn't armed then. You must have left the door open when you tried to arm it."

"I guess I did."

"All the doors have to be closed before you arm it."

"You mean I went through all that for nothing!" I cried.

"Sorry," he replied sympathetically.

A couple of days later I was visiting a relative and we got to talking about home security systems. He said he didn't have one but his son did. And, then he related this story.

"Once my son asked me to get something from his house while he was out of town. He then gave me the code to disarm the security system.

"I went over there, walked in and punched in the code. I was just about to enter the living room when sirens started wailing. I tell you, it was as if the house was celebrating the Fourth of July.

"On and on it went. Outside neighbors were gathering and giving the house strange looks. I entered the code repeatedly, but the thing refused to shut up.

"I even called the firm that installed the system. They said it was probably a malfunction and would have a serviceman over in about 90 minutes.

"Well, this went on for about an hour. Then, by lucky coincidence, my son called the house. He asked me what number I had punched in. I told him. Well, turns out I had written down the wrong number. I punched in the new number and silence finally came."

After hearing my relative's story I vowed never again to futz with electronic security.

* * * * *